The 3 Mistakes
of My Life

Chetan Bhagat is the author of four bestselling novels – *Five Point Someone* (2004), *One Night @ the Call Center* (2005), *The 3 Mistakes of My Life* (2008) and *2 States: The Story of My Marriage* (2009).

Chetan's books have remained bestsellers since their release, and have been adapted into major Bollywood films. *The New York Times* called him the 'the biggest selling English language novelist in India's history.' *Time* magazine named him as one amongst the '100 Most Influential People in the world' and Fast Company, USA, listed him as one of the world's '100 most creative people in business.'

Chetan writes for leading English and Hindi newspapers, focusing on youth and national development issues. He is also a motivational speaker.

Chetan quit his international investment banking career in 2009, to devote his entire time to writing and make change happen in the country. He lives in Mumbai with his wife Anusha, an ex-classmate from IIM-A, and his twin sons Shyam and Ishaan.

To know more about Chetan visit www.chetanbhagat.com or email him at info@chetanbhagat.com.

Praise for previous work

Many writers are successful at expressing what's in their hearts or articulating a particular point of view. Chetan Bhagat's books do both and more.

> – *A R Rahman, in TIME magazine, on Chetan's inclusion in the Time 100 Most Influential People in the world*

The voice of India's rising entrepreneurial class.

> – *Fast Company Magazine, on Chetan's inclusion in the 100 Most Creative People in business globally*

India's paperback king.

> – *The Guardian*

The biggest-selling English-language novelist in India's history.

> – *The New York Times*

A rockstar of Indian publishing.

> – *The Times of India*

Bhagat has touched a nerve with young Indian readers and acquired almost cult status.

> – *International Herald Tribune*

The 3 Mistakes of My Life

A Story about Business, Cricket and Religion

Chetan Bhagat

RUPA

Published by
Rupa Publications India Pvt. Ltd 2008
7/16, Ansari Road, Daryaganj
New Delhi 110002

Sales centres:

Allahabad Bengaluru Chennai
Hyderabad Jaipur Kathmandu
Kolkata Mumbai

ISBN: 978-81-291-3551-3

143rd impression 2016

148 147 146 145 144 143

The moral right of the author has been asserted.

Typeset by Mindways Design, New Delhi

Printed at Gopson Papers Ltd, Noida

To my country,
which called me back

Contents

Acknowledgements

My readers, you that is, to whom I owe all my success and motivation. My life belongs to you now, and serving you is the most meaningful thing I can do with my life. I want to share something with you. I am very ambitous in my writing goals. However, I don't want to be India's most admired writer. I just want to be India's most loved writer. Admiration passes, love endures.

To Shinie Antony, a friend who has been with me all these years and who critically reviews my work and ensures that it is fit for my reader's consumption. My family, which continues to support me in all my ventures. Specially, my brother Ketan Bhagat for his critical feedback from Sydney and cricket freak brother-in-law Anand Suryanaryan who told me more about cricket than anyone else would have.

The people of Gujarat, in particular Ahmedabad, where I spent some of the most wonderful and formative years of my life.

My publishers Rupa and Co, who have fulfilled all my dreams and continue to pursue the goal of making India read.

My friends in the film industry, who have given me a new platform to tell my stories from, and who teach me new things everyday, in particular Atul Agnihotri, Raju Hirani, Alvira Khan, Sharman Joshi, Vipul Shah, Imtiaz Ali, Shirish Kunder, Farah Khan and Salman Khan.

The Madras Players and Evam Theatre Group, who turned my stories into wonderful plays.

My friends in the media, especially those who have understood my intentions for my country and are with me.

My colleagues at Deutsche Bank, my friends in Mumbai and Hong Kong.

God, who continues to look after me despite my flaws.

Prologue

It is not everyday you sit in front of your computer on a Saturday morning and get an email like this:

From: Ahd_businessman@gmail.com
Sent: 12/28/2005 11.40 p.m.
To: info@chetanbhagat.com
Subject: A final note

Dear Chetan
This email is a combined suicide note and a confession letter. I have let people down and have no reason to live. You don't know me. I'm an ordinary boy in Ahmedabad who read your books. And somehow I felt I could write to you after that. I can't really tell anyone what I am doing to myself – which is taking a sleeping pill everytime I end a sentence – so I thought I would tell you.

I kept my coffeee cup down and counted. Five full stops already.

I made three mistakes; I don't want to go into details.

My suicide is not a sentimental decision. As many around me know, I am a good businessman because I have little emotion. This is no knee-jerk reaction. I waited over three years, watched Ish's silent face everyday. But after he refused my offer yesterday, I had no choice left.

I have no regrets either. Maybe I'd have wanted to talk to Vidya once more – but that doesn't seem like such a good idea right now.

Sorry to bother you with this. But I felt like I had to tell someone. You have ways to improve as an author but you do write decent books. Have a nice weekend.

Regards
Businessman

17, 18, 19. Somewhere, in Ahmedabad a young 'ordinary' boy had popped nineteen sleeping pills while typing out a mail to me. Yet, he expected me to have a nice weekend. The coffee refused to go down my throat. I broke into a cold sweat.

'One, you wake up late. Two, you plant yourself in front of the computer first thing in the morning. Are you even aware that you have a family?' Anusha said. In case it isn't obvious enough from the authoritative tone, Anusha is my wife.

I had promised to go furniture shopping with her – a promise that was made ten weekends ago.

She took my coffee mug away and jiggled the back of my chair. 'We need dining chairs. Hey, you look worried?' she said.

I pointed to the monitor.

'Businessman?' she said as she finished reading the mail. She looked pretty shaken up too.

'And it is from Ahmedabad,' I said, 'that is all we know.'

'You sure this is real?' she said, a quiver in her voice.

'This is not spam,' I said. 'It is addressed to me.'

My wife pulled a stool to sit down. I guess we really did need some extra chairs.

'Think,' she said. 'We've got to let someone know. His parents maybe.'

'How? I don't know where the hell it came from,' I said. 'And who do we know in Ahmedabad?'

'We met in Ahmedabad, remember?' Anusha said. A pointless statement, I thought. Yes, we'd been classmates at IIM-A years ago.

'So?'

'Call the institute. Prof Basant or someone,' she sniffed and left the room. 'Oh no, the daal is burning.'

There are advantages in having a wife smarter than you. I could never be a detective.

I searched the institute numbers on the Internet and called. An operator connected me to Prof Basant's residence. I checked the time, 10.00 a.m. in Singapore, 7.30 a.m. in India. It is a bad idea to mess with a prof early in the morning.

'Hello?' a sleepy voice answered. Had to be the prof.

'Prof Basant, Hi. This is Chetan Bhagat calling. Your old student, remember?'

'Who?' he said with a clear lack of curiosity in his voice. Bad start.

I told him about the course he took for us, and how we had voted him the friendliest professor in the campus. Flattery didn't help much either.

'Oh that Chetan Bhagat,' he said, like he knew a million of them. 'You are a writer now, no?'

'Yes sir,' I said, 'that one.'

'So why are you writing books?'

'Tough question, sir,' I stalled.

'Ok, a simple one. Why are you calling me so early on a Saturday?'

I told him why and forwarded the email to him.

'No name, eh?' he said as he read the mail.

'He could be in a hospital somewhere in Ahmedabad. He would have just checked in. Maybe he is dead. Or maybe he is at home and this was a hoax,' I said.

I was blabbering. I wanted help – for the boy and me. The prof had asked a good question. Why the hell did I write books – to get into this?

'We can check hospitals,' Prof said. 'I can ask a few students. But a name surely helps. Hey wait, this boy has a Gmail account, maybe he is on Orkut as well.'

'Or-what?' Life is tough when you are always talking to people smarter than you.

'You are so out of touch, Chetan. Orkut is a networking site. Gmail users sign up there. If he is a member and we are lucky, we can check his profile.'

I heard him clicking keys and sat before my own PC. I had just reached the Orkut site when Prof Basant exclaimed, 'Aha, Ahmedabad Businessman. There is a brief profile here. The name only says G. Patel. Interests are cricket, business, mathematics and friends. Doesn't seem like he uses Orkut much though.'

'What are you talking about Prof Basant? I woke up to a suicide note, written exclusively to me. Now you are telling me about his hobbies. Can you help me or…'

A pause, then, 'I will get some students. We will search for a new young patient called G. Patel, suspected of sleeping pill overdose. We will call you if we find anything, ok?'

'Yes, sir,' I said, breathing properly after a long time.

'And how is Anusha? You guys bunked my classes for dates and now forget me.'

'She is fine, sir.'

'Good, I always felt she was smarter than you. Anyway, let's find your boy,' the prof said and hung up.

Besides furniture shopping, I had to finish an office presentation. My boss, Michel's boss was due from New York. Hoping to impress him Michel had asked me to make a presentation of the group, with fifty charts. For three consecutive nights last week I had worked until 1:00 a.m., but had gotten only halfway.

'This is a suggestion. Don't take it the wrong way. But do consider taking a bath,' my wife said.

I looked at her.

'Just an option,' she said.

I think she is overcautious sometimes. I don't bite back.

'Yes, yes. I will,' I said and stared at the computer again.

Thoughts darted through my head. Should I call some hospitals myself? What if Prof Basant dozed off again? What if he could not collect the students? What if G. Patel was dead? And why am I becoming so involved here?

I took a reluctant shower. I opened the office presentation, but found myself unable to type a single word.

I refused breakfast, though regretted it moments later – as hunger and anxiety did not go well together.

My phone rang at 1.33 p.m.

'Hello,' Prof Basant's voice was unmistakable. 'We have a match at Civil Hospital. His name is Govind Patel, twenty-five years of age. A second-year student of mine found him.'

'And?'

'And he is alive. But won't talk. Even to his family. Must be in shock.'

'What are the doctors saying?' I said.

'Nothing. It is a government hospital. What do you expect? Anyway, they will flush his stomach and send him home. I won't worry too much now. Will ask a student to check again in the evening.'

'But what is his story? What happened?'

'All that I don't know. Listen, don't get too involved. India is a big country. These things happen all the time. The more you probe, the more the chances of the police harassing you.'

Next, I called the Civil Hospital. However, the operator did not know about the case and there was no facility to transfer line to the ward either.

Anusha, too, was relieved that the boy was safe. She then announced the plan for the day – the dining chair hunt. It would begin at Ikea on Alexandra Road.

We reached Ikea at around three o'clock and browsed through the space-saving dining sets. One dining table could fold four times over and become a coffee table – pretty neat.

'I want to know what happened to the twenty-fuve-year-old businessman,' I muttered.

'You will find out eventually. Let him recover. Must be one of those crazy reasons of youth – rejection in love, low marks or drugs.'

I stayed silent.

'C'mon, he just emailed you. Your ID is on your book cover. You really don't need to get involved. Should we take six or eight?' She moved towards an oak-wood set.

I protested that we rarely had so many guests at home. Six chairs would be enough.

'The marginal capacity utilisation of the two chairs would be less than ten per cent,' I said.

'You men are least helpful,' she tossed back and then selected six chairs.

My mind strayed back to the businessman.

Yes, everyone was right. I shouldn't get involved. But yet, of all the people in the world, this boy had sent me his last words. I couldn't help but get involved.

We ate lunch in the food court next to Ikea.

'I have to go,' I told my wife as I played with my lemon rice.

'Where? To the office. Ok, you are a free man now. I did my shopping,' my wife said.

'No. I want to go to Ahmedabad. I want to meet Govind Patel.' I did not meet her eye. Maybe I was sounding crazy.

'Are you nuts?'

I think it is only in my generation that Indian women started slamming their husbands.

'My mind keeps going back,' I said.

'What about your presentation? Michel will kill you.'

'I know. He won't get promoted unless he impresses his boss.'

My wife looked at me. My face was argument enough. She knew I would not talk sense until I had met the boy.

'Well, there is only one direct flight at 6 p.m. today. You can check the tickets.' She dialled the Singapore Airlines number and handed me the phone.

★

I entered the room the nurses had led me to. The eerie silence and the darkness made my footsteps sound loud. Ten different instruments beeped and LED lights flickered at regular intervals. Cables from the instruments disappeared into the man I had travelled thousands of miles to see – Govind Patel.

I noticed the curly hair first. He had a wheatish complexion and bushy eyebrows. His thin lips had turned dry because of the medicines.

'Hi, Chetan Bhagat ... the writer you wrote to,' I said, unsure if he could place me.

'O ... How did ... you find me?' he said, finding it difficult to speak.

'Destined to, I guess,' I said.

I shook hands and sat down. His mother came into the room. She looked so sleep-deprived, she could use a sleeping pill herself. I greeted her as she went out to get tea.

I looked at the boy again. I had two instant urges – one, to ask him what happened and two, to slap him.

'Don't look at me like that,' he said, shifting in his bed, 'you must be angry. Sorry, I should not have written that mail.'

'Forget the mail. You should not have done what you did.'

He sighed. He took a hard look at me and then turned his gaze sideways.

'I have no regrets,' he said.

'Shut up. There is nothing heroic in this. Cowards pop pills.'

'You would have done the same, if you were in my place.'

'Why? What happened to you?'

'It doesn't matter.'

We fell silent as his mother returned with tea. A nurse came in and told his mother to go home, but she refused to budge. Finally, the doctor had to intervene.

She left at 11.30 p.m. I stayed in the room, promising the doctor I would leave soon.

'So, tell me your story,' I said, once we were alone.

'Why? What can you do about it? You can't change what happened,' he said tiredly.

'You don't just listen to stories to change the past. Sometimes, it is important to know what happened.'

'I am a businessman. To me, people only do things out of self-interest. What's in it for you? And why should I waste my time telling you anything?'

I stared at the soft-skinned face that hid such hardness inside.

'Because I will want to tell others,' I said. There, that was my incentive.

'And why would anyone care? My story is not trendy or sexy like the IITs and call centres.'

He removed the quilt covering his chest. The heater and our conversation kept the room warm.

'I think they will care,' I said, 'a young person tried to kill himself. That does not seem right.'

'No one gives a fuck about me.'

I tried, but found it difficult to be patient. I considered slapping him again.

'Listen,' I said, pitching my voice to the maximum allowed in a hospital. 'You chose to send your last mail to me. That means at a certain level you trusted me. I located you and flew out within hours of your mail. You still question if I care? And now this cocky attitude, this arrogance is part of your business? Can't you talk to me like a friend? Do you even know what a friend is?'

A nurse came peeking into the room on hearing my loud voice. We became quiet. The clock showed midnight.

He sat there stunned. Everyone had behaved nicely with him today. I stood up and turned away from him.

'I know what a friend is,' he said at last.

I sat down next to him.

'I do know what a friend is. Because I had two, the best ones in the world.'

One

India vs South Africa
4th ODI, Vadodra
17 March 2000

Over 45

'Why the fuck did you have to move?' Ishaan's scream drowned out the stadium din on the TV. I had shifted up to a sofa from the floor.

'Huh?' I said. We were in Ishaan's house – Ishaan, Omi and I. Ishaan's mom had brought in tea and khakra for us. 'It is more comfortable to snack on the sofa. That is why I moved.'

'Tendulkar's gone. Fuck, now at *this* stage. Omi, don't you dare move now. Nobody moves for the next five overs.'

I looked at the TV. We were chasing 283 to win. India's score a ball ago was 256-2 after forty-five overs. Twenty-seven runs in five overs, with eight wickets to spare and Tendulkar on the crease. A cakewalk. The odds were still in India's favour, but Tendulkar was out. And that explained the frowns on Ishaan's forehead.

'The khakra's crispy,' Omi said. Ishaan glared at Omi, chiding him for his shallow sensory pleasure in a moment of national grief. Omi and I kept our tea cups aside and looked suitably mournful.

The crowd clapped as Tendulkar made his exit. Jadeja came to the crease and added six more runs. End of forty-six overs, India 262/3. Twenty-one more runs to win in four overs, with seven wickets in hand.

Over 46

'He made 122. The guy did his job. Just a few final closing shots left. Why are you getting so worked up?' I asked during a commercial break. I reached for my tea cup, but Ishaan signalled me to leave it alone. We were not going to indulge until the fate of the match was decided. Ishaan was pissed with us anyway. The match was in Vadodra, just two hours away from Ahmedabad. But we could not go – one, because we didn't have money, and two, because I had my correspondence exams in two days. Of course, I had wasted the whole day watching the match on TV instead, so reason number two did not really hold much weight.

'It is 5.25 runs required per over,' I said, not able to resist doing a mathematical calculation. That is one reason I like cricket, there is so much maths in it.

'You don't know this team. Tendulkar goes, they panic. It isn't about the average. It is like the queen bee is dead, and the hive loses order,' Ishaan said.

Omi nodded, as he normally does to whatever Ishaan has to say about cricket.

'Anyway, I hope you realise, we didn't meet today to see this match. We have to decide what Mr Ishaan is doing about his future, right?' I said.

Ishaan had always avoided this topic ever since he ran away from NDA a year ago. His dad had already sarcastically commented, 'Cut a cake today to celebrate one year of your uselessness.'

However, today I had a plan. I needed to sit them down to talk about our lives. Of course, against cricket, life is second priority.

'Later,' Ishaan said, staring avidly at a pimple cream commercial.

'Later when Ishaan? I have an idea that works for all of us. We don't have a lot of choice, do we?'

'All of us? Me, too?' Omi quizzed, already excited. Idiots like him love to be part of something, anything. However, this time we needed Omi.

'Yes, you play a critical role Omi. But later when Ish? When?'

'Oh, stop it! Look, the match is starting. Ok, over dinner. Let's go to Gopi,' Ish said.

'Gopi? Who's paying?' I was interrupted as the match began.

Beep, beep, beep. The horn of a car broke our conversation. A car zoomed outside the pol.

'What the hell! I am going to teach this bastard a lesson,' Ish said, looking out the window.

'What's up?'

'Bloody son of a rich dad. Comes and circles around our house everyday.'

'Why?' I said.

'For Vidya. He used to be in coaching classes with her. She complained about him there too,' Ish said.

Beep, beep, beep, the car came near the house again.

'Damn, I don't want to miss this match,' Ish said as he saw India hit a four. Ish picked up his bat. We ran out the house. The silver Esteem circled the pol and came back for another round of serenading. Ish stood in front of the car and asked the boy to stop. The Esteem halted in front of Ish. Ish went to the driver, an adolescent.

'Excuse me, your headlight is hanging out.'

'Really?' the boy said and shut off the ignition. He stepped outside and came to the front.

Ish grabbed the boy's head from behind and smashed his face into the bonnet. He proceeded to strike the headlight with his bat. The glass broke and the bulb hung out.

'What's your problem,' the boy said, blood spurting out of his nose.

'You tell me what's up? You like pressing horns?' Ish said.

Ish grabbed his collar and gave six non-stop slaps across his face. Omi picked up the bat and smashed the windscreen. The glass broke into a million pieces. People on the street gathered around as there is nothing quite as entertaining as a street fight.

The boy shivered in pain and fear. What would he tell his daddy about his broken car and face?

Ish's dad heard the commotion and came out of the house. Ish held the boy in an elbow lock. The boy was struggling to breathe.

'Leave him,' Ish's dad said.

Ish gripped him tighter.

'I said leave him,' Ish's dad shouted, 'what's going on here?'

'He has been troubling Vidya since last week,' Ish said. He kicked the boy's face with his knee and released him. The boy kneeled on the floor and sucked in air. The last kick from Ish had smeared the blood from his nose across his face.

'And what do you think you are doing?' Ish's dad asked him.

'Teaching him a lesson,' Ish said and unhooked his bat stuck in the windscreen.

'Really, when will you learn your lessons?' Ish's dad said to him.

Ish turned away.

'You go now,' Ish's dad said to the beeping driver, who folded his hands. Seeing that no one cared about his apology, he trudged back to his car.

Ish's dad turned to his neighbours. 'For one whole year he's been sitting at home. Ran away from the army of his own country and then wants to teach lessons to others! He and his loafer friends hanging around the house all day long.'

One sidelong glance at his dad and Ish walked back home.

'Where the hell are you going now?' Ish's dad said.

'Match. Why? You want to curse me some more?' Ish said.

'When you've wasted your entire life, what's another day?' Ish's father said and the neighbours half-nodded their heads in sympathy.

We missed the final five overs of the match. Luckily, India won and Ish didn't get that upset.

'Yes, yes, yes,' Ishaan jumped. 'Gopi on me tonight.' I love idiots.

Actually, Ishaan is not an idiot. At least not as much as Omi. It is just that both of them suck at studies, especially maths, and I am good at it. Hence, I have this chip on my shoulder. It does sound a bit conceited, but it is the only chip on my shoulder. For instance, I am easily the poorest of the three (though I will be the richest one day), even though Ishaan and Omi aren't particularly wealthy. Ishaan's dad works in the telephone exchange, and while they have lots of phones in the house, the salary is modest. Omi's dad is the priest of the Swamibhakti temple, which actually belongs to Omi's mom's family for generations. And that does not pay well either. But still, they are a lot better off than me and my mom. My mom runs a small Gujarati snacks business, and the little bit of money I make from tuitions helps us get by, but that's about it.

'We won, we won the series 3-1,' Omi repeated what he read on the TV screen. Of course, it would have been too much for him to express such original insight. Some say Omi was born stupid, while some say he became stupid after a cork ball hit him on the head in Class VI. I didn't know the reason, but I did know that maybe the best idea for him would be to become a priest. He wouldn't have much of a career otherwise, given that he barely scraped through Class XII, after repeating the maths compartment exam twice. But he didn't want to be a priest, so my plan was the best one.

I ate the khakra. My mother made it better than Ishaan's mom. We were professionals after all.

'I'll go home to change and then we will go to Gopi, ok?' I said as Ishaan and Omi were still dancing. Dancing after an Indian victory was a ritual we had started when we were eleven, one that should have stopped by thirteen. However, here we were at twenty-one, jigging like juveniles. Ok, so we won, someone had to. In mathematical terms, there was a pretty good probability – did it really need jumping around?

★

I walked back home.

The narrow lanes of the old city were bustling with the evening crowd. My house and Ishaan's were only half a kilometre apart. Everything in my world fell between this distance. I passed by the Nana Park, extra packed with kids playing cricket as India had won the match. I played here almost every day of my school life.

We still come here sometimes, but now we prefer the abandoned bank branch compound near my home.

A tennis ball landed at my feet. A sweaty twelve-year-old boy came running to me. I picked up the ball for him. Nana Park is where I had first met Ishaan and Omi, over fifteen years ago. There was no dramatic moment that marked the start of our friendship. Maybe we sized each other up as the only six-year-olds in the ground and started playing together.

Like most neighbourhood kids, we went to the Belrampur Municipal School, hundred metres down Nana Park. Of course, only I studied while Ish and Omi ran to the park at every opportunity.

Three bicycles tried to overtake each other in the narrow by lane. I had to step inside Qazi restaurant to let them pass. A scent of fried coriander and garlic filled the narrow room. The cook prepared dinner, a bigger feast than usual as India had won the match. Ishaan and I came here sometimes (without telling Omi, of course) for the cheap food and extraordinary mutton. The owner assured us 'small mutton', implying goat and not beef. I believed him, as he would not have survived in the neighbourhood if he served beef. I wanted to eat here instead of Gopi. But we had promised Gopi to Omi, and the food was fantastic there as well. Food is a passion here, especially as Gujarat is a dry state. People here get drunk on food.

Yes, Ahmedabad is my city. It is strange, but if you have had happy times in a city for a long time, you consider it the best city in the world. I feel the same about Ahmedabad. I know it is not one of those hip cities like Delhi, Bombay or Bangalore. I know people in these cities think of Ahmedabad as a small town, though that is not really the case. Ahmedabad is the sixth largest city in India, with a population of over five million. But I guess if you have to emphasise the importance of something, then it probably isn't as important in the first place. I could tell you that Ahmedabad has better multiplexes than Delhi or nicer roads than Bombay or better restaurants than Bangalore – but you will not believe me. Or even if you do, you won't give a damn. I know Belrampur is not Bandra, but why should I defend being called a small-town-person as if it is a bad thing? A funny thing about small towns is that people say it is the real India. I guess they do acknowledge that at one level the India of the big cities is fake. Yes, I am from the old city of Ambavad and proud of it. We don't have as many fashion shows and we still like our women to wear clothes. I don't see anything wrong with that.

I stepped out of Qazi and continued my way home, turning in the pol towards Omi's temple. Of course, we called it Omi's temple because he lived there, but the official name was the Swamibhakti temple. As I entered the by lane, two people fought over garbage disposal around the crammed pol.

There are things about my small town neighbourhood that I want to change. In some ways, it is way behind the rest of Ahmedabad. For one, the whole old city could be a lot cleaner. The new city across the other side of the Sabarmati river has gleaming glass and steel buildings, while the old city finds it difficult to get rubbish cleared on time.

I want to change another thing. I want to stop the gossip theories people come up with about other people. Like the theory about Omi becoming stupid because a cricket ball hit him. There is no basis for it, but every pol in Belrampur talks about it. Or the theory that Ish was thrown out of NDA and did not run away. I know for a fact that it is not true. Ish cannot handle unquestioned authority, and even though he was really excited about the army (which was his only option), he could not stand some Major ordering him around for the next two decades of his life. So he paid the penalty, cited personal reasons like ailing parents or something and ran right back to Belrampur.

And of course, what I want to stop the most – the weirdest theory that I became emotionless the day dad left us. Dad left mom and me over ten years ago, for we found out he had a second wife across town. As far as I can remember, I was never good with emotional stuff. I love maths, I love logic and those subjects have no place for emotion. I think human beings waste too much time on emotions. The prime example is my mother. Dad's departure was followed by months of crying with every lady in every pol coming down to sympathise with her. She spent another year consulting astrologers as to which planet caused dad to move out, and when will that position change. Thereafter, a string of grandaunts came to live with her as she could not bring herself to stay alone. It wasn't until I turned fifteen and understood how the world worked that I could coax her into opening the snacks business. Of course, my coaxing was part of it, the rest of it was that all her jewellery was officially sold by then.

Her snacks were great, but she was no businessman. Emotional people make terrible businessmen. She would sell on credit and buy on cash – the first mistake a small business can make. Next, she would keep no accounts. The home spending money was often mixed with the business money, and we frequently had months where the choice was to buy either rice for our consumption or black pepper for the papads.

Meanwhile, I studied as much as I could. Our school was not Oxford, and emphasis on studies was low with more teachers bunking classes than students. Still, I topped maths every single year. People thought I was gifted when I hit a hundred in maths in class X. For me, it was no big deal. For once, the gossip vine helped. The news of my score spread across pols, and we had a new source of income – tuitions. I was the only maths tutor in Belrampur, and bad maths scores had reached epidemic proportions. Along with khaman and khakra, trigonometry and algebra became sources of income in the Patel household. Of course, it was a poor neighbourhood, so people could not pay much. Still, another thousand bucks a month was a lifestyle changing event for us. From fan, we graduated to cooler. From chairs, we went to a secondhand sofa. Life became good.

I reached Omi's temple. The loud rhythmic chime of the bell interrupted my thoughts. I checked my watch, it was 6 p.m., the daily aarti time. I saw Omi's dad from a distance, his eyes closed as he chanted the mantras. Even though I was an agnostic, there was something amazing about his face – it had genuine feeling for the God he prayed to. No wonder he was among the most liked people in the community. Omi's mother was beside him, her maroon saree draped along her head and hands folded. Next to her was Bittoo Mama, Omi's maternal uncle. He was dressed in a white dhoti and saffron scarf. His huge biceps seemed even larger with his folded hands. His eyes, too, were transfixed in genuine admiration for the idols of Krishna and Radha.

Omi would get into trouble for reaching the aarti late. It would not be the first time though, as matches in Nana Park were at a crucial stage around 6 p.m.

★

'How was the match?' mom said as I reached home. She stood outside the house.

She had just finished loading a hired auto with fresh dhokla for a marriage party. Finally, my mother could delegate routine tasks like delivery and focus on her core competence – cooking. She took out a dhokla piece from the auto for me. Bad business – snucking out something from a customer order.

'Great match. Nail-biting finish, we won,' I said, walking in.

I switched on the tubelight inside. The homes in our pol required light even during daytime.

'If I have a good Diwali season, I will get you a colour TV,' mom vowed.

'No need,' I said. I removed my shoes to get ready for a shower, 'you need a bigger grinder urgently, the small one is all wobbly.'

'I will buy the TV if only the business makes extra money,' she said.

'No. If you make extra money, put it back in the business. Don't buy useless things. I can always see the match in colour in Ishaan's house.'

She left the room. My mother knew it was futile arguing with me. Without dad around, it was amazing how much say I had in the house. And I only hoped Ish and Omi would listen to my proposition as well.

My love for business began when I first started tuitions. It was amazing to see money build up. With money came not only things like coolers and sofas but also the most important stuff – respect. Shopkeepers no longer avoided us, relatives re-invited us to weddings and our landlord's visit did not throw us into turmoil. And then there was the thrill – I was *making* money, not earning it under some boss or getting a handout. I could decide my fate, how many students to teach, how many hours per class – it was *my* decision.

There is something about Gujaratis, we love business. And Ambavadis love it more than anything else. Gujarat is the only state in India where people tend to respect you more if you have a business than if you are in service. The rest of the country dreams about a cushy job that gives a steady salary and provides stability. In Ahmedabad, service is for the weak. That was why I dreamt my biggest dream – to be a big businessman one day. The only hitch was my lack of capital. But I would build it slowly and make my dream come true. Sure, Ish could not make his dream of being in the Indian cricket team real, but that was a stupid dream to begin with. To be in the top eleven of a country of a billion people was in many ways an impossible dream, and even though Ish was top class in Belrampur, he was no Tendulkar. My dream was more realistic, I would start slow and then grow my business. From a turnover of thousands, to lakhs, to crores and then to hundreds of crores.

I came out of the shower and dressed again.

'Want to eat anything?' my mother voiced her most quoted line from the kitchen.

'No, I am going out with Ish and Omi to Gopi.'

'Gopi? Why? I make the same things. What do you get at Gopi that I can't give you at home?'

Peace and quiet, I wanted to say.

'It's Ish's treat. And I want to talk to them about my new business.'

'So you are not repeating the engineering entrance,' my mother came out of the kitchen. She raised dough-covered hands, 'You can take a year to prepare. Stop taking tuitions for a while, we have money now.'

My mother felt guilty about a million things. One of them was me not making it to a good engineering college. Tuitions and supporting my mom's business meant I could study less for the entrance exams. I didn't make it to IIT or any of the top institutes. I did make it to a far-flung college in Kutch, but it wasn't worth it to leave my tuition income, friends, cricket at Nana Park and mom for that. Not that I felt any emotion, it just did not seem like the right trade. I could do maths honours right here in Ambavad University, continue tuitions and think about business. The Kutch college did not even guarantee a job.

'I don't want to be an engineer, mom. My heart is in business. Plus, I have already done two years of college. One more and I will be a graduate.'

'Yes, but who gives a job to a maths graduate?'

It was true. Maths honours was a stupid course to take from an economic point of view.

'It is ok. I needed a degree and I can get it without studying much,' I said. 'I am a businessman, mom. I can't change that.'

My mother pulled my cheeks. Chunks of dough stuck to my face.

'Be whatever. You are always my son first.'

She hugged me. I hated it. I hate a display of emotion more than emotion itself.

'I better go.'

★

'That is your tenth chapatti,' Ish told Omi.

'Ninth. Who cares? It is a buffet. Can you pass the ghee please?'

'All that food. It has to be bad for you,' Ish said.

'Two hundred push-ups.' Omi said. 'Ten rounds of Nana Park. One hour at Bittoo Mama's home gym. You do this everyday like me and you can hog without worry.'

People like Omi are no-profit customers. There is no way Gopi could make money off him.

'Aamras, and ras malai. Thanks,' Omi said to the waiter. Ish and I nodded for the same.

'So, what's up? I'm listening,' Ish said as he scooped up the last spoon of aamras.

'Eat your food first. We'll talk over tea,' I said. People argued less on a full stomach.

'I am not paying for tea. My treat is limited to a thali,' Ishaan protested.

'I'll pay for the tea,' I said.

'Relax, man. I was only joking. Mr Accounts can't even take a joke. Right, Omi?'

Omi laughed.

'Whatever. Guys, you really need to listen today. And stop calling me Mr Accounts.'

I ordered tea while the waiter cleared our plates.

'I am serious, Ish. What do you plan to do with your life? We are not kids anymore,' I said.

'Unfortunately,' Ish said and sighed. 'Ok, then. I will apply for jobs, maybe do an NIIT computer course first. Or should I take an insurance job? What do you think?'

I saw Ish's face. He tried to smile, but I saw the pain. The champion batsman of Belrampur would become an insurance salesman. Belrampur kids had grown up applauding his boundaries at Nana Park. But now, when he had no life ahead, he wanted to insure other people's lives.

Omi looked at me, hoping I'd come up with a great option from Santa's goodie bag. I was sick of parenting them.

'I want to start a business,' I began.

'Not again,' Ish said. 'I can't do that man. What was it the last time? A fruit dealership? Ugh! I can't be weighing watermelons all day. And the crazy one after that, Omi?'

'Car accessories. He said there is big money in that,' Omi said as he slurped his dessert.

'What? Put seat covers all day. No thanks. And the other one – stock broker. What is that anyway?' Ish shrugged.

'So what the fuck do you want to do? Beg people to buy insurance. Or sell credit cards at street corners? You, Ish, are a military school dropout,' I said and paused for breath. 'And you got a compartment in Class XII, twice. You can be a priest, Omi, but what about us?'

'I don't want to be a priest,' Omi said listlessly.

'Then, why do you oppose me even before I start? This time I have something that will interest you.'

'What?' Ish said.

'Cricket,' I said.

'What?' both of them said in unison.

'There you go, nice to get your attention. Now can I talk?'

'Sure,' Ish waved a hand.

'We are going to open a cricket shop,' I said.

I deliberately left for the restroom.

'But how?' Omi interrogated when I returned. 'What is a cricket shop?'

'A sports store really. But since cricket is the most popular game in Belrampur, we will focus on that.'

Ish's silence meant he was listening to me.

'It will be a small retail store. Money for a shop deposit is a problem, so I need Omi's help.'

'Mine?' Omi said.

'Yes, we will open the shop right inside the Swami temple complex. Next to the flower and puja shops. I noticed an empty shop there. And it is part of the temple land.'

'A cricket shop in a temple complex?' Ish questioned.

'Wait. Omi, do you think you can arrange that? Without that our plan is a non-starter.'

'You mean the Kuber sweet shop that just closed? The temple trust will rent it out soon. And normally they let it out to something related to temple activities,' Omi said.

'I know. But you have to convince your dad. After all he runs the temple trust.'

'He does, but Mama looks after the shops. Will we pay rent?'

'Yes,' I sighed. 'But not immediately. We need a two-month waiver. And we cannot pay the deposit.'

'I'll have to go through mom,' Omi said. Good, his mind was working.

'Sorry to ask again, but a cricket shop in a temple complex? Who will buy? Seventy-year-old aunties who come for kirtan will want willow bats?' Ish scoffed.

The waiter had cleared our tea and presented the bill. By Gopi protocol, we had to be out of the restaurant in two minutes.

'Good question. A cricket shop by a temple does sound strange. But think – is there any sports shop in Belrampur?'

'Not really. You don't even get leather balls. Ellis Bridge is the nearest,' Ish said.

'See, that's number one. Number two, the temple is a family place. Kids are among the most bored people in temples. Where are they going to hang out?'

'It is true,' Omi said. 'That is why so many balloon wallahs hover outside.'

'And that is where Ish comes in. People know you were a good player. And you can give playing tips to every kid who comes to buy from us. Slowly, our reputation will build.'

'But what about Christian or Muslim kids? They won't come, right?' Ish said.

'Not at first but the shop is outside the temple. As word spreads, they will come. What choice do they have anyway?'

'Where will we get what we sell?' Ish said.

'There's a sports equipment supplier in Vastrapur who will give us a month's credit. If we have the space, we are good to go without cash.'

'But what if it doesn't run?' Ish asked with scepticism.

'Worst case, we sell the stock at a loss and I'll cover the rest through my tuition savings. But it will work, man. If you put your heart into it, it will.'

Both of them remained silent.

'Guys, please. I need you for this. I really want to run a business. I can't do it without partners. It's cricket,' I appealed to Ish.

'I'm in,' Omi smiled. 'I don't have to be a priest and I get to work from home. I'm so in.'

'I won't handle money. I'll focus on the cricket,' Ish said.

I smiled. Yes, he was coming around.

'Of course. You think I will let you handle cash? So, are we partners?' I stretched out my hand.

Omi hi-fived me and Ish joined in.

'What are we going to call it?' Omi said in the auto.

'Ask Ish,' I said. If Ish named it, he would feel more connected to the project.

'How about Team India Cricket Shop?' Ish suggested.

'Great name,' I said and watched Ish smile for the first time that evening.

'Two rupees fifty paise each, guys,' I said as the auto stopped near my pol in Belrampur.

'Here you go Mr Accounts,' Ish said and passed his share.

Two

The Team India Cricket Shop opened with the smashing of a coconut on the morning of 29 April 2000. All our immediate families had come. My mother and Omi's family were visibly happy while Ish's parents were silent. They still visualised Ish as an army officer, not a shopkeeper in Belrampur.

'May Laxmi shower all blessings on you hardworking boys,' Omi's mother said before she left.

Soon, it was just us in our twenty-feet-by-ten-feet shop.

'Move the counter in, the shutter won't close,' Ish screamed at Omi. Omi's forehead broke into sweat as he lifted the bulky countertop yet again to move it back an inch.

I stepped out of the shop and crossed the road for the tenth time to look at the board. It was six feet wide and two feet tall. We had painted it blue – the colour of the Indian team. In the centre, we had the letters 'Team India Cricket Shop' in the colours of the Indian flag. The excited painter from Shahpur had thrown in the faces of Tendulkar and Ganguly for free. Ganguly had a squint and Tendulkar's lips looked bee-stung, but it all added to the charm.

'It's beautiful,' Omi said as he joined me in looking at the board.

Our first customer came at 12 noon. An under-ten boy strolled to the front of our store as his mother bought puja flowers. The three of us sprung into action.

'Should I ask him what he wants?' Omi whispered to me.

I shook my head. Pushy meant desperate.

The boy looked at tennis balls and bounced a few of them. While no one played tennis in Belrampur, kids played cricket with them.

'How much for the balls?' The boy moved to local balls. Clearly this was a price-sensitive customer. He bounced five different ones on the ground.

'Eight bucks. You want one?' I said.

He nodded.

'You have money?'

'Mummy has,' he said.

'Where is mummy?'

'There,' he pointed in the general direction of the other temple shops. I picked up the balls he had bounced and placed them in the basket.

His mother came running into our shop.

'There you are Sonu, stupid boy,' she pulled his elbow and took him out.

'Mummy, ball' was all he could say about his potential purchase.

'Don't worry, we will sell,' I told my business partners.

We made our first sale soon after. Two young brothers wearing branded clothes came to the shop.

'How much for tennis balls?' one boy said.

'Eight bucks for Arrow, six bucks for the local basket there,' Ish said.

The boys moved to the local basket. They started the ball-bouncing routine again as my heart wept.

'So where do you play cricket?' Ish asked them.

'Satellite,' the elder boy said.

Satellite was an upmarket neighbourhood on the other side of the Sabarmati river.

'What are you doing in the old city?' Ish said.

'We came to the temple. It is Harsh bhaiya's birthday,' the younger boy said.

I realised we had struck real-estate gold. The temple was ancient and drew in people from the new city, too. And it was a birthday, every chance of pockets being loaded.

'You want to see bats?' I asked from the cash counter.

The boys shook their heads.

Ish turned to me and signalled silence.

'Happy birthday, Harsh. You bowler or batsman?' Ish said.

Harsh looked up at Ishaan. A grown-up man asking an eleven-year-old if he was a bowler or batsman was a huge honour. It meant he was now old enough to be specialised, even though he may not have thought about it.

'Er, I am more of a batsman,' Harsh said.

'Defensive or attack?' Ish asked as if he was interviewing Tendulkar on ESPN.

'Huh?' Harsh said.

'You like shots?' Ish asked. Which kid didn't? Harsh nodded.

'Show me your stance,' Ish said. He turned to me and asked for a bat. I went to the stack of willow bats. I had bought them directly from a Kashmiri supplier in Law Garden. I picked the right size for the boy. Size six and two hundred bucks. Not top of the line, of course, but the best we could hope to sell here.

Harsh took a stance on the empty space in front of the shop. Like every kid, he leaned his entire weight on the bat while standing. Ish moved over and gently straightened Harsh's back. He moved his wrist upwards, and told him to balance the weight evenly on the legs.

'And now, whenever you attack, use the front leg to move forward but do not forget the back leg. That is your support, your anchor. Notice Tendulkar, he keeps one leg fixed.'

An awestruck Harsh air-struck a few strokes.

'Give me some tips, too,' the younger one whined.

'First me, Chinu,' Harsh said.

Ish turned to Chinu. 'What are you, Chinu?'

'All-rounder,' Chinu said promptly.

'Great. Show me your bowling grip.'

Their parents finally found our shop. It was time to go to the temple.

'Mummy, I want the ball,' Chinu said.

'How much?' his mother said.

'Six rupees,' Ish said.

She took out a twenty-rupee note and asked me to give two.

'I want the bat, mummy,' Harsh said.

'You already have a bat.'

'This one is better for my stance, mummy. Please.' Harsh took a stance again. He had improved with the lesson but his mother ignored him.

'How much is this?' she said.

'Two hundred rupees,' I said.

'Too expensive. No Harsh, we are not getting a bat.'

'My birthday present, mummy, please.' Harsh cajoled.

'Yes but beta, why buy something from this temple shop. Old city doesn't have good quality. We will go to the Navrangpura market.'

'It is excellent quality, aunty. We source from Kashmiri suppliers. Take my word,' Ish said.

'Aunty' eyed us with suspicion.

'I was the team captain for all municipal schools in the area, aunty. I have personally chosen the bats,' Ish said with as much heart as Omi's dad said his prayers.

'Please, mummy,' Harsh said and tugged at her saree. The tug connected to aunty's purse, which opened and brought out two hundred-rupee notes.

Done. We had closed the deal of the day. The bat cost us a hundred and sixty, so forty bucks profit, I exclaimed mentally.

'Goodbye, champ.' Ish waved to Harsh.

'I'll come to your shop on my happy birthday,' Chinu said.

'Yes! You are amazing, Ish,' I said and hi-fived everyone.

'The kid is a quick learner. If he practices, he will be good. Of course, his mother will stuff him with studies the moment he reaches Class X. The only stance he will take is to sit on a desk with his books,' Ish said.

'Don't be depressing, man,' I said. 'We made forty bucks on the bat and four on the two balls. We are forty-four bucks in profit, sir.'

We sold some candy and two more balls in the next two hours. Our total profit for the day was fifty bucks. We moved the bats and the ball baskets inside and closed shop at 7.00 p.m., after the puja. To celebrate our opening we chose the chana-bhatura stall. At four bucks a plate, I could expense it to the business.

'Do I get to take some money home? I really want to give mom my first salary,' Omi said as he tucked in half a chili with his hot bhatura.

'Wait, this isn't real profit. This is contribution. We earn the rent first and then we will see.' I placed my empty plate back at the stall. 'Congrats guys, we are in business.'

Three Months Later

'Eight thousand three, four and five hundred,' I said as I emptied the cashier's box. 'This is our profit for the first three months after paying rent. Not bad, not bad at all.'

I was super-pleased. Our shop had opened at an opportune time. The summer vacations had started and India had won the one-day series with South Africa. Kids with lots of time and patriotism flocked to Team India Cricket Shop the day they received their pocket money.

Some came even without money, if only to meet Ish and get tips on cricket. I didn't mind as it helped us pass the time. The dull aspect of opening a shop is boredom. We opened from nine to seven, and even with twenty customers a day it meant only around two customers an hour.

'So we get our share now?' Omi said excitedly.

I divided the money into four stacks. The first three stacks were fifteen hundred rupees each – the money each of us could take home. The remaining four thousand was to be retained in the business.

'What do you mean retained? What do we need to retain it for?' Ish questioned even as Omi happily counted his notes.

'Ish, we need to keep a war chest in case we want to renovate the store. Don't you want a better glass countertop? Or nicer lighting?'

Ish shook his head.

'Sure we do. And … I have expansion plans,' I said.

'What?'

'There is a new shopping mall under construction at Navrangpura char rasta. If you book early, you can get a discount on renting a shop.'

'Renting? But we already have a shop,' Ish said, puzzled and irritated at the same time.

I knew why Ish grumbled. He wanted to buy a TV for the shop. Listening to matches on radio during shop hours was no fun.

'No Ish, a proper shop. Young people like to shop in swanky malls. That is the future. Our shop has been doing good business, but we can't grow unless we move to a new city location.'

'I like it here,' Omi said. 'This is our neighbourhood. What we sell is being used by kids in Nana Park.'

'I don't want this short-sighted mentality. I will open a store in a mall, and by next year have one more store. If you don't grow in business, you stagnate.'

'Another shop? What? We will not be working together?' Omi said.

'It is Govind's bullshit. We have only started and he already aspires to be Ambani. Can't we just buy a TV?' Ish said, 'Shah Electronics will give us on instalment if we pay a downpayment of four thousand.'

'No way. We keep the four thousand for business.'

'Well, the TV belongs to the business, no?' Ish said.

'Yes, but it is a dead asset. It doesn't earn. We have a long way to go. Three thousand a month is nothing. And Ish doesn't let me keep notebooks and pencils…'

'I said this is a sports store. I don't want kids to think about studies when they come here.'

Ish and I had argued about this before. I saw an easy opportunity, but Ish protested every time.

'Ok, here is a deal,' Ish said, 'I agree to the notebooks, not textbooks mind you, only notebooks. But we buy a TV. I have to watch matches. I don't care, here take my fifteen hundred.'

He threw his share of cash at me.

Omi tossed in his money as well. As usual, I had to surrender to fools.

'Ok, but we need to increase the revenue. Target for next quarter is twenty thousand bucks.'

They ignored me as they discussed TV brands. I shook my head and outlined my strategy for increasing revenues.

'Will you do coaching classes?' I asked Ish.

'What?'

'Kids love your cricket tips. Why not do cricket coaching for a fee?'

'Me? I am not that good man. And where? In the temple?'

'No, we will do it in the abandoned SBI compound.'

'Why? Aren't we making enough?' Omi said.

'We can never make enough. I want to get to fifty thousand a quarter. Omi, you can give fitness training to the students.'

'So more work for us. What about you?' Ish said.

'I am going to start offering maths tuitions again.'

'Here?'

'Yes, a couple here, or in the SBI compound itself while you guys give cricket coaching.'

Omi and Ish looked at me like I was the hungriest shark in the world.

'C'mon guys. I am making sure we have a solid healthy business.'

'It is ok. Just the shop is so boring, Ish,' Omi said. He was excited about making kids do pushups.

'Yeah, at least I will get to hit the pitch,' Ish said.

I tossed in my fifteen hundred, too, and we bought a TV the same day. We set it permanently at the sports channel. Omi brought mats and cushions and spread them in front of the TV. On match days, we would all sit there until a customer arrived. I had to admit, it made the day go by much quicker.

I changed the board on the shop. Under the 'Team India Cricket Shop', it also said 'Stationery, Cricket Coaching and Maths Tuitions available'. I may not have diversified geographically, but I had diversified my product offering.

Three

A part from cricket, badminton was the other popular game in Belrampur. In fact, the girls only played badminton. It was an excellent turnover business. Shuttle cocks needed to be replaced, rackets needed rewiring and badminton rackets didn't last as long as cricket bats.

School stationery became the other hit item in the following weeks. Only some kids played sports, but every kid needed notebooks, pens and pencils, and parents never said no to that. Many times, someone buying a ball would buy a notebook, or the other way round. We offered a total solution. Soon, suppliers came to us themselves. They kept stuff on credit and returnable basis – chart paper, gum bottles, maps of India, water bottles and tiffin boxes. It is only after you open a shop that you realise the length and breadth of the Indian student industry.

We kept the cricket coaching and tuitions at the same price – 250 rupees a month. Customers for maths tuitions were easier to get, given the higher demand and my track record. I taught at the SBI compound building in the mornings. Ish used the compound grounds for the two students who signed up for cricket tuitions.

They were the best players in the Belrampur Municipal School and had fought with their parents to let them try coaching for three months.

Of course, we still spent most of our time in the shop.

'Should we do greeting cards?' I wondered as I opened a sample packet left by a supplier. At five-rupee retail price and two-rupee cost price, cards had solid margins. However, people in Belrampur did not give each other greeting cards.

'This is in-swinger, and this is off-swinger. By the way, this is the third ball in two weeks. What's up Tapan?' Ish asked a regular customer. Thirteen-year-old Tapan was one of the best bowlers of his age in the Belrampur Municipal School. Ish gripped the cricket ball and showed him the wrist movement.

'It is that nightmare Ali. Ball keeps getting lost with his shots. Why did he move to our school?' Tapan grumbled as he rubbed the ball on his shorts.

'Ali? New student? Haven't seen him here,' Ish said. All good players visited our store and Ish knew them personally.

'Yes, batsman. Just joined our school. You should come see him. He wouldn't come here, right?' Tapan said.

Ish nodded. We had few Muslim customers. Most of them used other Hindu boys to make their purchases.

'You want to sign up for cricket tuitions. Ish will teach you, he played at the district level,' I could not help pitching our other service.

'Mummy will not allow. She said I can only take tuitions for studies. No sports coaching,' Tapan said.

'It is ok, have a good game,' Ish said, ruffling the boy's hair.

'You see this. That is why India doesn't win every match,' Ish said after Tapan left.

Yes, Ish has this ridiculous theory that India should win every match. 'Well, we don't have to. It won't be much of a game otherwise,' I said and closed the cash box.

'Our country has a billion people. We should always win,' Ish insisted.

'Statistically impossible.'

'Why? Australia has twenty million people. Yet they win almost every match. We have fifty times the people, so fifty times the talent. Plus, cricket is India's only game while Australia has rugby and football and whatever. So there is no way we should be defeated by them. Statistically, my friend, Australia should be a rounding error.'

'Then why?' I said.

'Well, you saw that kid. Parents will spend thousands teaching kids useless trigonometry and calculus they will never use in real life. But if it is sports coaching, it is considered a waste of money.'

'Don't worry, we have them covered. Our shop now offers both.'

'It is not about the business Govind. Really, is this just about money for you?'

'Money is nice…'

'These kids, Govind. Look at them, thirteen-year-olds holding their bats with pride. Or the way they want to learn to bowl better. They have a fire in their eyes before every little match at Nana Park. When India wins, they dance. They are they only people I see with passion. I like being with them.'

'Whatever,' I shrugged.

'Of course, in two years time they will reach Class X. Their bats will be replaced with physics books. And then the spark will begin to die. Soon, they will turn into depressed adults.'

'That is not true, Ish. Everyone needs a passion. I have mine.'

'Then why are most grown-ups so grumpy? Why can't they smile more often and be excited like those kids at Nana Park?'

'Can you stop being grumpy now and help me clean the shop?'

★

'Ok, ok, we will do a booze party,' I laughed. Omi and Ish had gripped me tight from both sides until I relented.

'Where is my son Omi?' Bittoo Mama entered our shop at closing time and proceeded to hug his nephew. He held a box of sweets in a red velvet cloth.

'Where were you, Mama?' Omi said. Since the shop opened, he had never visited us.

'I toured all over Gujarat, with Parekh-ji. What an experience! Here, have some besan ladoos. Fresh from Baroda,' Bittoo Mama said. I ordered a Frooti. Ish pulled out stools and we sat outside. I picked a ladoo.

'What is this, Omi? Wearing shoes?' Bittoo Mama's eyes were lined with kohl. He had a red tikka in the middle of his forehead.

'Mama?' Omi squeaked. I looked at my feet. I wore fake Reebok slippers. Ish wore his old sneakers.

'Your shop is in a temple, and you are wearing shoes? A Brahmin priest's boy?'

'Mama, c'mon this is outside the temple. None of the other shopkeepers wear…'

'Other shopkeepers are useless baniyas so you will also become like them? Do you do puja every morning before you open?'

'Yes, Mama,' Omi lied point-blank.

'You also,' Mama said, referring to Ish and me. 'You are Hindu boys. You have your shop in such a pure place. At least remove your shoes, light a lamp.'

'We come here to work, not to perform rituals,' I said. I now paid full rent every month to be in this shop. Nobody told me how to run my business.

Mama looked surprised. 'What is your name?'

'Govind.'

'Govind what?'

'Govind Patel.'

'Hindu, no?'

'I am agnostic,' I said, irritated as I wanted to shut the shop and go home.

'Agno…?'

'He is not sure if there is God or not,' Ish explained.

'Doesn't believe in God? What kind of friends do you have, Omi?' Mama was aghast.

'No, that is an atheist,' I clarified. 'Agnostic means maybe God exists, maybe he doesn't. I don't know.'

'You young kids,' Bittoo said, 'such a shame. I had come to invite you and look at you.'

Omi looked at me. I turned my gaze away.

'Don't worry about Govind, Mama. He is confused.' I hate it when people take my religious status for confusion. Why did I have to or not have to believe in something?

Ish offered the Frooti to Bittoo Mama. It softened him a little.

'What about you?' Mama asked Ish.

'Hindu, Mama. I pray and everything.' Ish said. Yeah right, only when six balls were left in a match.

Mama took a large sip and shifted his gaze to Omi and Ish. As far as he was concerned I did not exist.

'What did you want to invite us for Mama?' Omi said.

He lifted the red velvet cloth and unwrapped a three-foot-long brass trishul. Its sharp blades glinted under the shop's tubelight.

'It's beautiful. Where did you get it from?' Omi queried.

'It is a gift from Parekh-ji. He said in me he sees the party's future. I worked day and night. We visited every district in Gujarat. He said, "if we have more people like Bittoo, people will be proud to be Hindu again." He made me the recruitment in-charge for young people in Ahmedabad.'

Ish and I looked at Omi for footnotes.

'Parekh-ji is a senior Hindu party leader. And he heads the biggest temple trust in Baroda,' Omi said. 'What, he knows the CM or something, Mama?'

'Parekh-ji not only knows the CM, but also talks to him twice a day,' Bittoo Mama said. 'And I told Parekh-ji about you, Omi. I see in you the potential to teach Hindu pride to young people.'

'But Mama, I'm working full time…'

'I am not telling you to leave everything. But get in touch with the greater responsibilities we have. We are not just priests who speak memorised lines at ceremonies. We have to make sure India's future generation understands Hindutva properly. I want to invite you to a grand feast to Parekh-ji's house. You should come too, Ish. Next Monday in Gandhinagar.'

Of course, blasphemous me got no invitation.

'Thanks, Mama. It sounds great, but I don't know if we can,' Ish said. How come some people are so good at being polite.

'Why? Don't worry, it is not just priests. Many young, working people will also come.'

'I don't like politics,' Ish said.

'Huh? This isn't politics, son. This is a way of life.'

'I will come,' Omi said.

'But you should come too, Ish. We need young blood.'

Ish stayed hesitant.

'Oh, you think Parekh-ji is some old, traditional man who will force you to read scriptures. Do you know where Parekh-ji went to college? Cambridge, and then Harvard. He had a big hotel business in America, which he sold and came back. He talks your language. Oh, and he used to play cricket too, for the Cambridge college team.'

'I will come if Govind comes,' said Ish the idiot.

Mama looked at me. In his eyes, I was the reason why Hindu culture had deteriorated lately.

'Well, I came to invite the three of you in the first place. He only said he doesn't believe in God.'

'I didn't say that,' I said. Oh, forget it, I thought.

'Then come.' Mama stood up. 'All three of you. I'll give Omi the address. It is the grandest house in Gandhinagar.'

★

People called me Mr Accounts; greedy, miser, anything. But the fact is, I did organise an all-expense-paid booze party to motivate my partners at the shop. It is bloody hard to get alcohol in Ahmedabad, let alone bulky bottles of beer. One of my contacts – Romy Bhai – agreed to supply a crate of extra strong beer for a thousand bucks.

At 7 p.m. on the day of the party, Romi Bhai left the beer – wrapped in rags – at the SBI compound entrance. I came to the gate and gave Romi Bhai the day's newspaper. On the third page of the newspaper, I had stapled ten hundred-rupee notes. He nodded and left.

I dragged the cloth package inside and placed the bottles in the three ice-filled buckets I had kept in the kitchen. I took out the bottle opener from the kitchen shelf, where we kept everything from Maggi noodles to boxes of crackers to burst when India won a match.

Another person may see the abandoned SBI branch as an eerie party venue. This used to be an old man's haveli. The owner could not repay and the bank foreclosed the property. Thereafter, the bank opened a branch in the haveli. The owner's family filed a lawsuit after he died. The dispute still unresolved, the family obtained a court injunction that the bank could not use the property for profit. Meanwhile, SBI realised that a tiny by lane in Belrampur was a terrible branch location. They vacated the premises and gave the keys to the court. The court official kept a key with Omi's dad, a trustworthy man in the area. This was done in case officials needed to view it and the court was closed. Of course, no one ever came and Omi had access to the keys.

The property was a six-hundred square yard plot, huge by Belrampur standards. The front entrance directly opened into the living room, now an abandoned bank customer service area. The three bedrooms on the first floor were the branch manager's office, the data room and the locker room. The branch manager's office had a giant six-feet vault. We kept our cricket kit in the otherwise empty safe.

We hung out most in the haveli's backyard. In its prime, it was the lawn of a rich family. As part of the bank branch, it was an under-utilised parking lot and now, our practice pitch.

I rotated the beer bottles in the ice bucket to make them equally cold.

Ish walked into the bank.

'So late,' I said. 'It is 8.30.'

'Sorry, watching cricket highlights. Wow, strong beer,' Ish said as he picked up a bottle. We had parked ourselves on the sofas in the old customer waiting area downstairs. I reclined on the sofa. Ish went to the kitchen to get some bhujia.

'Omi here?' Ish said as he opened the packet.

'No, I am the only fool. I take delivery, clean up the place and wait for my lords to arrive.'

'Partners, man, partners,' Ish corrected. 'Should we open a bottle?'

'No, wait.'

Omi arrived in ten minutes. He made apologies about his dad holding him back to clean the temple. Omi then prayed for forgiveness before drinking alcohol.

'Cheers!' all of us said as we took a big sip. It was bitter, and tasted only slightly better than phenyl.

'What is this? Is this genuine stuff?' Ish asked.

We paused for a moment. Spurious alcohol is a real issue in Ahmedabad.

'Nah, nobody makes fake beer. It is just strong,' I said.

If you filled your mouth with bhujia, the beer did not taste half as bad. In fact, the taste improved considerably after half a bottle. As did everyone's mood.

'I want to see this Ali kid. Three customers have mentioned him,' Ish said.

'The Muslim boy?' Omi said.

'Stop talking like your Mama?' Ish scolded. 'Is that relevant? They say he has excellent timing.'

'Where does he play?' I enquired through a mouthful of bhujia.

'In our school. Kids say his most common shot is a six.'

'Let's go check him out. Looks like the school has your worthy successor,' I said.

Ish turned silent. It was a sensitive topic and if it was not for the beer, I would not have said it.

'Succeeding Ish is hard,' Omi said. 'Remember the hundred against Mahip Municipal School, in sixty-three balls? No one forgets that innings.' Omi stood up and patted Ish's back again, as if the ten-year-old match had ended minutes ago.

'No one forgets the two ducks in the state selection trials either,' Ish said and paused again.

'Screw that, you were out of form, man,' Omi said.

'But those are the matches that fucking mattered, right? Now can we flip the topic?'

Omi backed off and I gladly changed the subject. 'I think we should thank our sponsors for tonight – The Team India Cricket Shop. In seven months of operation, our profit is 42,600 rupees. Of which, we have distributed 18,000 to the partners and 22,000 is for the Navrangpura shop deposit. And the remaining 2,600 is for entertainment like tonight. So, thank you, dear shareholders and partners, and let's say cheers to the second bottle.'

I took out the second bottle for each of us from the ice bucket.

'Stud-boy,' Ish slurred, standing up, 'This business and its profit is all owed to Stud-boy, Mr Govind Patel. Thank you, buddy. Because of you this dropout military cadet has a future. And so does this fool who'd be otherwise jingling bells in the temple all his life. Give me a hug, Stud-boy.'

He came forward to give me a hug. It was drunk affection, but genuine enough.

'Will you do me one more favour buddy?' Ish said.

'What?'

'There is someone who wants maths tuitions,' Ish said.

'No, I am full, Ish. Seven students already…,' I said as Ish interrupted me.

'It is Vidya.'

'Your sister?'

'She finished Class XII. She is dropping a year now to prepare for the medical entrance.'

'You don't need maths to become a doctor.'

'No, but the entrance exams do. And she is awful at it. You are the best man, who else can I trust?'

'If it is your sister, then I mean…,' I took a breath. 'Wow, Vidya to join medical college? Is she that old now?'

'Almost eighteen, dude.'

'I teach younger kids though, class five to eight. Her course is more advanced. I am not in touch.'

'But you got a fucking century in that subject, dude. Just try, she needs any help she can get.'

I said nothing for a while, trying to remember what I knew of Vidya, which was little.

'What are you thinking. Oh, I know, Mr Accounts. Don't worry, we will pay you,' Ish said and took a big sip.

'Shut up, man. It is for your sister. Ok, I'll do it. When do we start?'

'Can you start Monday … no Monday is Parekh-ji's feast. Damn, Omi what the fuck are we going to do there?'

'The things we do to keep your Mama happy.' I couldn't wait to move to Navrangpura.

'Parekh-ji is supposed to be a great man,' Omi said. 'And I always listen to you guys. Come for me this time.'

'Anyway, Tuesday then,' I said to Ish. 'So is she going to come to the bank?'

'Dad will never send her out alone. You come home.'

'What?' I said. Maybe I should have accepted a fee. 'Ok, I'll move some classes. Say seven in the evening?'

'Sure, now can you answer one maths question, Mr Accounts,' Ish said.

'What?'

'You ordered a crate with ten bottles. We drank three each. Where is the tenth one?' Ish stood up swaying.

I stood as well. 'The question is not where the tenth one is, but who does it belong to.' I lunged for the ice bucket. Ish dived in as well. Cold water splashed on the floor as we tugged at the bottle. After a ten-second tiff, he released it.

'Take it, dude. What would I do without you?'

Four

We reached Parekh-ji's residence at around eight in the evening. Two armed guards manning the front gate let us in after checking our names. The entrance of the house had an elaborate rangoli, dozens of lamps and fresh flowers.

'See, what a gathering,' Bittoo Mama met us at the door. 'Have dinner before the talk begins.' From an aarti plate, he put big red tikkas on our foreheads. He told us Parekh-ji would make a speech after dinner.

We moved to the massive food counter. A Gujarati feast, consisted of every vegetarian snack known to man. There was no alcohol, but there was juice of every fruit imaginable. At parties like this, you regret you have only one stomach. I took a Jain pizza and looked around the massive living room. There were fifty guests dressed in either white or saffron. Parekh-ji wore a saffron dhoti and white shirt, sort of a perfect crowd blend. Ish looked oddly out of place with his skull and crossbones, black Metallica T-shirt. Apart from us, every one had either grey hair or no hair. It looked like a marriage party where only the priests were invited.

Most of them carried some form of accessory like a trishul or a rudraksha or a holy book.

Ish and I exchanged a what-are-we-doing-here glance.

Omi went to meet a group of two bald-whites, one grey-saffron and one bald-saffron. He touched their feet and everyone blessed him. Considering Omi met these kind of people often, he had one of the highest per-capita-blessings ratio in India.

'The food is excellent, no?' Omi returned. Food in Gujarat was always good. But still people keep saying it. Ish passed his Jain-dimsum to Omi.

'Who are these people?' I asked idly.

'It is quite simple,' Omi said. 'The people in saffron are priests or other holy men from around the city. The people in white are the political party people. Why aren't you eating any dimsums?'

'I don't like Chinese,' Ish said. 'And who is Parekh-ji?'

'Well, he is a guide,' Omi said. 'Or that is what he says to be humble. But actually, he is the chairperson of the main temple trust. He knows the politicians really well, too.'

'So he is a hybrid, a poli-priest,' I deduced.

'Can you be more respectful? And what is this T-shirt, Ish?'

Everyone shushed as Parekh-ji came to the centre of the living room. He carried a red velvet cushion with him, which looked quite comfortable. He signalled everyone to sit down on the carpet. Like a shoal of fishes, the saffrons separated from the whites and sat down in two neat sections.

'Where the hell do we sit?' Ish said as he turned to me. I had worn a blue T-shirt and couldn't find my colour zone. Bittoo Mama tugged at Omi's elbow and asked us to join the saffron set. We sat there, looking like the protagonists of those ugly duckling stories in our mismatched clothes. Bittoo Mama came with three saffron scarves and handed them to us.

'What? I am not...,' I protested to Omi.

'Shh ... just wear it,' Omi said and showed us how to wrap it around our neck.

Parekh-ji sat on his wonderful magic cushion. There was pin-drop silence. Ish cracked his knuckle once. Omi gave him a dirty look. Everyone closed their eyes, apart from me. I looked around while everyone chanted in Sanskrit. They ended their chants after a minute and Parekh-ji began his speech.

'Welcome devotees, welcome to my humble home. I want to especially welcome the team on the right from the Sindhipur temple. They have returned from kar seva in Ayodhya for over a month. Let us bow to them and seek blessings.'

Everyone bowed to a group of six saffrons holding trishuls.

Parekh-ji continued, 'We also have some young people today. We need them badly. Thanks to Bittoo Mama, who brought them. Bittoo is working hard for the party. He will support our candidate Hasmukh-ji for the election next year.'

Everyone looked at us and gave smiling nods. We nodded back.

'Devotees, the Hindu religion teaches us to bear a lot. And we do bear a lot. So, today's discussion is "How much bearing is enough? Until when does a Hindu keep bearing pain?"'

Everyone nodded. My knees were stiff with pain from sitting cross-legged. I wondered if I should stop bearing pain right then and stretch my legs.

'Our scriptures tell us not to harm others,' Parekh-ji said. 'They teach us acceptance of all faiths, even if those faiths do not accept us. They teach us patience. Thousands of years ago, our wise men thought of such wonderful values, valid even today. And today you great men pass on these values to society,' Parekh-ji said, gesturing at the priests. The priests nodded.

'At the same time, the scriptures also tell us not to bear injustice. The Gita tells Arjun to fight a virtuous war. So at some point we are meant to fight back. When is that point is something to think about.'

Vigorous nods shook the crowd. Even though I found the whole gathering and the magic red cushion a bit over the top, Parekh-ji's logic was flawless.

'And right now, I see that injustice again. Hindus being asked to compromise, to accept, to bear. Hindus asked for the resurrection of one temple. Not any temple, a temple where one of our most revered gods was born. But they won't give it to us. We said we will move the mosque respectfully, round the corner. But no, that was considered unreasonable. We tried to submit proof, but that was suppressed. Is this justice? Should we keep bearing it? I am just an old man, I don't have the answers.'

Ish whispered in my ear, 'It is politics, man. Just pure simple politics.'

Parekh-ji continued: 'I don't even want to go into who this country belongs to. Because the poor Hindu is accustomed to being ruled by someone else – 700 years by Muslims, 250 years by the British. We are independent now, but the Hindu does not assert himself. But what makes me sad is that we are not even treated as equals. They call themselves secular, but they give preference to the Muslims? We fight for equal treatment and are called communal? The most brutal terrorists are Muslim, but they say we are hardliners. More Hindu kids sleep hungry every night than Muslim, but they say Muslims are downtrodden.'

Parekh-ji stopped to have a glass of water. 'They say to me, Parekh-ji, why do you know so many politicians? I say, I am a servant of God. I didn't want to join politics. But if I as a Hindu want justice, I need to get involved in how the country is run. And what other way is there to get involved than join politics? So, here I am half saffron, half white – at your service.'

The audience gave a mini applause, including Omi. Ish and I were too overfed to react.

'But there is hope. You know where this hope comes from – Gujarat. We are a state of businessmen. And you might say a hundred bad things about a businessman, but you cannot deny that a businessman sees reality. He knows how the parts add up, how the world works. We won't stand for hypocrisy or unfairness. That is why, we don't elect the pseudo-secular parties. We are not communal, we are honest. And if we react, it is because we have been bearing pain for a long time.'

The audience broke into full applause. I used the break to step out into the front garden of Parekh-ji's house and sit on an intricately carved swing. Parekh-ji spoke inside for ten more minutes, inaudible to me. I looked at the stars above and thought of the man on the velvet cushion. It was strange, I was both attracted to and repelled by him. He had charisma and lunacy at the same time.

After his speech there were a few more closing mantras, followed by two bhajans by a couple of priests from Bhuj. Ish came out. 'You here?'

'Can we go home?' I said.

★

I reached Ishaan's house at 7 p.m. on Tuesday. She sat at her study table. Her room had the typical girlie look – extra clean, extra cute and extra pink. Stuffed toys and posters with cheesy messages like 'I am the boss' adorned the walls of the room. I sat on the chair. Her brown eyes looked at me with full attention. I couldn't help but notice that her childlike face was in the process of turning into a beautiful woman's.

'So which areas of maths are you strong in?'

'None really,' she said.

'Algebra?'

'Nope.'

'Trigonometry?'

'Whatever.'

'Calculus?'

She raised her eyebrows as if I had mentioned a horror movie.

'Really?' I said, disturbed at such indifference to my favourite subject.

'Actually, I don't like maths much.'

'Hmmm,' I said and tried to be like a thoughtful professor. 'You don't like it much or you don't understand a few things and so you don't like it yet? Maths can be fun you know.'

'Fun?' she said with a disgusted expression.

'Yes.'

She sat up straight and shook her head. 'Let me make myself clear. I positively hate maths. For me it occupies a place right up there with cockroaches and lizards. I get disgusted, nauseated, and depressed by it. Between an electric shock or a maths test, I will choose the former. I heard some people have to walk two miles to get water in Rajasthan. I would trade my maths problems for that walk, everyday. Maths is the worst thing ever invented by man. What were they thinking? Language is too easy, so let's make up some creepy symbols and manipulate them to haunt every generation of kids. Who cares if sin theta is different from cos theta? Who wants to know the expansion of the sum of cubes?'

'Wow, that's some reaction,' I said, my mouth still open.

'And fun? If maths is fun, then getting a tooth extraction is fun. A viral infection is fun. Rabies shots are fun.'

'I think you are approaching it the wrong way.'

'Oh ho ho, don't go there. I am not just approaching it. I have lived, compromised, struggled with it. It is a troubled relationship we have shared for years. From classes one to twelve, this subject does not go away. People have nightmares about monsters. I have nightmares about surprise maths tests. I know you scored a hundred and you are in love with it. But remember, in most parts of the world maths means only one thing to students.'

She stopped to breathe. I had the urge to get up and run away. *How can I tame a wild beast?*

'What?'

'Goosebumps. See I already have them,' she said, pulling her kameez sleeve up to her elbow. I thought the little pink dots on her skin were more from her emotional outburst than maths.

I also noticed her thin arm. It was so fair you could see three veins running across. Her hand had deep lines, with an exceptionally long lifeline. Her fingers seemed long as they were so thin. She had applied a glittery silver-white nailpolish only on the outer edge of the nails. How do women come up with these ideas?

'What?' she said as I checked out her arm for a moment too long.

I immediately opened a textbook.

'Nothing. My job is to teach you maths, not to make you like it. You want to be a doctor I heard.'

'I want to go to a college in Mumbai.'

'Excuse me?'

'I want to get out of Ahmedabad. But mom and dad won't let me. Unless, of course, it is for a prestigious course like medicine or engineering. Engineering has maths, maths means vomit so that is ruled out. Medicine is the other choice and my exit pass. But they have this medical entrance exam and...'

I realised that Vidya did not have an internal pause button. And since I had only an hour and the tutorial equivalent of climbing Everest barefoot, I wanted to come to the point.

'So, which topic would you like to start with?'

'Anything without equations.'

'I saw your medical entrance exam course. Looks like there are a few scoring areas that are relatively easier.'

I opened the medical exam entrance guide and turned it towards her.

'See this, probability,' I said. 'This and permutations will be twenty-five per cent of the maths exam. Statistics is another ten per cent. No equations here, so can we start with this?'

'Sure,' she said and took out a brand new exercise book. She kept two pens parallel to the notebook. She opened the first page of the probability chapter like she was the most diligent student in India. Most clueless, probably.

'Probability,' I said, 'is easily the most fun. I say this because you can actually use the concepts in probability to solve everyday problems.'

'Like what?'

'Like what what?'

'What everyday problems can you solve?' she quizzed, brushing aside a strand of hair.

'Well, you are going ahead, but let's see.' I looked around for an easy example. I noticed her impeccably done-up room, tucked in pink bedsheets. On the opposite wall were posters of Westlife,

Backstreet Boys, Hrithik Roshan. Next to them was a wall of greeting cards. 'See those cards?'

'They are birthday cards from my school friends. I had my birthday two months ago.'

I ignored the information overload. 'Say there are twenty of them. Most are white, though. Some are coloured. How many?'

'Five coloured ones,' she said, scanning the cards, her eyes asking 'so?'

'Cool, five. Now let's say I take all the cards and put them in a sack. Then I pull out one card, what is the probability the card is coloured?'

'Why would you put them in a sack?' she said.

'Hypothetical. What is the chance?'

'I don't know.'

'Ok, so let's use this example to start the basic premise of probability. Probability can be defined as,' I said as I wrote the lines:

Probability = No of times something you want happens/ No of times something can happen

'How come there are no symbols?' she said.

'See, I told you probability is interesting. Let's look at the denominator. How many different cards can come out if I pull out one card from the stack of twenty?'

'Er ... twenty?'

'Yes, of course. Good.'

'Duh!' she said.

I controlled my irritation. I dumbed down the problem for her and she duh-ed me. Some attitude, there.

'And now the numerator. I want a coloured card. How many different coloured cards can come out if I pull one?'

'Five?'

'Yep. And so let's apply our wordy formula,' I said and wrote down.

Probability = No of times something you want happens (5) / No of times something can happen (20)

So, probability = 5/20 = 0.25

'There you go. The probability is 0.25, or twenty-five per cent.' I said and placed the pen back on the table. She reread what I wrote for a few moments.

'That is simple. But the exam problems are harder,' she said at last.

'We will get there. But the basic concept needs to be understood first. And you didn't vomit.'

I was interrupted by two beeps on her cellphone. She rushed to her bedside table to pick up the phone. She sat on the bed and read her message. 'My school friend. She's stupid,' she smiled fondly at the phone.

I kept silent and waited for her to come back. 'Ok, let's do another one,' I said. 'Let us say we have a jar with four red and six blue marbles.'

I finished three more problems in the next half an hour. 'See, it's not that hard when you focus. Good job!' I praised her as she solved a problem.

'You want tea?' she said, ignoring my compliment.

'No thanks, I don't like to have too much tea.'

'Oh me neither. I like coffee. You like coffee?'

'I like probability and you should too. Can we do the next problem?'

Her cellphone beeped again. She dropped her pen and leaped to her phone.

'Leave it. No SMS-ing in my class,' I said.

'It's just…,' she said as she stopped her hand midway.

'I will go if you don't concentrate. I have turned down many students for this class.'

She was zapped at my firmness. But I am no Mr Nice, and I hate people who are not focused. Especially those who hate maths.

'Sorry,' she said.

'We only have an hour. Do your fun activities later.'

'I said sorry.' She picked up her pen again and opened the cap in disgust.

Five

'**Y**ou. Must. Come. Now.' The kid sucked in air after every word. 'Ali. Is…'

'Relax Paras,' Ish told the panting boy. He had come running from the Belrampur Municipal School and was insisting we go with him.

'Now? It is only four, how can I close business?' I said.

'He doesn't play cricket that often. He always plays marbles. Please come today, Ish bhaiya.'

'Let's go. It is a slow day anyway,' Ish said as he slipped on his chappals.

Omi had already stepped out. I locked the cashbox and told the owner of the flower shop next to ours to keep watch.

We reached our school's familiar grounds. Twenty boys circled Ali.

'I don't want to play now,' a voice said from the centre of the crowd.

A thin, almost malnourished boy sat on the ground, his face covered with his hands.

'No, Ish bhaiya has to see you play,' Paras joined the cajoling crowd and tugged at Ali's elbow.

'I don't like cricket. It gives me a headache,' Ali said, his hands still covering his face.

'I have heard a lot about you,' Ish said as he bent down on one knee to Ali's level.

Ali parted his fingers to see Ish's face. His eyes were a startling green.

'Hi, I am Ish. I studied in this school for thirteen years. And I teach cricket too,' Ish said and extended a handshake to Ali.

Ali studied Ish's face. He brought his hand forward with reluctance.

Ali's long hair was neatly parted. His young and fragile body resembled a girl's. He looked like an arts or music prodigy, not a cricketer.

'How old is he?' I asked a spectacled kid in the crowd.

'He is in Class VII C,' the kid sniffed due to a cold.

I calculated, he could be no more than twelve.

'He just joined, no? Where from?' I said.

'He was in Shahpur Madrasa before. His daddy moved him here. Since then, every bowler has lost confidence,' he sneezed. I narrowly escaped a mucous spray.

Ish and Omi sat cross-legged on the ground with Ali.

'I can't play long. I get a headache,' Ali said.

'It's ok if you don't want to play,' Ish said. 'Let's go, Omi.'

Ish and Omi stood up and dusted their pants.

'I can play an over, if you will bowl,' Ali said as we turned to leave.

'Sure,' Ish said casually. Another kid tossed a ball into his hand.

The crowd backed off. Some kids volunteered to be fielders. Omi became the wicket keeper. I stood near the bowler's end, at the umpire's slot. Ali took the crease. He strained hard to look at the bowler. The crowd clapped as Ish took a short run-up. I couldn't understand the fuss in seeing this delicate, doe-eyed boy play. The bat reached almost two-thirds his height.

Ish's run-up was fake, as he stopped near me. A grown man bowling pace to a twelve-year-old is silly. Ish looked at the boy and bowled a simple lollipop delivery.

The slow ball pitched midway and took its time to reach the crease. Thwack, Ali moved his bat in a smooth movement and connected. The ball surged high as Ish and I looked at it for its three seconds of flight – six!

Ish looked at Ali and nodded in appreciation. Ali took a stance again and scrunched his face, partially due to the sun but also in irritation for not receiving a real delivery.

For the next ball, Ish took an eight step run-up. The boy could play, girlie features be damned! The medium pace ball rose high on the bounce and smash! Another six.

Ish gave a half smile. Ali's bat had not hit the ball, but his pride. The crowd clapped.

Ish took an eleven-step run-up for the next ball. He grunted when the ball left his hand. The ball bounced to Ali's shoulder. Ali spun on one leg as if in a dance and connected – six!

Three balls, three sixes – Ish looked molested. Omi's mouth was open but he focused on wicket-keeping. I think he was trying to control his reaction for Ish's sake.

'He is a freak. Ali the freak, Ali the freak,' a kid fielding at mid-on shouted and distracted Ali.

'Just play,' Ish said to Ali and gave the fielder a glare.

Ish rubbed the ball on his pants thrice. He changed his grip and did some upper body twists. He took his longest run-up yet and ran forward with full force. The ball went fast, but was a full toss. Ish's frustration showed in this delivery. It deserved punishment. Ali took two steps forward and smash! The ball went high and reached past the ground, almost hitting a classroom window.

I laughed. I knew I shouldn't have, but I did. To see the school cricket champion of my batch raped so in public by a mere boy of twelve was too funny. At least to me. Actually, only to me.

'What?' Ish demanded in disgust.

'Nothing,' I said.

'Where is the fucking ball?'

'They are trying to find it. You want to buy one from my shop, coach?' I jeered lightly.

'Shut up,' Ish hissed as the ball came rolling back to him.

Ish was about to take a run-up when Ali sat down at his crease.

'What happened?' Omi was the first to reach him.

'I told you. I get a headache. Can I go back now?' Ali said, his childish voice almost in tears.

Omi looked at Ish and me. I shrugged.

'I told you, no? Freak!' Paras ran up to us.

Ali stood. 'Can I go?'

We nodded. From his pocket, Ali took out some marbles that resembled his eyes. Rolling them in his hand, he left the ground.

★

'I cannot believe it,' Ish declared as he finished his fifty morning push-ups. He came and sat next to me on the bank's backyard floor.

Omi continued to complete his hundred.

'Tea,' I announced and handed Ish his cup. My best friend had faced serious mental trauma yesterday. I couldn't do much apart from making my best cup of ginger tea in the bank kitchen.

'It can't be just luck, right? No way,' Ish answered his own questions.

I nodded my head towards a plate of biscuits, which he ignored. I wondered if the Ali episode would cause permanent damage to Ish's appetite. Ish continued to talk to himself as I tuned myself out. Omi moved on to sit-ups. He also belted out Hanuman-ji's forty verses along with the exercise. I loved this little morning break – between the students' leaving and the shop's opening. It gave me time to think. And these days I only thought about the new shop. 'Twenty-five thousand rupees saved already, and fifteen thousand more by December,' I mumbled, 'If the builder accepts forty as deposit, I can secure the Navrangpura lease by year end.'

I poured myself another cup of tea. 'Here are your shop's keys, Mama. We are moving to our shop in Navrangpura, in the air-conditioned mall,' I repeated my dream dialogue inside my head for the hundredth time. Three more months, I assured myself.

'You guys ate all the biscuits?' Omi came to us as he finished his exercise.

'Sorry, tea?' I offered.

Omi shook his head. He opened a polypack of milk and put it to his mouth. Like me, he didn't have much tea. Caffeine ran in Ish's family veins though. I remembered Vidya offering me tea. Stupid girl, duh-ing me.

'Still thinking of Ali?' Omi said to Ish, wiping his milk moustache.

'He is amazing, man. I didn't bowl my best, but not so bad either. But he just, just…,' Words failed Ish.

'Four sixes. Incredible!' Omi said, 'No wonder they call him a freak.'

'Don't know if he is a freak. But he is good,' Ish said.

'These Muslim kids man. You never know what...,' Omi said and gulped the remainder of his milk.

'Shut up. He is just fucking good. I have never seen anyone play like that. I want to coach him.'

'Sure, as long as he pays. He can't play beyond four balls. You could help him,' I told Ish.

'What? You will teach that mullah kid?' Omi's face turned worrisome.

'I will teach the best player in Belrampur. That kid has serious potential. You know like...'

'Team India?' I suggested.

'Shh, don't tempt fate, but yes. I want to teach him. They'll ruin him in that school. They can barely teach the course there, forget sports.'

'We are not teaching a Muslim kid,' Omi vetoed. 'Bittoo Mama will kill me.'

'Don't overreact. He won't know. We just teach him at the bank,' Ish said. For the rest of the argument, Ish and Omi just exchanged stares. Ultimately, like always, Omi gave in to Ish.

'Your choice. Make sure he never comes near the temple. If Bittoo Mama finds out, he will kick us out of the shop.'

'Omi is right. We need the shop for a few more months,' I said.

'We also need to go to the doctor,' Ish said.

'Doctor?' I said.

'His head was hurting after four balls. I want a doctor to see him before we begin practicing.'

'You'll have to talk to his parents if you want him to pay,' I said.

'I'll teach him for free,' Ish said.

'But still, for Indian parents cricket equals time waste.'

'Then we'll go to his house,' Ish said.

'I am not going to any Muslim house,' Omi said almost hysterically. 'I am not going.'

'Let's go open the shop first. It's business time,' I said.

★

'No cricket, I like marbles,' Ali protested for the fifth time. Ish took four chocolates (at the shop's expense, idiot) for him, a reward for every sixer. Ali accepted the chocolates but said no to cricket coaching, and a foot-stomping no to meeting the doctor.

'Our shop has marbles,' I cajoled. 'Special blue ones from Jaipur. One dozen for you if you come to the doctor. He is just across the street.'

Ali looked at me with his two green marbles.

'Two dozen if you come for one cricket coaching class in the morning,' I said.

'Doctor is fine. For coaching class, ask abba.'

'Give me abba's name and address,' I said.

'Naseer Alam, seventh pol, third house on the ground floor.'

'What name did you say?' Omi said.

'Naseer Alam,' Ali repeated.

'I have heard the name somewhere. But I can't recall…' Omi murmured, but Ish ignored him.

'Dr Verma's clinic is in the next pol. Let's go,' Ish said.

★

'Welcome, nice to have someone young in my clinic for a change.' Dr Verma removed his spectacles. He rubbed his fifty-year-old eyes.

His wrinkles had multiplied since I last met him three years ago. His once black hair had turned white. Old age sucks.

'And who is this little tiger? Open your mouth, baba,' Dr Verma said and switched on his torch out of habit. 'What happened?'

'Nothing's wrong. We have some questions,' Ish said.

The doctor put his torch down. 'Questions?'

'This boy is gifted in cricket. I want to know how he does it,' Ish said.

'Does what?' Dr Verma said. 'Some people are just talented.'

'I bowled four balls to him. He slammed sixes on all of them,' Ish said.

'What?' Dr Verma said. He knew Ish was one of the best players in the neighbourhood.

'Unbelievable but true,' I chimed in. 'Also, he sat down after four balls. He said his head hurt.'

Dr Verma turned to Ali. 'You like cricket, baba?'

'No,' Ali said.

'This is more complicated than the usual viral fever. What happened after the four balls, baba?'

'Whenever I play with concentration, my head starts hurting,' Ali said. He slid his hands into his pocket. I heard the rustle of marbles.

'Let us check your eyes,' Dr Verma said and stood up to go to the testing room.

'Eyesight is fantastic,' Dr Verma said, returning. 'I recommend you meet my friend Dr Multani from the city hospital. He is an eye specialist and used to be a team doctor for a baseball team in USA. In fact, I haven't met him for a year. I can take you tomorrow if you want.'

We nodded. I reached for my wallet. Dr Verma gave me a stern glance to stop.

'Fascinating,' Dr Multani said only one word as he held up Ali's MRI scan. He had spent two hours with Ali. He did every test imaginable – a fitness check, a blood test, retinal scans, a computerised hand-eye coordination exam. The Matrix style MRI, where Ali had to lie down head first inside a chamber, proved most useful.

'I miss my sports-doctor days, Verma. This love for Ambavad made me give up a lot,' Dr Multani said. He ordered tea and khakra for all of us.

'Are we done?' Ali said and yawned.

'Almost. Play marbles in the garden outside if you want,' Dr Multani said. He kept quiet until Ali left.

'That was some work, Multani, for a little headache,' Dr Verma said.

'It is not just a headache,' Dr Multani said and munched a khakra. 'Ish is right, the boy is exceptionally gifted.'

'How?' I blurted. What was in those tests that said Ali could smash any bowler to bits.

'The boy has hyper-reflex. It is an aberration in medical terms, but proving to be a gift for cricket.'

'Hyper what?' Omi echoed.

'Hyper reflex,' Dr Multani lifted a round glass paper weight from his table and pretended to hurl it at Omi. Omi ducked. 'When I throw this at you, what do you do? You reflexively try to prevent the attack. I didn't give you an advance warning and everything happened in a split second. Thus, you didn't do a conscious *think* to duck away, it just happened.'

Dr Multani paused for a sip of water and continued, 'It matters little in everyday life, except if we touch something too hot or too cold. However, in sports it is crucial.' Dr Multani paused to open a few reports and picked up another khakra.

I looked at Ali outside from the window. He was using a catapult to shoot one marble to hit another one.

'So Ali has good reflexes. That's it?' Ish said.

'His reflexes are at least ten times better than ours. But there is more. Apart from reflex action, the human brain makes decisions in two other ways. One is the long, analysed mode – the problem goes through a rigorous analysis in our brain and we decide the course of action. And then there is a separate, second way that's faster but less accurate. Normally, the long way is used and we are aware of it. But sometimes, in urgent situations, the brain chooses the shortcut way. Call it a quick-think mode.'

We nodded as Dr Multani continued:

'In reflex action, the brain short-circuits the thinking process and acts. He can just about duck, forget try to catch it. However, the response time is superfast. Sports has moments that requires you to think in every possible way – analysed, quick-think or reflex.'

'And Ali?' Ish said.

Dr Multani picked up the MRI scan again. 'Ali's brain is fascinating. His first, second and even the third reflex way of thinking is fused. His response time is as fast as that of a reflex action, yet his decision making is as accurate as the analysed mode. You may think he hit that superfast delivery of yours by luck, but his brain saw its path easily. Like it was a soft throw.'

'But I bowled fast.'

'Yes, but his brain can register it and act accordingly. If it is hard to visualise ... imagine that Ali sees the ball in slow motion. A normal player will use the second or third way of thinking to hit a fast ball. Ali uses the first. A normal player needs years of practice to ensure his second way gets as accurate to play well. Ali doesn't need to. That is his gift.'

It look us a minute to digest Dr Multani's words. We definitely had to use the first way of thinking to understand it.

'To him a pace delivery is slow motion?' Ish tried again.

'Only to his brain, as it analyses fast. Of course, if you hit him with a fast ball he will get hurt.'

'But how can he hit so far?' Ish said.

'He doesn't hit much. He changes direction of the already fast ball. The energy in that ball is mostly yours.'

'Have you seen other gifted players like him?' I wanted to know.

'Not to this degree, this boy's brain is wired differently. Some may call it a defect, so I suggest you don't make a big noise about it.'

'He is Indian team material,' Ish said. 'Dr Multani, you know he is.'

Dr Multani sighed. 'Well, not at the moment. His headaches are a problem, for instance. While his brain can analyse fast, it also tires quickly. He needs to stay in the game. He has to survive until his brain gets refreshed to use the gift again.'

'Can that happen?' Ish said.

'Yes, under a training regimen. And he has to learn the other aspects of cricket. I don't think he ever runs between the wickets. The boy has no stamina. He is weak, almost malnourished,' the doctor said.

'I am going to coach him,' Ish vowed. 'And Omi will help. Omi will make him eat and make him fit.'

'No, I can't,' Omi refused as all looked at him. 'Dr Verma, tell them why I can't.'

'Because he's a Muslim. Multani, remember Nasser from the Muslim University? Ali is his son.'

'Oh, that Nasser? Yes, he used to campaign in the university elections. Used to be a firebrand once, but I have heard that he has toned down.'

'Yes, he is in politics full time now. Moved from a pure Muslim to a secular party,' Dr Verma said.

Ish looked at Dr Verma, surprised.

'I found out after you guys left yesterday. Sometimes I feel I run a gossip centre, not a clinic.' Dr Verma chuckled. 'Anyway, that's the issue then. A priest's son teaching a Muslim boy.'

'I don't want to teach him,' Omi said quickly.

'Shut up, Omi. You see what we have here?' Ish spoke.

Omi stood up, gave Ish a disapproving glance and left the room.

'How about the state academy?' Dr Verma said.

'They'll ruin him,' Ish said.

'I agree.' Dr Multani paused. 'He is too young, Muslim and poor. And he is untrained. I'd suggest you keep this boy and his talent under wraps for now. When the time comes, we will see.'

We left the clinic. I took out four marbles from my pocket and called Ali.

'Ali, time to go. Here, catch.'

I threw the four marbles high in the air towards him. I had thrown them purposely apart.

Ali looked away from his game and saw the marbles midair. He remained in his squat position and raised his left hand high. One, two, three, four – like a magic wand his left hand moved. He caught every single one of them.

Six

'He won't agree, I spoke to him already,' Ali huffed. We reached the end of Belrampur to get to his house. He lived in a particularly squalid pol. Ali pressed the bell. I noticed his father's nameplate had a motif of the secular political party.

'Ali, so late again,' his dad said as he opened the door. He wore an impeccable black achkan, which contrasted with his white beard and a tight skullcap of lace material. He looked around sixty, which meant Ali came late in his life.

'And who are you gentlemen?' he said.

'I am Ishaan,' Ish said. 'And this is Govind and Omi. We are Ali's friends.'

'Friends?' Ali's dad said, underlining the absurd age difference.

'Yes abba, they came to play cricket at the school. They have a sports shop. I told you, remember?'

'Come in,' Ali's dad said.

We sat in the living room. Ali's mother, wearing a brown-coloured salwar suit, brought in glasses of roohafza. Even though a dupatta covered most of her face, I could make out that she must've been at least twenty years younger than her husband. She scolded Ali for not studying for his test the next day. I think Indian mothers have two tasks – to tell children to eat more or study more.

'We wanted to talk about coaching Ali,' Ish began after Ali left the room with his mom.

'Cricket coaching? No, thanks. We are not interested,' Ali's dad said in a tone that was more conclusive than discussion oriented.

'But uncle…,' Ish protested.

'Look above,' Ali's dad said and pointed to the roof, 'look, there are cracks on the ceiling. There is this room and one other tiny room that I have taken on rent. Does it look like the house of a person who can afford cricket coaching?'

'We won't be charging Ali,' Ish said.

I glared at Ish. I hate it when he gives discounts at the shop, but a hundred per cent off is insane.

'What will he do with cricket coaching? Already school is difficult for him after the madrasa. This is the first time Ali is studying maths. And I can't even afford a maths tutor…'

'Govind teaches maths,' Ish said.

'What?' Ali's dad and I said together.

'Really, he is the best in Belrampur. He got hundred per cent marks in the Class XII board exam.'

I double glared at Ish. I was fully booked in tuitions and I already taught his clown of a sister for free. 'But Ish, I can't,' I said.

'Maybe we can do a combined deal. If you allow him cricket coaching with us, we will teach him maths for free,' Ish said ignoring my words.

'How can I teach for free? I have paying students waiting,' I said.

Ish glanced at me with disdain as if I had shot down his mission to Mars.

'For *free*?' I mouthed to him.

'I will pay whatever I can,' Ali's dad said in a muffled voice.

'I am sorry, but this is how I earn my living. I can't...' I said, in a desperate attempt to salvage my asshole image.

'Just take it from my salary, ok? Can you let me talk?' Ish said with great politeness.

I wanted to get up and leave.

'I get a small retirement pension. How much do you charge?'

'Four hun...,' I started to say but Ish interrupted with 'Why don't we start and see how it goes?'

Everyone nodded, even Omi because he did whatever everyone else was doing anyway.

'Right, Govind?' he said to me last.

I gave the briefest nod possible, a five-degree tilt.

'Stay for dinner, please,' Ali's dad implored as we stood up to leave.

'No, no,' Omi said, horrified at the idea of eating in a Muslim home.

'Please, I insist. For us, hospitality is important. You are our mehmaan.'

I would have disagreed, but I wanted to get something for the free maths-and-cricket coaching programme.

We sat on the living room floor. Ali's mom brought us two extra large plates, one for the three of us and another for Ali's dad. The plates had simple food – chapattis, daal and a potato-cauliflower vegetable.

Omi sat down. He did not touch the food.

'Sorry I can't offer you meat. This is all we have today.'

'I don't eat meat. I am a priest's son,' Omi said.

An awkward pause followed. Ish jumped in, 'The food looks great. Dig in guys.'

To share a single plate is strangely intimate. Ish and I broke off the same chapatti. His long fingers reminded me of his sister's. Damn, I had to teach her again the next day.

'They don't teach maths in madrasas?' I asked for the sake of conversation and mathematics.

'Not in this one,' Ali's dad said as he spooned in daal. 'Maths and science are forbidden.'

'That's strange. In this day and age,' I said. I thought of a business opportunity, a massive maths tuition chain outside every madrasa.

'Not really,' Ali's dad said. 'Madrasas were not even supposed to be schools. Their role is confined to teaching Islamic culture. Here, have some more chapattis.'

'And that's why you had him switch schools?' Ish said.

'Yes. I would have done it earlier, but my father was adamant Ali goes to a madrasa. He died six months ago.'

'Oh, I am sorry,' Ish said.

'He was unwell for a long time. I miss him, but not the years of medical expenses that wiped me out,' Ali's father said. He drank a glass of water. 'When I retired from university, I had to leave the campus quarters. The party wanted me to move here. The Belrampur Municipal School was close, so I put him there. Is it good?'

'Yes, we studied there for twelve years,' I said.

'Omi, you didn't eat anything. At least have some fruit,' Ali's dad said, offering him some bananas. Omi took one, examined it, and gobbled it in three bites.

'Why are you so keen to teach Ali cricket?' Ali's dad said.

The question was enough to light up Ish's face. He spoke animatedly. 'Ali has a gift. You see how he blossoms with my training.'

'You play cricket?' Ali's father said.

'In school and now I have a sports store. I've seen players, but none like Ali,' Ish said passionately.

'But it's just a game. One guy hits a ball with a stick, the rest run around to stop it.'

'It's more than that,' Ish said, offended. 'But if you have never played it, you will never understand.'

Ali's dad said, 'You know I am a member of the secular party?'

'We saw the sign,' I said.

'Would you like to come and visit our party sometime?'

Omi suddenly stood up. 'Do you know who you are talking to? I am Pandit Shastri's son. You have seen the Swami temple in Belrampur or not?' His voice was loud.

Ish pulled Omi's elbow to make him sit down.

'How does that matter, son?' Ali's dad said.

'You are telling me to come visit your party? I am a Hindu.'

'We won't hold that against you,' Ali's father grinned. 'Ours is a secular party.'

'It is not secular. It is suck-ular party. Suck-up politics, that is all you know. No wonder Muslims like you flock there. Now Ish, we are leaving or not?'

'Omi, behave yourself, we came for Ali.'

'I don't care. Let him play marbles and fail maths. If Bittoo Mama finds out I am here...'

'Bittoo is your Mama?' Ali's dad said.

'He is your opposition. And a suck-up party will never win in Belrampur.'

'Calm down, son. Sit down,' Ali's dad said.

Omi sat down and Ish massaged his shoulder. Omi rarely flared up, but when he did, it took several pacifying tactics to get him back to normal.

'Here, have a banana. I know you are hungry,' Ish soothed.

Omi resisted, but took the banana.

'I am also new to secular politics, son. I was in a hardline party,' Ali's dad said and paused to reflect, 'yes, I made a few mistakes too.'

'Whatever. Don't even try to convert people from our party to yours,' Omi said fiercely.

'I won't. But why are you so against us? The party has ruled the country for forty years, we must be doing something right.'

'You won't rule Gujarat anymore. Because we can see through your hypocrisy,' Omi said.

'Omi, stop,' Ish said.

'It's ok, Ish. I rarely get young people to talk to. Let him speak his mind,' Ali's dad said.

'I don't have anything to say. Let's go,' Omi said.

'The communal parties aren't perfect either,' Ali's dad said.

I guess even Ali's dad loved to argue.

'There you go. Here is the bias, you call us communal. Your party gives preference to Muslims, but it is secular. Why?' Omi said.

'What preference have we given?' Ali's dad said.

'Why can't you let us make a temple in Ayodhya?' Omi said.

'Because there is a mosque there already.'

'But there was a temple there before.'

'That is not proven.'

'It has. The government keeps hiding those reports.'

'Incorrect.'

'Whatever. It is not an ordinary place. We believe it is the birthplace of our lord. We said, "Give us that site, and we will move the mosque respectfully next door." But you can't even do that. And we, the majority, can't have that one little request fulfilled. Parekh-ji is right, what hope does a Hindu have in this country?'

'Oh, so it is Parekh-ji. He taught you all this?' Ali's dad almost smirked.

'He didn't teach us. Our cause is labelled communal, it is not cool to talk about it. But because Hindus don't talk, you think they don't feel anything? Why do you think people listen to Parekh-ji? Because somewhere deep down, he strikes a chord. A common chord of resentment is brewing Mr Nasser, even if it is not talked about.'

'A lot of Hindus vote for us, you should know,' Ali's father said.

'But slowly they will see the truth.'

'Son, India is a free country. You have a right to your views. My only advice is Hinduism is a great religion, but don't get extreme.'

'Hah, don't tell me about being extreme. We know which religion is extreme.'

I wasn't sure if Omi really believed in what he said, or if he was revising lessons given by Parekh-ji. He never spoke about this to Ish and me, but, somewhere deep down, did he also feel like Bittoo Mama? If Ish's passion was cricket and my passion was business, was Omi's passion religion? Or maybe, like most people, he was confused and trying to find his passion. And unlike us who never took him seriously, perhaps Parekh-ji gave him a sense of purpose and importance.

'Can we please make a pact to not discuss politics?' Ish pleaded as he signalled a timeout.

'You still fine with sending your son?' I asked Ali's dad, wondering if he had changed his mind after Omi's outbursts.

'Don't be silly. We are communicating our differences. That is what is missing in this country. It's ok, I trust you with my son.'

We stood up to leave and reached the door. Ish confirmed the practice time – 7 a.m.

'Come, I will walk you boys to the main road. I like to take a walk after dinner,' Ali's dad said.

We walked out of Ali's house. Omi held his head down, probably feeling ashamed at having raised his voice. Ali's dad spoke again.'I am not particularly fond of my own party.'

'Really?' I said when no one said anything.

'Yes, because at one level, they too, like all political parties, spend more time playing politics than working for the country. Creating differences, taking sides, causing divides – they know this too well.'

All of us nodded to say goodnight. But Ali's dad was not finished. 'It is like two customers go to a restaurant and the manager gives them only one plate of food. And if you want to eat, you must fight the other guy. The two guys get busy fighting, and some people tell them to make amends and eat half plate each. In all this, they forget the real issue – why didn't the manager provide two plates of food?'

I noticed Ali's dad's face. Behind the beard and the moustache, there was a wise man somewhere.

'Good point, the fight is created. That is why I am never big on religion or politics,' I said.

'Once a fight is created, it leads to another and so on. You can't really check it,' Ish said.

'You know I used to teach zoology in college,' Ali's dad said. 'And I once read about chimpanzee fights that may be relevant here.'

'Chimpanzee fights?'

'Yes, male chimpanzees of the same pack fight violently with each other – for food, females, whatever. However, after the fight, they go through a strange ritual. They kiss each other, on the lips.'

Even Omi had to laugh.

'So Hindus and Muslims should kiss?' I said.

'No, the point is this ritual was created by nature. To make sure the fight gets resolved and the pack stays together. In fact, any long-term relationship requires this.'

'Any?' Ish said.

'Yes, take any husband and wife. They will fight, and hurt each other emotionally. However, later they will make up, with hugs, presents or kind understanding words. These reconciliatory mechanisms are essential. The problem in Indian Hindu-Muslim rivalry is not that that one is right and the other is wrong. It is...'

'That there are no reconciliatory mechanisms,' Ish said.

'Yes, so that means if politicians fuel a fire, there is no fire brigade to check it. It sounds harsh, but Omi is right. People feel inside. Just by not talking about it, the differences do not go away. The resentment brews and brews, and doesn't come out until it is too late.'

We had reached the main road and stopped next to a paan shop. I figured out why Ali's dad had come with us. He wanted his after-dinner paan.

'Tell Ali to be on time,' Ish said as we waved goodbye.

The image of kissing chimpanzees stayed with me all night.

Ali came on time in a white kurta pajama. He held his maths books in one hand and his cricket bat in the other.

'Cricket first. Keep the books away,' Ish said.

The boy looked startled by the sudden instruction. I took him upstairs and opened the vault. Ali chose an empty locker and put down his books. Paresh and Naveen, two other kids had also come for cricket practice. They were both Ali's age but looked stronger.

'Boys, run around the backyard twenty times,' Ish ordered in his drill sergeant voice. His decision on how many rounds the kids must run was arbitrary. I think he enjoyed this first dose of power everyday.

I went upstairs to the vault to look at Ali's books. The notebooks were blank. The maths textbook was for Class VII, but looked untouched.

I came out to the first floor balcony. The students were on their morning jog.

'What?' Ish said as Ali stopped after five rounds.

'I ... can't ... run,' Ali heaved.

Omi smirked. 'Buddy, people here do hundred rounds. How are you going to run between the wickets? How are you going to field?'

'That is why ... I don't ... like cricket,' Ali said, still trying to catch his breath. 'Can't we just play?' Ali said. 'You have to warm up, buddy,' Ish said. Ali had more than warmed up. His face was hot and red.

After exercises, Ish did catch and field practice. Ish stood in the middle with the bat as everyone bowled to him. He lobbed the ball high and expected everyone to catch. Ali never moved from his position. He could catch only when the ball came close to him.

'All right, let's play,' Ish clapped his hands. 'Paresh, you are with me. We'll bowl first. Naveen you be in Ali's team and bat first.'

Naveen took the crease and Ali became the runner. Naveen struck on Paresh's fourth ball. Ish ran to get the ball. It was an easy two runs, but Ali's laziness meant they could score only one. Paresh took a three-step run-up and bowled. Ali struck, the ball rose and hurled towards the first floor. I ducked in the first floor balcony. The ball went past me and hit the branch manager's office window.

Paresh had the same shocked expression as Ish, when Ali had hit a six off his first ball.

'Hey, what? You hero or something?' Ish ran to Ali.

Ali looked puzzled at the reprimand.

'This is not a cricket ground. We are playing in a bank. If the ball goes out and hits someone, who will be responsible? What if things break? Who will pay?' Ish shouted.

Ali still looked surprised.

'That was a good shot,' Paresh said.

'Shut up. Hey Ali, I know you can do that. Learn the other aspects of the game.'

Ali froze, very near tears.

'Ok, listen. I am sorry. I did not mean to…,' Ish said.

'That is all I know. I can't do anything else,' Ali's voice cracked.

'We will teach you. Now why don't you bowl?'

Ali didn't bat anymore that day. Ish kept the practice simple for the next half an hour and tried not to scream. The latter was tough, especially because he was an animal when it came to cricket.

'Get your books from upstairs. We will study in the backyard,' I told a sweaty Ali.

He brought his books down and opened the first chapter of his maths book. It was on fractions and decimals.

Omi brought two polypacks of milk. 'Here,' he gave one to Ish.

'Thanks,' Ish said, and tore it open with his mouth.

'And here, one more,' Omi said.

'For what?' Ish said, after taking a big sip.

'Give it to your stick insect,' Omi said. 'Have you seen his arms? They are thinner than the wicket. You want to make him a player or not?'

'You give him yourself,' Ish smiled.

Omi shoved the milk packet near Ali and left.

'You have done some fractions before?' I said.

He nodded.

I told him to simplify 24/64 and he started dividing the numerator and denominator by two again and again. Of course, he lacked the intuition he had in hitting sixes in mathematics. However, his father had tried his best.

'See you at the shop,' Ish told me and turned to Ali, 'Any questions on cricket, champ?'

'Why do people run between the wickets to score runs?' Ali said, nibbling the end of his pen.

'That's how you score. It's the rule,' Ish said.

'No, not that way. I mean why run across and risk getting out for one or two runs when you can hit six with one shot?'

Ish scratched his head. 'Keep your questions to maths,' he said and left.

★

'I have figured it out. The young generation from the Sixties to the Eighties is the worst India ever had. These thirty years are an embarrassment for India,' Ish said as we lay down in the shop.

We had spread a mat on the shop's floor. A nap was a great way to kill time during slow afternoons. It was exam time and business was modest. Omi snoozed while Ish and I had our usual philosophical discussion.

'Not all that bad,' I said. 'We won the World Cup in 1983.'

'Yeah, we played good cricket, but that's about it. We remained poor, kept fighting wars, electing the same control freaks who did nothing for the country. People's dream job was a government job, yuck. Nobody took risks or stuck their neck out. Just one corrupt banana republic marketed by the leaders as this new socialist, intellectual nation. Tanks and thinktanks, nothing else,' Ish said.

'And guess who was at the top? Which party? Secular nonsense again,' Omi joined in, opening one eye.

'Well, your right-wing types didn't exactly get their act together either,' Ish said.

'We will, man. We are so ready. You wait and see, elections next year and Gujarat is ours,' Omi said.

'Anyway, screw politics. My point is, that the clueless Sixties to Eighties generation is now old, and running the country. But the Nineties and the, what do they say...'

'Zeroes.'

'Yeah, whatever. The Zeroes think different. But we are being run by old fogeys who never did anything worthwhile in their primetime. The Doordarshan generation is running the Star TV generation,' Ish said.

I clapped. 'Wow, wisdom is free at the Team India Cricket Shop.'

'Fuck off. Can't have a discussion around here. You think only you are the intellectual type. I am just a cricket coach,' Ish grumbled.

'No, you are the intellectual, bro. I am the sleepy type. Now can we rest until the next pesky kid comes,' I said, closing my eyes.

Our nap was soon interrupted.

'Lying down, well done. When rent is cheap, shopkeepers will sleep,' Bittoo Mama's voice made us all sit up. Now what the hell was he doing here?

'It is slow this time of the day, Mama,' Omi said as he pulled out a stool. He signalled me to get tea. I opened the cash box and took some coins.

'Get something to eat as well,' Mama said. I nodded. Now who the fuck pays for Mama's snacks? The rent is not that cheap, I thought as I left the shop with a fake smile. I returned with tea for everyone.

Mama was telling Omi, 'You come help me if it is slow in the afternoons. Your friends can come too. Winning a seat is not that easy. These secular guys are good.'

'What do you want me to do, Mama?' Omi said as he took the tea glasses off the crate and passed them around.

'We have to mobilise young people. Tell them our philosophy, warn them against the hypocrites. During campaign time, we need people to help us in publicity, organising rallies. There is work to be done.'

'I'll come next time, Mama,' Omi said.

'Tell others, too. If you see young people at the temple, tell them about our party. Tell them about me.'

I stood up, disgusted. Yes, I could see the point in targeting temple visitors, given the philosophy of the party. But when someone comes to pray, should they be pitched to join politics? I opened the accounts register to distract myself.

'You will come?' Mama turned to Ish.

'Someone has to man the shop. At least one person, even if it is slow,' Ish said. Smartass, that was supposed to be my excuse.

'And you, Govind?' Mama said.

'I am not into that sort of stuff. I am agnostic, remember?' I said, still reading the register.

'But this isn't about religion. It is about justice. And considering we gave you this shop at such a low rent, you owe us something.'

'It is not your shop. Omi's mother gave it to us. And given the location, the rent we pay is fair,' I said.

'I alone am enough, Mama. Dhiraj will come as well, right?' Omi said, to break the ever escalating tension between Mama and me. Dhiraj was Mama's fourteen-year-old son and Omi's cousin.

'Look at his pride! This two-bit shop and a giant ego,' Mama said. 'If Omi wasn't there, I'd get you kicked out.'

'There will be no need. We are leaving soon anyway,' I said without thinking. I couldn't help it. I wanted to tell him only at the last minute, just before we moved to the Navrangpura mall. But I was sick of his patronising tone.

'Oh, really? Where, you will pull a hand-cart with these bats and balls?' Mama said.

'We are moving to Navrangpura mall. You can take your shop back then.'

'What?' Mama exclaimed.

'We will make the deposit next month. Possession when it opens in three months. This two-bit shop is about to move to a prime location sports store,' I said.

Mama's mouth remained open. I had dreamt of this expression for months.

'Really?' Mama turned to Omi.

Omi nodded.

'How much is the deposit?' Mama said.

'Forty thousand. We saved it,' I said.

'You pay one thousand a month for this shop. If you were paying the market rent of two, you wouldn't be able to save this much,' Mama said.

I kept quiet.

'What? Now you are quiet, eh?' Mama stood up.

What was I supposed to do? Jump and grab his feet? I was also giving his nephew employment and an equal share in my business. Sure, Omi was a friend, but given his qualifications, nobody would give him that stature. A cheaper rent was the least he could do.

'Let me know when you want me, Mama,' Omi said.

'Good, I'll see you,' he said. 'continue your rest.'

Ish raised his middle finger as Mama left. Then we lay down and went back to sleep.

Seven

'Have you done the sums I gave you?'

Vidya nodded. I couldn't see her face as we sat side by side, but I knew she'd just cried when she lifted a hand to wipe an eye.

I opened her tuition notebook. I am a tutor, not a consoler.

'You did them all?'

She shook her head.

'How many did you do?'

She showed me seven fingers. Ok, seven out of ten weren't bad. But why wasn't she saying anything.

'What's up?' I said, more to improve communication than the sight of her smudged eyes.

'Nothing,' she said in a broken voice.

A girl's 'nothing' usually means 'a lot'. Actually, it meant 'a lot and don't get me started'. I thought of a suitable response to a fake 'nothing'.

'You want to go wash your face?' I said.

'I am fine. Let's get started.'

I looked at her eyes. Her eyelashes were wet. She had the same eyes as her brother. However, the brown was more prominent on her fair face.

'Your second problem is correct too,' I said, and ticked her notebook. I almost wrote 'good' out of habit. I normally taught young kids, and they loved it if I made comments like 'good', 'well done' or made a 'star' against their answers. But Vidya was no kid.

'You did quite well,' I said as I finished reviewing her work.

'Excuse me,' she said and ran to the bathroom. She probably had an outburst of tears. She came back, this time her eyeliner gone and the whole face wet.

'Listen, we can't have a productive class if you are disturbed. We have to do more complex problems today and...'

'But I am not disturbed. It's Garima and her, well, forget it.'

'Garima?'

'Yes, my cousin and best friend in Bombay. I told you last time.'

'I don't remember,' I said.

'She told me last night she would SMS me in the morning. It is afternoon already, and she hasn't. She always does that.'

'Why don't you SMS her instead?'

'I am not doing that. She said she would. And so she should, right?'

I looked at her blankly, unable to respond.

'She is in this hi-fi PR job, so she is too busy to type a line?' I wished that woman would SMS her so we could start class.

'Next time I will tell her I have something really important to talk about and not call her for two days,' she said.

Some, I repeat only some girls, measure the strength of their friendship by the power of the emotionally manipulative games they could play with each other.

'Should we start?'

'Yeah, I am feeling better. Thanks for listening.'

'No problem. So what happened in problem eight?' I said.

We immersed ourselves into probability for the next half an hour. When she applied her mind, she wasn't dumb at maths as she came across on first impression. But she rarely applied it for more than five minutes. Once, she had to change her pen. Then she had to reopen and fasten her hairclip. In fifteen minutes, she needed a cushion behind her back. After that her mother sent in tea and biscuits and she had to sip it every thirty seconds. Still, we plowed along. Forty minutes into the class, she pulled her chair back.

'My head is throbbing now. I have never done so much maths continuously in my life. Can we take a break?'

'Vidya, we only have twenty minutes more,' I said.

She stood up straight and blinked her eyes. 'Can we agree to a five-minute break during class? One shouldn't study maths that long. It has to be bad for you.'

She kept her pen aside and opened her hair. A strand fell on my arm. I pulled my hand away.

'How is your preparation for other subjects? You don't hate science, do you?' I said. I wanted to keep the break productive.

'I like science. But the way they teach it, it sucks,' Vidya said.

'Like what?'

'Like the medical entrance guides, they have thousands of multiple choice questions. You figure them out and then you are good enough to be a doctor. That's not how I look at science.'

'Well, we have no choice. There are very few good colleges and competition is tough.'

'I know. But the people who set these exam papers, I wonder if they ever are curious about chemistry anymore. Do they just cram up reactions? Or do they ever get fascinated by it? Do they ever see a marble statue and wonder, it all appears static, but inside this statue there are protons buzzing and electrons madly spinning.'

I looked into her bright eyes. I wished they would be as lit up when I taught her probability.

'That's quite amazing, isn't it?' I said.

'Or let's talk of biology. Think about this,' she said and touched my arm. 'What is this?'

'What?' I said, taken aback by her contact.

'This is your skin. Do you know there are communities of bacteria living here? There are millions of individual life forms – eating, reproducing and dying right on us. Yet, we never wonder. Why? We only care about cramming up an epidermal layer diagram, because that comes in the exam every single year.'

I didn't know what to say to this girl. Maybe I should have stuck to teaching seven-year-olds.

'There are some good reference books outside your textbooks for science,' I told her.

'Are there?'

'Yes, you get them in the Law Garden book market. They go into concepts. I can get them for you if you want. Ask your parents if they will pay for them.'

'Of course, they will pay. If it is for studies, they spend like crazy. But can I come along with you?'

'No, you don't have to. I'll get the bill.'

'What?'

'In case you are thinking how much I will spend.'

'You silly or what? It will be a nice break. We'll go together.'

'Fine. Let's do the rest of the sums. We have taken a fifteen-minute break.'

I finished a set of exercises and gave her ten problems as homework. Her phone beeped as I stood up to leave. She rushed to grab it. 'Garima,' she said and I shut the door behind me.

I was walking out when Ish came home.

'Hey, good class? She is a duffer, must be tough,' said Ish, his body covered in sweat after practice.

'Not bad, she is a quick learner,' I said. I didn't know why, but looking at Ish right then made my heart beat fast. I wondered if I should tell him about my plan to go to Law Garden with Vidya to buy books. But that would be stupid, I thought. I didn't have to explain everything to him.

'I figured out a way to rein in Ali,' Ish said.

'How?'

'I let him hit his four sixes first. Then he is like any of us.'

I nodded.

'The other boys get pissed though. They think I have a special place for this student.' Ish added.

'They are kids. Don't worry,' I said and wondered how much longer I had to be with him and why the hell did I feel so guilty?

'Yeah. Some students *are* special, right?' Ish chuckled. For a nanosecond I felt he was making a dig at me. No, this was about Ali. I didn't have a special student.

'You bet. Listen, have to go. Mom needs help with a big wedding order.'

With that, I took rapid strides and was out of his sight. My head buzzed like those electrons inside the marble statue in Omi's temple.

★

She was dressed in a white chikan salwar kameez on the day of our Law Garden trip. Her bandhini orange and red dupatta had tiny brass bells at the end. They made a sound everytime she moved her hand. There was a hint of extra make-up. Her lips shone and I couldn't help staring at them.

'It's lip gloss. Is it too much?' she said self-consciously, rubbing her lips with her fingers. Her upper lip had a near invisible mole on the right. I pulled my gaze away and looked for autos on the street. Never, ever look at her face, I scolded myself.

'That's the bookshop,' I said as we reached the store.

The University Bookstore in Navrangpura was a temple for all muggers in the city. Nearly all customers were sleep deprived, over zealous students who'd never have enough of quantum physics or calculus. They don't provide statistics, but I am sure anyone who clears the engineering and medical entrance exams in the city has visited the bookstore.

The middle-aged shopkeeper looked at Vidya through his glasses. She was probably the best looking customer to visit that month. Students who prepared for medical entrance don't exactly wear coloured lip gloss.

'Ahem, excuse me,' I said as the shopkeeper scanned Vidya up and down.

'Govind beta, so nice to see you,' he said. One good way old people get away with leching is by branding you their son or daughter. He knew my name ever since I scored a hundred in the board exam. In the newspaper interview I had recommended his shop. He displayed the cutting for two years after that. I still get a twenty-five per cent discount on every purchase.

'You have organic chemistry by L.G.Wade?' I said. I would have done more small talk, but I wanted to avoid talking about Vidya. In fact, I didn't even want him to look at Vidya.

'Well, yes,' the shopkeeper said, taken aback by my abruptness.

'Chemistry book, red and white balls on the cover,' he screamed at one of his five assistants.

'This is a good book,' I said as I tapped the cover and gave it to Vidya. 'Other organic chemistry books have too much to memorise. This one explains the principles.'

Vidya took the book in her hand. Her red nail polish was the same colour as the atoms on the cover.

'Flip through it, see if you like it,' I said.

She turned a few pages. The shopkeeper raised an eyebrow. He was asking me about the girl. See this is the reason why people think Ahmedabad is a small town despite the multiplexes. It is the mentality of the people.

'Student, I take tuitions,' I whispered to satisfy his curiosity lest he gave up sleeping for the rest of his life. He nodded his head in approval. *Why do these old people poke their nose in our affairs so much? Like, would we care if he hung out with three grandmas?*

'If you say it is good, I am fine,' she said, finishing her scan.

'Good, and in physics, have you ever read Resnick and Halliday?'

'Oh, I saw that book at my friend's place once. Just the table of contents depressed me. It's too hi-fi for me.'

'What is this "hi-fi"? It is in your course, you have to study it,' I said, my voice stern.

'Don't they have some guides or something?' she said, totally ignoring my comment.

'Guides are a short cut. They solve a certain number of problems. You need to understand the concepts.'

The shopkeeper brought out the orange and black cover Resnick and Halliday. Yes, the cover was scary and dull at the same time, something possible only in physics books.

'I won't understand it. But if you want to, let's buy it,' Vidya agreed.

'Of course, you will understand it. And uncle, for maths do you have M.L. Khanna?'

I could see his displeasure in me calling him uncle, but someone needed to remind him.

'Maths Khanna,' the shopkeeper shouted. His assistants pulled out the yellow and black tome. Now if Resnick and Halliday is scary, M.L. Khanna is the Exorcist. I haven't seen a thicker book and every page is filled with the hardest maths problems in the world. It was amusing that a person with a friendly name like M.L. Khanna could do this to the students of our country.

'What is this?' Vidya said and tried to lift the book with her left hand. She couldn't. She used both hands and finally took it six inches off the ground. 'No, seriously, what is this? An assault weapon?'

'It covers every topic,' I said and measured the thickness with the fingers of my right hand, the four fingers fell short.

She held her hand sideways over mine to assist.

'Six, it is six fingers thick,' she said softly.

I pulled my hand out, lest uncle raise his eyebrows again, or worst case join his hand to ours to check the thickness.

'Don't worry, for the medical entrance you only have to study a few topics,' I reassured her.

We paid for the books and came out of the shop.

We walked on the Navrangpura main road. My new shop was two hundred metres away. I had the urge to go see it.

'Now what?' she said.

'Nothing, let's go home,' I said and looked for an auto.

'You are a big bore, aren't you?' she said.

'Excuse me?' I said.

'Dairy Den is round the corner. I'm hungry,' she said.

'I am starving. Seriously, I am famished.' She kept a hand on her stomach. She wore three rings, each with different designs and tiny, multi-coloured stones.

I took the least visible seat in Dairy Den. Sure, no one from our gossip-loving pol came to this hip teen joint, but one could never be too careful. If a supplier saw me at Dairy Den, I would be like any other trendy young boy in Ahmedabad. I would never get a good price for cricket balls.

I felt hungry too. But I couldn't match the drama-queen in histrionics. She ordered a Den's special pizza, which had every topping available in Dairy Den's kitchen. All dishes were vegetarian, as preferred by Ambavadis.

'These books look really advanced,' she said, pointing to the plastic bag.

'They are MSc books,' I said.

She raised her eyebrows. 'Can someone explain to me why seventeen-year-olds are made to read MSc books in this country?'

I shrugged. I had no answers for lazy students.

The pizza arrived. We kept quiet and started eating it. I looked at her. She tied her hair, so that it would not fall on the pizza and touch the cheese. She kept her dupatta away from the table and on the chair. The great thing about girls is that even during pauses in the conversation you can look at them and not get bored.

She looked sideways as she became conscious of two boys on a faraway table staring at her. It wasn't surprising, considering she was the best looking girl in Dairy Den by a huge margin. Why are there so few pretty girls? Why hadn't evolution figured it out that men liked pretty women and turned them all out that way?

She checked her phone for any new SMSs. She didn't need to as her phone beeped louder than a fire alarm everytime there was one. She pulled back her sleeve and lifted a slice of pizza. She used her fingers to lift the strands of cheese that had fallen out and placed them back on the slice. Finally she took a bite.

'So, what's up?' she broke the silence. 'Are we allowed to talk about anything apart from science subjects?'

'Of course,' I said. I glared at the boys at the other table. They didn't notice me.

'We are not that far apart in age. We could be friends, you know,' she said.

'Well,' I said, 'tough, isn't it?'

'Tough? Give me one reason why?'

'I will give you four – (1) I am your teacher (2) you are my best friend's sister (3) you are younger than me, and (4) you are a girl.'

I felt stupid stating my reasons in bullet points. There is a reason why nerds can't impress girls. They don't know how to talk.

She laughed at me rather than with me.

'Sorry for the list. Can't get numbers out of my system,' I said.

She laughed. 'It tells me something. You have thought it out. That means, you have considered a potential friendship.'

I remained silent.

'I am kidding,' she said and tapped my hand. She had this habit of soothing people by touching them. With normal people it would've been ok, but with sick people like me, female touches excite more than soothe. I felt the urge to look at her face again. I turned determinedly to the pizza instead.

'But seriously, you should have a backup friend,' she said.

'Backup what?'

'You, Ish and Omi are really close. Like you have known each other since you were sperm.'

My mouth fell open at her last word. Vidya was supposed to be Ish's little sister who played with dolls. Where did she learn to talk like that?

'Sorry, I meant Ish and Omi are your best friends. But if you have to bitch … oops, rant about them, who do you do it with?'

'I don't need to rant about my friends,' I said.

'C'mon, are they perfect?'

'No one is perfect.'

'Like Garima and I are really close. We talk twice a day. But sometimes she ignores me, or talks to me like I am some naive small town girl. I hate it, but she is still my best friend.'

'And?' I said. Girls talk in circles. Like an algebra problem, it takes a few steps to get them to the point.

'And, talking about it to you, venting, like this, makes me feel better. And I can forgive her. So, even though she is a much closer friend of mine, you became a backup friend.'

If she applied as much brain in maths, no one could stop her from becoming a surgeon. But Vidya who could micro-analyse relationships for hours, would not open M.L. Khanna to save her life.

'So, c'mon, what's the one rant you have about your best friends?'

'My friends are my business partners, too. So it's complicated,' I paused. 'Sometimes I don't think they understand business. Or may be they do, but they don't understand the passion I bring to it.'

She nodded. I loved that nod. For once, someone had nodded at something I felt so deeply about.

'How?' she egged me on.

Over the last few scraps of pizza, I told her everything. I told her about our shop, and how I managed everything. How I had expanded the business to offer tuitions and coaching. I told her about Ish's irritating habit of giving discounts to kids and Omi's dumbness in anything remotely connected to numbers. And finally, I told her about my dream – to get out of the old city and have a new shop in an air-conditioned mall.

'Navrangpura,' she said, 'near here?'

'Yes,' I said, as my chest expanded four inches.

She saw the glitter in my eyes, as I could see it reflected in hers.

'Good you never did engineering. Though I am sure you would have got in,' she said.

'I can't see myself in an office. And leaving mom and her business alone was not an option.'

I had opened up more than I ever had to anyone in my life. This wasn't right, I chided myself. I mentally repeated the four reasons and poked the pile of books.

'More than me, you need to be friends with these books,' I said and asked for the bill.

★

'Coming,' a girl responded as Ishaan rang the bell of our supplier's home. We had come to purchase new bats and get old ones repaired.

Saira, supplier Pandit-ji's eighteen-year-old daughter, opened the door.

'Papa is getting dressed, you can wait in the garage,' she said, handing us the key to Pandit-ji's warehouse store. We went to the garage and sat on wooden stools. Ish dumped the bats for repair on the floor.

The Pandit Sports Goods Suppliers was located in Ellisbridge. The owner, Giriraj Pandit, had his one-room house right next to it. Until five years ago, he owned a large bat factory in Kashmir. That was before he was kicked out of his hometown by militants who gave him the choice of saving his neck or his factory. Today he felt blessed being a small supplier in Ahmedabad with his family still alive.

'Kashmiris are so fair complexioned,' I said to make innocuous conversation.

'You like her,' Ish grinned.

'Are you nuts?'

'Fair-complexioned, eh?' Ish began to laugh.

'Govind bhai, my best customer,' Pandit-ji said as he came into the warehouse, fresh after a bath. He offered us green almonds. It is nice to be a buyer in business. Everybody welcomes you.

'We need six bats, and these need repairs,' I said.

'Take a dozen Govind bhai,' he said and opened a wooden trunk, 'the India-Australia series is coming, demand will be good.'

'Not in the old city,' I said.

He opened the wooden trunk and took out a bat wrapped in plastic. He opened the bat. It smelled of fresh willow. Sometimes bat makers used artificial fragrance to make new bats smell good, but Pandit-ji was the real deal.

Ish examined the bat. He went to the box and checked the other bats for cracks and chips.

'The best of the lot for you Govind bhai,' Pandit-ji smiled heartily.

'How much,' I said.

'Three hundred.'

'Joking?'

'Never,' he swore.

'Two hundred fifty,' I said, 'last and final.'

'Govind bhai, it is a bit tough right now. My cousin's family has arrived from Kashmir, they've lost everything. I have five more mouths to feed until he finds a job and place.'

'They are all living in that room?' Ish was curious.

'What to do? He had a bungalow in Srinagar and a fifty-year-old almond business. Now, see what times have come to, kicked out of our own homes,' Pandit-ji sighed and took out the bats for repair from the gunny bag.

I hated sympathy in business deals. We settled for two hundred and seventy after some more haggling. 'Done,' I said and took out the money. I dealt in thousands now, but imagined that transacting in lakhs and crores wouldn't be that different.

Pandit-ji took the money, brushed it against the mini-temple in his godown and put it in his pocket. His God had made him pay a big price in life, but he still felt grateful to him. I could never understand this absolute faith that believers possess. Maybe I missed something by being agnostic.

Eight

Ali reached practice twenty minutes late. Every delayed minute made Ish more pissed.

'You are wearing kurta pajama, where is your kit?' Ish screamed as Ali walked in at 7.20 a.m.

'Sorry, woke up late. I didn't get time and...'

'Do your rounds,' Ish said and stood in the centre of the bank's courtyard.

When Ali finished his rounds, Ish unwrapped a new bat for him.

'For you, brand new from Kashmir. Like it?'

Ali nodded without interest. 'Can I leave early today?'

'Why?' Ish snapped.

'There is a marble competition in my pol.'

'And what about cricket?'

Ali shrugged.

'First you come late, then you want to go early. What is the point of marbles?' Ish said as he signalled him to take the crease. One of the three other boys became the bowler.

'We will start with catching practice. Ali, no shots, give them catches.'

Ali's self-control had become better after training for a few months. Ish had taught him to play defensive and avoid getting out. With better diet and exercise, Ali's stamina had improved. He gained the strength to hit the ball rather than rely on momentum. Once Ali faced five balls in a restrained manner, he could sharpen his focus to use his gift. The trick was to use his ability at a level that scored yet sustained him at the crease. One ball an over worked well. Ish now wanted him to get to two balls an over.

'Switch. Paras to bat, Ali to field,' Ish shouted after three overs. Ali didn't hit any big shots. Disappointed, he threw the bat on the crease.

'Hey, watch it. It is a new bat,' Ish said.

Paras batted a catch towards Ali, whose hands were busy tightening the cords of his pajama. The ball thunked down on the ground.

'You sleeping or what?' Ish said but Ali ignored him.

Three balls later, Paras set up a catch for Ali again.

'Hey, Ali, catch,' Ish screamed from his position at the umpire.

Ali had one hand in his pocket. He noticed Ish staring at him and lifted up his hand in a cursory manner. Two steps and he could have caught the ball. He didn't, and the ball landed on the ground.

'Hey,' Ish shook Ali's shoulder hard. 'You dreaming?'

'I want to leave early,' Ali said, rubbing his shoulder.

'Finish practice first.'

'Here Ali, bat,' Paras said as he came close to Ali.

'No he has to field,' Ish said.

'It is ok, Ish bhaiya. I know he wants to bat,' Paras said and gave Ali the bat. 'And I want to practice more catches. I need to get good before my school match.'

Ali took the bat, walked to the crease without looking up. Disconcerted by this insolence, Ish rued spoiling the boy with gifts – sometimes kits, sometimes bats.

Ish allowed Ali to bat again upon Paras' insistence. 'Lift it for Paras, gentle to the left.'

The ball arrived, Ali whacked it hard. Like his spirit, the ball flew out of the bank. 'I want to go.' Ali stared at Ish with his green eyes.

'I don't care about your stupid marble tournament. No marble player ever became great,' Ish shouted.

'Well, you also never became great,' Ali said.

Ouch, kids and their bitter truth.

Ish froze. His arm trembled. With perfect timing like Ali's bat, Ish's right hand swung and slapped Ali's face hard. The impact and shock made Ali fall on the ground.

Everyone stood erect as they heard the slap.

Ali sat up on the ground and sucked his breath to fight tears.

'Go play your fucking marbles,' Ish said and deposited a slap again. I ran behind to pull Ish's elbow. Ali broke into tears. I bent down to pick up Ali. I tried to hug him, as his less-strict maths tutor. He pushed me away.

'Go away,' Ali said, crying as he kicked me with his tiny legs, 'I don't want you.'

'Ali, quiet buddy. Come, let's go up, we will do some fun sums,' I said. Oops, wrong thing to say to a kid who had just been whacked.

'I don't want to do sums,' Ali glared back at me.

'Yeah, don't want to field. Don't want to do sums. Lazy freak show wants to play marbles all day,' Ish spat out.

I felt it was stupid of Ish to argue with a twelve-year-old.

'Everyone go home, we practice tomorrow,' I said.

'No, we have to…,' Ish to said.

'Ish, go inside the bank,' I said.

'I don't like him,' Ali said, still in tears.

'Ali behave. This is no way to speak to your coach. Now go home,' I said.

I exhaled a deep breath as everyone left. Maybe God sent me here to be everyone's parent.

★

'What the fuck is wrong with you? He is a kid,' I said to Ish after everyone left. I made lemonade in the kitchen to calm Ish down. Ish stood next to me.

'Brat, thinks he has a gift,' Ish said.

'He does,' I said and passed him his drink, 'hey, can you order another LPG cylinder. This one is almost over,' I said. We did have a kerosene stove, but it was a pain to cook on that.

We came to the cashier's waiting area to sit on the sofas.

Ish kept quiet. He held back something. I wasn't sure if it was tears, as I had never seen Ish cry.

'I shouldn't have hit him,' he said after drinking half a glass. I nodded.

'But did you see his attitude? "You never became great." Can you imagine if I had said it to my coach?'

'He is just a twelve-year-old. Don't take him seriously,'

'He doesn't care man. He has it in him to make to the national team. But all he wants to do is play his fucking marbles.'

'He enjoys marbles. He doesn't enjoy cricket, yet.'

Ish finished his drink and tossed the plastic glass in the kitchen sink. We locked the bank's main door and the gate and walked towards our shop.

'It is so fucking unfair,' Ish said, 'I slaved for years. I gave up my future for this game. Nothing came of it. And you have this kid who is born with this talent he doesn't even care about.'

'What do you mean nothing came of it? You were the best player in school for years.'

'Yeah, in Belrampur Municipal School, that's like saying Vidya is the Preity Zinta of our pol. Who cares?'

'What?' I said and couldn't control a smile.

'Nothing, our aunt once called her that, and I keep teasing her on it,' Ish said. His mood lightened up a little. We came close to our shop. The temple dome became visible.

'Why does God do this Govind?' Ish said.

'Do what?'

'Give so much talent to some people. And people like me have none.'

'You are talented.'

'Not enough. Not as much as Ali. I love this game, but have no gifts. I pushed myself – woke up at 4 a.m. everyday, training for hours, practice and more practice. I gave up studies, and now that I think of it, even my future. And then comes this marble player who has this freakish gift. I could never see the ball and whack it like Ali. Why Govind?'

Continuing my job as the parent of my friends, I had to try and answer every silly question of his. 'I don't know. God gives talent so that the ordinary person can become extraordinary. Talent is the only way the poor can become rich. Otherwise, in this world the rich would remain rich and the poor would remain poor. This unfair talent actually creates a balance, helps to make the world fair,' I said. I reflected on my own statement a little.

'So why doesn't he care? Marbles? Can you believe the boy is more interested in marbles?'

'He hasn't seen what he can get out of cricket. Right now he is the marble champ in his pol and loves that position. Once he experiences the same success in cricket, he will value his gift. Until now, he was a four ball freak show. You will turn him into a player Ish,' I said.

We reached the shop. Omi had reached before us and swept the floor. He missed coming to coaching, but he had promised his Mama to attend the morning rallies at least twice a week. Today was one of those days.

'Good practice?' Omi asked idly as he ordered tea.

Ish went inside. I put a finger on my lips to signal Omi to be quiet.

A ten-year-old came with thirty coins to buy a cricket ball.

'A leather ball is twenty-five bucks. You only have twenty-one,' I said as I finished the painful task of counting the coins.

'I broke the piggy bank. I don't have anymore,' the boy said very seriously.

'Then come later,' I said as Ish interrupted me.

'Take it,' Ish said and gave the boy the ball.

The boy grabbed it and ran away.

'Fuck you Ish,' I said.

'Fuck you businessman,' Ish said and continued to sulk about Ali in the corner.

★

It took Ish one box of chocolates, two dozen marbles and a new sports cap to woo Ali back. Ali missed us, too. His mother told us he cried for two hours that day and never attended the marble tournament. He hadn't come for practice the next two days either. Ish's guilt pangs had turned into an obsession. Ali had an apology ready – probably stage-managed by his mother. He touched Ish's feet and said sorry for insulting his guru. Ish hugged him and gave the gifts. Ish said he'd cut off his hand rather than hit him again. All too melodramatic if you ask me. The point was Ali came back, this time more serious, and Ish mellowed somewhat. Ali's cricket improved, and other students suggested we take him to the district trials.

Ish vetoed the idea. 'No way, the selection people will destroy him. If they reject him, he is going to be disappointed forever. If they accept him, they will make him play useless matches for several years. He will go for selections, but only the big one – the national team.'

'Really? You confident he will make it,' Omi said, passing us lassi in steel glasses after practice.

'He will be a player like India never had,' Ish announced. It sounded a bit mad, but we had seen Ali demolish the best of bowlers, even if for a few balls. Two more years and Ish could well be right.

'Don't talk about Ali's gift at all. I don't trust anyone.' Ish wiped his lassi moustache.

★

'Excuses don't clear exams, Vidya. If you study this, it will help. Nothing else will.' I opened the chemistry book again.

'I tried,' she said and pushed back her open hair. She had not bathed. She had a track pant on that I think she had been wearing since she was thirteen and a pink T-shirt that said 'fairy queen' or something. How can a grown-up woman wear something that says 'fairy queen'? How can anyone wear something that says 'fairy queen'?

'I pray everyday. That should help,' she said.

I didn't know whether to laugh or flip my fuse again at her nonchalance. Maybe if she didn't look like a cute ragdoll in those clothes, I would have lost my temper again.

'Don't leave it to God, nothing like reading organic chemistry yourself,' I said.

She nodded and moved her chair, as a bottle fell over on the ground.

'Oops,' she said and bent down.

'What?' I stood up in reflex. It was a bottle of coconut oil, fortunately closed.

'Nothing, I thought I'll oil my hair,' she said and lifted the blue bottle.

I looked at her face. My gaze lasted a quarter second more than necessary. There is an optimal time for looking at women before it gets counted as a stare. I had crossed that threshold. Self-consciously she tugged at the T-shirt's neckline as she sat back up. The tug was totally due to me. I didn't look there at all, but she thought I did. I felt sick.

'Coconut oil,' I said, probably the dumbest thing to say but it changed the topic.

'Yes, a bit of organic chemistry for my head. Maybe this will help.'

I flipped the book's pages to see how benzene became oxidised.

'When is your birthday?' she said.

'14 March,' I replied. 'Pi Day.'

'What day?'

'Pi Day. You see, Pi approximates to 3.14 so 14 March is the same date. It is Einstein's birthday, too. Cool, isn't it?'

'A day for Pi? How can you have a day for something so horrible?'

'Excuse me? It is an important day for maths lovers. We never make it public though. You can say you love literature, you can say you love music but you can't say you feel the same way for maths.'

'Why not?'

'People label you a geek.'

'That you are,' she giggled.

She pulled the oil bottle cap close.

'Can you help me oil my hair? I can't reach the back.'

My tongue slipped like it was coated in that oil as I tried to speak. 'Vidya, we should study now.'

'Yeah, yeah, almost done. Just above the back of my neck, please.'

She twisted on her chair so her back faced me. She held up the cap of the oil bottle.

What the hell, I thought. I dipped my index finger in the oil and brought it to her neck.

'Not here,' she giggled again. 'It tickles. Higher, yes at the roots.'

She told me to dip three fingers instead of one and press harder. I followed her instructions in a daze. The best maths tutor in town had become a champi man.

'How's the new shop coming?' she said.

'Great, I paid the deposit and three months advance rent,' I said. 'Fifty thousand bucks, cash. We will have the best location in the mall.'

'I can't wait,' she said.

'Two more months,' I said. 'Ok, that's enough. You do it yourself now, I will hold the cap for you.'

She turned to look at me, dipped her fingers in the oil and applied it to her head.

'I wish I were a boy,' she said, rubbing oil vigorously.

'Why? Easier to oil hair?' I said, holding up the cap in my hand even though my wrist ached.

'So much easier for you to achieve your passions. I won't be allowed to open such a shop,' she said.

I kept quiet.

'There, hopefully my brain would have woken up now,' she said, tying back her hair and placing the chemistry book at the centre of the table.

'I don't want to study this,' she said.

'Vidya, as your teacher my role is…'

'Yeah, what is your role as my teacher? Teach me how to reach my dreams or how to be a drone?'

I kept quiet. She placed her left foot on her lap. I noticed the tiny teddy bears all over her pajamas.

'Well, I am not your teacher. I am your tutor, your maths tutor. And as far as I know, there are no dream tutors.'

'Are you not my friend?'

'Well, sort of.'

'Ok, sort-of-friend, what do you think I should do? Crush my passion and surround myself with hydrocarbon molecules forever?'

I kept quiet.

'Say something. I should lump these lessons even if I have no interest in them whatsoever as that is what all good Indian students do?'

I kept quiet.

'What?' she prodded me again.

'The problem is you think I am this geek who solves probability problems for thrills. Well, maybe I do, but that is not all of me. I am a tutor, it is a job. But never fucking accuse me of crushing your passion.' Too late I realised I had used the F-word. 'Sorry for the language.'

'Cursing is an act of passion.'

I smiled and turned away from her.

'So there you go,' she said, 'my tutor-friend, I want to make an admission to you. I want to go to Mumbai, but not to cut cadavers. I want to study PR.'

I banged my fist on the table. 'Then do it. Don't give me this wish-I-was–a-boy and I'm-trapped-in-a-cage nonsense. Ok, so you are in a cage, but you have a nice, big, oiled brain that is not pea-sized like a bird's. So use it to find the key out.'

'Medical college is one key, but not for me,' she said.

'In that case, break the cage,' I said.

'How?'

'What makes the cage? Your parents, right? Do you have to listen to them all the time?'

'Of course not. I've been lying to them since I was five.'

'Really? Wow,' I said and collected myself. 'Passion versus parents is a tough call. But if you have to choose, passion should win. Humanity wouldn't have progressed if people listened to their parents all the time.'

'Exactly. Our parents are not innocent either. Weren't we all conceived in a moment of passion?' I looked at her innocent-looking face, shocked. This girl is out of control. Maybe it isn't such a good idea to get her out of her cage.

Nine

26 January is a happy day for all Indians. Whether or not you feel patriotic, it is a guaranteed holiday in the first month of the year. I remember thinking it would be the last holiday at our temple shop since we were scheduled to move to the new mall on Valentine's Day. Apart from the deposit, we had spent another sixty thousand to fit out the interiors. I borrowed ten thousand from my mother, purely as a loan. Ish's dad refused to give any money. Omi, even though I had said no, took the rest in loan from Bittoo Mama.

The night before Republic Day, I lay in bed with my thoughts. I had invested a hundred and ten thousand rupees. My business had already reached lakhs. Should we do a turf carpet throughout? Now that would be cool for a sports shop. I dreamed of my chain of stores the whole night.

'Stop shaking me mom, I want to sleep,' I screamed. Can't the world let a businessman sleep on a rare holiday.

But mom didn't shake me. I moved on my own. I opened my eyes. My bed went back and forth too. I looked at the wall clock. It had fallen on the floor. The room furniture, fan and windows vibrated violently.

I rubbed my eyes, what was this? Nightmares?

I stood up and went to the window. People on the street ran haphazardly in random directions.

'Govind,' my mother screamed from the other room, 'hide under the table. It is an earthquake.'

'What?' I said and ducked under the side table kept by the window in reflex. I could see the havoc outside. Three TV antennas from the opposite building fell down. A telephone pole broke and collapsed on the ground.

The tremors lasted for forty-five seconds, the most destructive and longest forty-five seconds of my life. Of course, I did not know it then. A strange silence followed the earthquake.

'Mom,' I screamed.

'Govind, don't move,' she screamed back.

'It is gone,' I said after ten more minutes had passed, 'you ok?'

I came out to the living room. Everything on the wall – calendars, paintings and lampshades, lay on the floor.

'Govind,' my mother came and hugged me. Yes, I was fine. My mother was fine too.

'Let's get out,' she said.

'Why?'

'The building might collapse.'

'I don't think so,' I said as my mother dragged me out in my pajamas. The street was full of people.

'Is it a bomb?' a man spoke to the other in whispers.

'Earthquake. It's coming on TV. It started in Bhuj,' a man on the street said.

'Bad?' the other man said.

'We felt the tremors hundreds of kilometres away, imagine the situation in Bhuj,' another old man said.

We stood out for an hour. No, the foundation of our building, or for that matter any in our pol had not come loose. Meanwhile, rumours and gossip spread fast. Some said more earthquakes could come. Some said India had tested a nuclear bomb. A few parts of Ahmedabad reported property damage. Stories rippled through the street.

I re-entered my house after two hours and switched on the TV. Every channel covered the earthquake. It epicentred in Bhuj, though it affected many parts of Gujarat.

'Reports suggest that while most of Ahmedabad is safe, many new and upcoming buildings have suffered severe damage…,' the reporter said as tingles went down my spine.

'No, no, no…,' I mumbled to myself.

'What?' my mother said as she brought me tea and toast.

'I have to go out.'

'Where?'

'Navrangpura … now,' I said and wore my slippers.

'Are you mad?' she said.

'My shop mom, my shop,' is all I said as I ran out of the house.

The whole city was shut. I couldn't find any autos or buses. I decided to run the seven-kilometre stretch. I had to see if my new store was ok. Yes, I just wanted that to be ok.

It took me an hour to get there. I saw the devastation en-route. The new city areas like Satellite suffered heavy damage. Almost every building had their windows broken. Those buildings that were under construction had crumbled to rubble. I entered Navrangpura. Signs of plush shops lay on the road. I reasoned that my new, ultra-modern building would have earthquake safety features. I gasped for breath as I ran the last hundred metres. Sweat covered my entire body.

Did I miss the building? I said as I reached my lane. The mayhem on the street and the broken signs made it hard to identify addresses.

I retreated, catching my breath.

'Where is the building?' I said to myself as I kept circling my lane.

I found it, finally. Only that the six storeys that were intact a day ago had now turned into a concrete heap. I could not concentrate. I felt intense thirst. I looked for water, but I only saw rubble, rubble and more rubble. My stomach hurt. I grabbed it with my left hand and sat on a broken bench to keep my consciousness.

The police pulled out a labourer, with bruises all over. Cement bags had fallen on him and crushed his legs. The sight of blood made me vomit. No one in the crowd noticed me. One lakh and ten thousand, the number spun in my head.

Unrelated images of the day my dad left us flashed in my head. Those images had not come for years. The look on his face as he shut the living room door on the way out. My mother's silent tears for the next few hours, which continued for the next few years. I don't know why that past scene came to me. I think the brain has a special box where it keeps crappy memories. It stays shut, but everytime a new entry has to be added, it opens and you can look at what is inside. I felt anger at my dad, totally misplaced as I should have felt anger at the earthquake. Or at myself, for betting so much money. Anger for making the *first big mistake* of my life.

My body trembled with violent intensity.

'Don't worry, God will protect us,' someone tapped my shoulder.

'Oh really, then who the hell sent it in the first place?' I said and pushed the stranger away. I didn't need sympathy, I wanted my shop.

Two years of scrimping and saving, twenty years of dreams – all wiped away in twenty seconds. The 'Navrangpura Mall's' neon sign, once placed at the top of the six floor building, now licked the ground. Maybe this was God's way of saying something – that we shouldn't have these malls. We were destined to remain a small town and we shouldn't even try to be like the big cities. I don't know why I thought of God, I was agnostic. But who else do you blame earthquakes on?

Of course, I could blame the builder of the Navrangpura mall. For the hundred-year-old buildings in the old city pols remained standing. Omi's two-hundred-year-old temple stood intact. Then why did my fucking mall collapse? What did he make it with? Sand?

I needed someone to blame. I needed to hit someone, something. I lifted a brick, and threw it at an already smashed window. The remaining glass broke into little bits.

'What are you doing? Haven't we seen enough destruction?' said someone next to me.

I couldn't make out his face, or anyone's face. My heart beat at double the normal rate. Surely, we could sue the builder, my heart said. The builder would have run away, my head said. And no one would get their money back.

'Govind, Govind,' Ish said. He screamed in my ear when I finally noticed him.

'What the hell are you doing here man? It is dangerous to be out, let's go home' Ish said.

I kept looking at the rubble like I had for the last four hours.

'Govind,' Ish said, 'we can't do anything. Let's go.'

'We are finished Ish,' I said, feeling moist in my eyes for the first time in a decade.

'It's ok buddy. We have to go,' Ish said.

'We lost everything. Look, our business collapsed even before it opened…'

I broke down. I never cried the day my father left us. I never cried when my hand had got burnt one Diwali and Dr Verma had to give me sedatives to go to sleep. I never cried when India lost a match. I never cried when I couldn't join engineering college. I never cried when we barely made any money for the first three months of business. But that day, when God slapped my city for no reason, I cried and cried. Ish held me and let me use his shirt to absorb my tears.

'Govi, let's go home,' Ish said. He never shortened my name before. He'd never seen me like that too. Their CEO and parent had broken down.

'We are cursed man. I saved, and I saved and I fucking saved. And we took loans. But then, this? Ish, I don't want to see that smug look on Bittoo Mama's face. I will work on the roadside,' I said as Ish dragged me away to an auto.

People must have thought I had lost a child. But when a businessman loses his business, it is similar. It is one thing when you take a business risk and suffer a loss, but this was unfair. Someone out there needed to realise this was fucking unfair.

Ish bought a Frooti to calm me. It helped, especially since I didn't eat anything else for the next two days. I think the rest of the Ambavadis didn't either.

I found out later that over thirty thousand people lost their lives. That is a stadium full of people. In Bhuj, ninety per cent of homes were destroyed. Schools and hospitals flattened to the ground. Overall in Gujarat, the quake damaged a million structures. One of those million structures included my future shop. In the large scheme of things, my loss was statistically irrelevant. In the narrow, selfish scheme of things, I suffered the most. The old city fared better than the new city. Somehow our grandfathers believed in cement more than the new mall owners.

Compared to Gujarat, Ahmedabad had better luck, the TV channels said. The new city lost only fifty multi-storey buildings. They said only a few hundred people died in Ahmedabad compared to tens of thousands elsewhere. It is funny when hundreds of people dying is tagged with 'only'. Each of those people would have had families, and hopes and aspirations all shattered in forty-five seconds. But that is how maths works – compared to thirty thousand, hundreds is a rounding error.

★

I had not left home for a week. For the first three days I had burning fever, and for the next four my body felt stone cold.

'Your fever is gone.' Dr Verma checked my pulse.

I lay on the bed, staring at the ceiling.

'You haven't gone to the shop?'

I shook my head, still horizontal on bed.

'I didn't expect this from you. You have heard of Navaldharis?' Dr Verma said.

I kept quiet.

'You can talk. I haven't put a thermometer in your mouth.'

'No, who are they?'

'Navaldharis is a hardcore entrepreneur community in Gujarat. Everyone there does business. And they say, a true Navaldhari businessman is one who can rise after being razed to the ground nine times.'

'I am in debt, Doctor. I lost more money in one stroke than my business ever earned.'

'There is no businessman in this world who has never lost money. There is no one who has learnt to ride a bicycle without falling off. There is no one who has loved without getting hurt. It's all part of the game.' Dr Verma shrugged.

'I'm scared,' I said, turning my face to the wall.

'Stop talking like middle-class parents. So scared of losing money, they want their kids to serve others all their lives to get a safe salary.'

'I have lost a lot.'

'Yes, but age is on your side. You are young, you will earn it all back. You have no kids to feed, you have no household to maintain. And the other thing is, you have seen less money. You can live without it. '

'I don't feel like doing anything. This earthquake, why did this happen? Do you know our school is now a refugee camp?'

'Yes, and what are the refugees doing? Lying in bed or trying to recover?'

I tuned out the doctor. Everyone around me was giving me advice, good advice actually. But I was in no mood to listen. I was in no mood for anything. The shop? It would remain closed for a week more. Who would buy sports stuff after an earthquake?

'Hope to see you out of bed tomorrow,' Dr Verma said and left. The clock showed three in the afternoon. I kept staring at it until four.

'May I come in, Govind sir,' Vidya's cheeky voice in my home sounded so strange that I sprang up on bed. And what was with the sir?

She had the thick M.L. Khanna book and a notebook in her hand.

'What are you doing here?' I pulled up my quilt to hide my pajamas and vest attire.

She, of course, looked impeccable in her maroon and orange salwar kameez with matching mirror-work dupatta.

'I got stuck with some sums. Thought I'd come here and ask since you were not well,' she said, sitting down on a chair next to my bed.

My mother came in the room with two cups of tea. I mimed to her for a shirt.

'You want a shirt?' she said, making my entire signalling exercise futile.

'What sums?' I asked curtly after mom left.

'Maths is what I told my mom. Actually, I wanted to give you this.' She extended the voluminous M.L. Khanna tome to me.

What was that for? To solve problems while bedridden?

My mother returned with a shirt and left. I held my shirt in one hand and the M.L. Khanna in another. Modesty *vs* Curiosity. I shoved the shirt aside and opened the book. A handmade, pink greeting card fell out.

The card had a hand-drawn cartoon of a boy lying in bed. She had labelled it Govind, in case it wasn't clear to me. Inside it said: 'Get Well Soon' in the cheesiest kiddy font imaginable. A poem underneath said:

To my maths tutor/ passion guide/ sort-of-friend,
I cannot fully understand your loss, but I can try.
Sometimes life throws curve balls and you question why.
There may be no answers, but I assure time will heal the
wound.
Here is wishing you a heartfelt 'get well soon'.

Your poorest performing student,
Vidya

'It's not very good,' she murmured.

'I like it. I am sorry about the sort-of friend. I am just...,' I said.

'It's ok. I like the tag. Makes it clear that studies are first, right?'

I nodded.

'How are you doing?'

I overcame my urge to turn to the wall. 'Life goes on. It has to. Maybe an air-conditioned mall is not for me.'

'Of course, it is. It isn't your fault. I am sure you will get there one day. Think about this, aren't you lucky you weren't in the shop already when it happened? Imagine the lives lost if the mall was open?'

She had a point. I had to get over this. I had to re-accept Bittoo Mama's smug face.

I returned her M.L. Khanna and kept the card under my pillow.

'Ish said you haven't come to the shop.'

'The shop is open?' I said. Ish and Omi met me every evening but never mentioned it.

'Yeah, you should see bhaiya struggle with the accounts at home. Take tuitions for him, too,' she giggled. 'I'll leave now. About my classes, no rush really.'

'I'll be there next Wednesday,' I called out.

'Nice girl,' my mother said carefully. 'You like her?'

'No. Horrible student.'

Ish and Omi came at night when I had finished my unappetising dinner of boiled vegetables.

'How are you running the shop?' my energetic voice surprised them.

'You sound better,' Ish said.

'Who is doing the accounts?' I said and sat up.

Omi pointed at Ish.

'And? What is it? A two for one sale?'

'We haven't given any discounts all week,' Ish said and sat next to me on the bed.

Ish pulled at my pillow to be more comfortable. 'Wait,' I said, jamming the pillow with my elbow.

'What's that?' Ish said and smiled as he saw an inch of pink paper under my pillow.

'Nothing. None of your business,' I said. Of course it was his business, it was his sister.

'Card?' Omi said.

'Yes, from my cousin,' I said.

'Are you sure?' Ish came to tickle me, to release my death grip on the pillow.

'Stop it', I said, trying to appear light hearted. My heart beat fast as I pinned the pillow down hard.

'Pandit's daughter, isn't it?' Omi chuckled.

'Whatever,' I said, sitting on the pillow as a desperate measure.

'Mixing business with pleasure?' Ish said and laughed.

I joined in the laughter to encourage the deception.

'Come back,' Ish said.

'The loans ... It's all my fault,' I told the wall.

'Mama said we can continue to use the shop,' Omi said.

'No conditions?' I said, surprised.

'Not really,' Omi said.

'And that means?'

'It is understood we need to help him in his campaign,' Ish said. 'Don't worry, you don't have to do anything. Omi and I will help.'

'We have to pay his loan back fast. We have to,' I said.

'We'll get over this,' Ish looked me in the eye. Brave words, but for the first time believable.

'I am sorry I invested...,' I felt I had to apologise, but Omi interrupted me.

'We did it together as business partners. And you are the smartest of us.'

I was not sure if his last line was correct anymore. I was a disaster as a businessman.

'See you tomorrow,' I said.

After they left, I pulled out the card again and smoothed the creases. I read the card eight times before falling asleep.

My break from work brought out hidden skills in my friends. Save a few calculation errors, they managed the accounts just fine. They tabulated daily sales, had their prices right and had offered no discounts. The shop was clean and things were easy to find. Maybe one day I could create businesses and be hands-off. I checked myself from dreaming again. India is not a place for dreams. Especially when you have failed once. I finally saw the sense inherent in the Hindu philosophy of being satisfied with what one had, rather than yearn for more. It wasn't some cool philosophy that ancient sages invented, but a survival mantra in a country where desires are routinely crushed. This shop in the temple was my destiny, and earning that meagre income from it my karma. More was not meant to be. I breathed out, felt better and opened the cash drawer.

'Pretty low for two weeks. But first the earthquake, and now the India-Australia series,' Ish said from his corner.

'People really don't have a reason to play anymore,' Omi said.

'No, no. It's fine. What's happening in the series?' I said. I had lost track of the cricket schedule.

'India lost the first test. Two more to go. The next one is in Calcutta,' Ish said.

'Damn. One-days?'

'Five of them, yet to start,' Omi said. 'I wouldn't get my hopes high. These Australians are made of something else.'

'I'd love to know how the Australians do it,' Ish said.

Mama's arrival broke up our chat. 'Samosas, hot, careful,' he said, placing a brown bag on the counter.

In my earlier avatar, this was my cue to frown, to comment about the grease spoiling the counter. However, the new post-quake Govind no longer saw Mama as hostile. We sat in the sunny courtyard having tea and samosas. They tasted delicious, I think samosas are the best snack known to man.

'Try to forget what happened,' Mama sighed. 'I have never seen such devastation.'

'How was your trip?' Omi said. Mama had just returned from Bhuj. 'Misery everywhere. We need camps all over Gujarat. But how much can Parekh-ji do?'

Mama had stayed up nights to set up the makeshift relief camp at the Belrampur school. Parekh-ji had sent truckloads of grain, pulses and other supplies. People had finally begun to move out and regain their lives.

'We'll close the camp in three weeks,' Mama said to Omi, 'and I can go back to my main cause, Ayodhya.'

The camp had won Mama many fans in the neighbourhood. Technically, anyone could seek refuge. However, a Muslim family would rarely go there for help. Even if they did, camp managers handed out rations but emphasised that everyone in the camp was a Hindu. Despite this soft discrimination, the new-me found it a noble exercise.

'Mama, about your loan,' I turned to him, but he did not hear me.

'My son is coming with me to Ayodhya. You guys should join,' he said. He saw our reluctant faces and added, 'I mean after you restore the business.'

'We can help here, Mama,' Omi said. 'Is there any project after the camp?'

'Oh yes, the spoonful of mud campaign,' Mama said.

We looked puzzled.

'We are going to Ayodhya for a reason. We will get gunnybags full of soil from there. We will go to every Hindu house in Belrampur and ask them if they want a spoon of mud from Rama's birthplace in their house. They can put it in their backyard, mix it with plants or whatever. A great idea from Parekh-ji.'

I saw Parekh-ji's twisted but impeccable logic. No one would say no to a spoonful of soil from Ayodhya. But with that, they were inadvertently buying into the cause. Sympathy for people fighting for Ayodhya would be automatic. And sympathy converted well into votes.

Mama noted the cynicism in my expression.

'Only a marketing strategy for a small campaign. The other party does it at a far bigger scale.'

I picked up another samosa.

'It's ok, Mama. Politics confuses me,' I said. 'I can't comment. We will help you. You have saved our livelihood, we are forever indebted.'

'You are my kids. How can you be indebted to your father?'

'Business is down, but on the revised loan instalments...,' but Mama cut me again.

'Forget it, sons. You faced a calamity. Pay when you can. And now you are members of our party, right?'

Mama stood up to hug us. I half-heartedly hugged him back. I felt sick owing people money. 'Mama, I am sorry. I was arrogant, rude and disrespectful. I realise my destiny is this shop. Maybe God intended it this way and I accept it,' I said.

'We are all like that when young. But you have started believing in God?' Mama said and beamed.

'I'm just less agnostic now.'

'Son, this is the best news I've heard today,' Mama said. 'Something good has come out of all this loss.'

A man dragged a heavy wooden trunk into our shop. 'Who's that? Oh, Pandit-ji?' I said.

Pandit-ji panted, his white face a rosy red. He arranged the trunk on the floor. 'A sports shop closed down. The guy could not pay. He paid me with trunks full of goods. I need cash, so I thought I will bring this to you.'

'I have no cash either,' I said as I offered him a samosa. 'Pandit-ji, business is terrible.'

'Who's asking you for cash now? Just keep it in your shop. I'll send one more trunk. Whatever sells, you keep half and give me half. Just this one trunk is worth ten thousand. I have six more at home. What say?'

I took in the trunks as I had no risk. We needed a miracle to move that many goods. Of course, I wasn't aware that the second test match of the India Australia series would be one.

Mama introduced himself to Pandit-ji. They started talking like grown-ups do, exchanging hometowns, castes and sub-castes.

'We are late,' Ish whispered, but loud enough for Mama and Pandit-ji to hear.

'You have to go somewhere?' Mama said.

'Yes, to a cricket match. One of the students we coach is playing,' Ish said, avoiding Ali's name.

Omi downed the shutters of the shop. Omi signalled and all of us bent to touch Mama's feet.

'My sons,' Mama said as he held a palm over our heads and blessed us.

'Don't worry about that idiot from that stupid team. You creamed them,' Ish said to Ali.

We returned from a neighbourhood match. Ali's side had won with him scoring the highest. Ali lasted eight overs. Ish looked pleased that the training was finally showing results. However, our celebratory mood dampened as the opposing team's captain kicked Ali in the knee before running away.

'Will they hurt me again?' Ali said.

'No, because I will hurt them before anyone touches you,' Ish said, kissing Ali's forehead, Ish would make a good father. Not like his own father who never said one pleasant sentence.

Omi picked up a limping Ali. 'I'll take him to the shop,' Omi said. 'And ask ma to make him some turmeric milk. You guys get dinner, whatever he wants.'

'I want kebabs,' Ali said promptly.

'Kebabs? In the shop?' I hesitated.

'Fine, just don't tell anyone,' Omi said.

'He's ready,' Ish said. His face glowed behind the smoke of roasting kebabs at Qazi dhaba. 'Did you see him play? He can wait, run and support others. He plays along until time comes for the big hits. Fielding sucks, but other than that, he is perfect. He is ready, man.' The smell of chicken tikka filled my nostrils. Omi was really missing a lot in life. 'For what?' I asked.

'Australia is touring India at present, right?' Ish said as the waiter packed our order of rumali rotis, lamb skewers and chicken tikka with onions and green chutney.

'So?' I said.

'He is ready to meet the Australians.'

Ten

India vs Australia Test Match
Kolkata, 11-15 March 2001

Day 1

Most of the time crap happens in life. However, sometimes miracles do too. To us, the second test match of the India-Australia series was the magic cure for the quake. I remember every day of that match. Ish continued with his weird and highly improbable ideas of making Ali meet the Australian team.

'Meet the Australians?' Omi said as he dusted the counter. Ish and I sat on the floor in front of the TV.

'They are in India,' Ish said. He pointed to the Australian team batting on the screen. 'When are we ever going to get a chance like this?'

'Is he mad?' Omi asked me.

'Of course, he is. What will you do by meeting them? Really?' I joined in.

'I want to get their opinion on Ali.'

'How?' Omi said as he sat down with us.

'We will go see a match. Maybe a one-day,' Ish said.

'There is no money for trips,' I said.

'The one-day series will continue for the next two months. If business picks up, then we could,' Ish said.

'They are raping us again. Fuck, business is never going to pick up,' I said as I saw the score. On the first day at tea, Australia's score was 193/1.

'If it does. I said *if*,' Ish said, upset at the score more than me.

'So we go see a match. Then what? Knock on Hayden's door and say, "Hey, check this kid out." How do you intend to meet them?' I mocked.

'I don't know,' Ish turned to the screen, scowling. 'Bowl better, guys.'

'Excuse me, are you watching the India-Australia match?' a lady's voice interrupted us.

An elderly woman stood at the counter with a puja thali in her hand.

'Yes?'

'Can my grandson watch it with you for a while?' she said.

I stood up from the floor. A small boy accompanied the lady. I was never keen on random people coming into our shop to spend their time. She sensed my hesitation. 'We'll buy something. I want to attend the bhajans inside and Babloo wants to see the match.'

'Of course, he can come in.' Ish opened the door wider. The boy came in and sat before the TV. Ish and I exchanged a round of dirty looks.

'Don't watch from so close Babloo. Hello, I am Mrs Ganguly by the way. I also need advice on buying cricket equipment for my school, if you can visit me sometime.'

'School?' I said.

'Yes, I am the principal of the Kendriya Vidyalaya on Ellisbridge. We never had good suppliers for sports. Everybody thinks we are government so they try and rip us off. You supply to schools, no?'

The answer was no. We did not supply to schools.

'Yes,' I said. 'In fact, we have our inhouse advisor Ishaan. He is an ex-district level player.'

'Great. I will see you then,' Mrs Ganguly said and left us to ponder over her business proposition.

'You want candy, Babloo?' Omi said as we tried our best to impress anyone related to Mrs Ganguly.

'But we are not suppliers,' Ish said later.

'So what? You have to swing this for me, Ish. This is a regular income business.'

'If I get you this, will you come to Goa?'

'Goa?' I raised my eyebrows.

'It's the last one-day. I am stretching it out as far as I can. If we save enough, let's go with Ali.'

'But...'

'Say yes.'

'Yes,' I said. After the mall fiasco, I wanted to make Ish happy. I stood up to check the day's accounts.

'Cool. Hey, see the match?' Ish said. 'It has totally turned.'

I looked at the TV. Perhaps God listened to Mrs Ganguly's prayers inside. A little known Surd called Harbhajan Singh had bowled after tea. Wickets crumbled and from 193/1, Australia ended the day at 291/8.

'Bhajji, you are great,' Ish bent forward to kiss the TV.

'Don't watch the TV from so close,' Babloo said.

'Don't listen to grown-ups all the time. Nobody went blind watching TV from close. Don't people work on computers?' Ish was jumping up and down in excitement.

Mrs Ganguly came in two hours later to pick up Babloo. She bought him two tennis balls. I was tempted to throw them in for free, but she might take it the wrong way.

'Here,' she said, giving me her card. 'We have a board meeting every Monday. Why don't you come and tell us how you can help?'

We had four days to prepare. The board would be in a better mood if India won this match.

'Sure, we will see you then,' I said and slipped a candy to Babloo.

Day 2

The only way to describe the second day of the match was 'depressing'. From 291/8, Australia dragged on their first innings to end at a healthy 445 all out. The Indians came out to bat and opener Ramesh got out for no score.

'Who the fuck is this Ramesh? Connection quota,' Ish said.

But it wasn't only Ramesh who sucked. Tendulkar scored ten, others even less. Dravid scored the highest at twenty-five. The second day ended with India at 128/8.

Ish tore his chapattis with anger over dinner. 'These Australians must be thinking – why even bother to come and play with India.'

'Pray for a draw. With a draw there is hope of sales. Else we should change our business. Sports is the wrong choice in our country.' I passed the daal to Omi.

'They have twenty million people. We have one billion, growing at two per cent a year. Heck, we create an Australia every year. Still, they cream us. Something is wrong about this.'

'Should we open another flower shop? There will always be a demand for that in a temple,' I said.

Ish ignored me. He mumbled something about avoiding a follow-on, which looked pretty difficult.

Day 3
The next morning I don't know why we even bothered to switch on the TV. India struggled to stretch their first innings, but packed up before lunch at 171 all out. 'And the Australians have asked India to follow on,' the commentator said and I slapped my forehead. A defeat in a test match was one thing, but an innings defeat meant empty parks for weeks. Kids would rather read textbooks than play cricket and be reminded of India's humiliation. *Why on earth had I started this business? What an idiot I am? Why couldn't I open a sweet shop instead? Indians would always eat sweets. Why sports? Why cricket?*

'That's fucking-follow-on-fantastic,' Ish said, inventing his own phrases for the moment. He clenched his fist and came dangerously close to the TV. 'We had them by their balls at 291/8, and now they ask us to follow on?'

'Should we turn off the TV?' I said. Should we close the shop for good? I thought.

'Wait, I want to see this. I want to see how our team makes eye contact when they lose so badly,' Ish said.

'They are not making eye contact. You are just watching them on TV,' Omi said.

'If this match is a draw, I will treat you all to dinner. Ok, two dinners,' Ish said.

For its second innings, India made one change. It replaced the opener Ramesh with another new guy called Laxman.

'The team is full of people with contacts. Everyone is getting their turn today,' Ish said as the Indian openers took the crease for the second follow-on innings.

But Laxman connected with the ball and bat. He slammed four after four. At the end of the third day, India stood at a respectable 254/4. Adding that to the first innings score of 171, India needed only 20 runs to match Australia's first innings of 445. An innings defeat looked unlikely, and, yes, we could even draw now.

'See, that's what the Indian team does. Right when you give up hope, they get you involved again,' Ish said at dinner.

'You were going to see all days anyway. Please think about our Monday meeting,' I said.

'Laxman's job is not done. He needs to be around if we want a draw,' Ish said.

I sighed. I would have to prepare for the school meeting by myself.

Day 4

If there was a day that India dominated world cricket, it was on the fourth day of the match. Yes, India won the World Cup on 25 June 1983 and so that counted, too. But the day I'm talking about was when two Indian batsmen made eleven Australian cricketers dance to their tune. They did it in public and they did it the whole day. That's right. On the fourth day of the Test, Ish didn't leave the TV even to pee.

Here is what happened. Laxman and Dravid continued to play and added 357 runs for the fifth wicket. Day 4 started at 274/4 and ended at 589/4. Nine of the eleven members of the Australian team took turns bowling, but none of them succeeded in getting a wicket. The crowd at Eden Gardens became possessed. They chanted Laxman's name enough times to make Steve Waugh visibly grumpy. The team that had given us a follow-on could not bowl one batsman out.

Laxman ended the day at 275 not out, scoring more than what the entire Indian team did in their first innings. Dravid made 155 not out. We had lots of wickets left, had 337 runs more than Australia and only one day left in the match.

'I can finally sleep in peace. I'll buy the draw dinners,' Ish said as we downed the shutters of the shop.

'Hope we have some kids back in the park again,' I said.

Day 5

Human expectations have no limit. While we were praying only for a draw two days ago, the start of the fifth day raised new hopes. Laxman left at 281 and everyone in the stadium stood up to applaud for his eleven-hour innings.

The Indian captain Ganguly made a surprise decision. After an hour's play for the day, he declared the Indian innings at 657/7. It meant Australia would have to come back and bat. And that they had to make 384 runs in the rest of the day to win the match.

'Is Ganguly mad? It's too risky. We should have continued to play. Get the draw done and over with,' I said.

'Maybe he has something else in mind,' Ish said.

'What?' Omi scratched his head.

I wasn't sure of Ganguly's intentions either. Ok, so we lucked out and made a big total to take the game to a draw. But why did the captain declare when he could have played on until there was no time left? Unless, of course, he wanted a decision. That was, an Indian victory.

'He can't be serious. We had a follow-on. We could have had an innings defeat. Now, Ganguly really thinks he has a chance to bowl these Australians out?' I said.

Ish nodded as the Australian batsman reverted to the crease. Ganguly had kept the winning score of 384 required by the

Australians at a tantalising level – difficult yet possible. Australians could have played safe and taken the game to a draw, but that is not how Australians play.

'Hey Mr Mathematician, has it happened? Has it ever happened that the side facing a follow-on actually won the match?' Ish said. He signalled Omi to start urgent, special prayers.

I pulled out the cricket data book from the top shelf. We hardly sold any of these, but the publisher insisted we keep a few copies. 'Ok, so it has happened earlier,' I said after a ten-minute search.

'How many times?' Ish said, eyes glued to screen.

'Twice,' I said and noticed Omi close his eyes and chant silently.

'See, it happens. Twice in how long?' Ish said.

'Twice in the last hundred and ten years.'

Ish turned to me. 'Only twice?'

'Once in 1894 and then in 1981,' I read out loud from the page. 'Both times, England won against, guess who, Australia. Sorry buddy, but statistically speaking, this match is so over.'

Ish nodded.

'Like the probability is so low that I'd say if India wins, I will sponsor the Goa trip,' I joked.

'Or like if India wins, you will start believing in God?' Omi played along.

'Yep,' I said.

I told Omi to stop praying too much. A draw would be fine. Ganguly probably did not know the odds. The worst would be if Australia did score the runs.

'161/3,' Omi read Australia's score at tea, which coincided with our own break.

'Let's clean up the shop, guys. The match gets over in a few hours. We may have some customers,' I said.

'A draw is fine. We will take the Australians another time.' Ish reluctantly picked up the mop.

Day 5 – Post-tea

The Indian team must have mixed something special in their tea. Australia came back and continued to cruise at 166/3. Then came five deadly overs that included a hattrick from Harbhajan Singh. Next stop, Australia 174/8. In eight runs, half of the Australian team was gone.

'Ish, don't fucking stand in front of the TV,' I said. But Ish wasn't standing, only jumping.

'Fuck your statistics man, fuck the probability,' Ish shouted in jubilation. I don't like it when people insult mathematics, but I gave Ish the benefit of doubt. You are allowed a few celebratory curses when you witness history.

Pretty soon, the last two batsmen were scalped as well. Harbhajan, the Surd that Ish kissed on screen (and left saliva marks all over), took six wickets, and India won the match in the most spectacular way ever.

In Eden Gardens, every placard, every poster and anything combustible besides people was on fire. It was impossible to hear the TV commentary, as the crowds roared everytime an Indian team member's name was announced.

Ish stood tall, his hands on his hips and looked at the screen. I could see genuine love in his eyes. Every now and then, I had seen Ish watch the men in blue as if he wished he was one of them. But today, he didn't have any of his own regrets. I think more than wanting to be them, he wanted them to win. He saw Harbhajan jump and jumped along. He clapped when Ganguly came to accept the trophy.

'Two balls quickly please, we have a match,' a boy plonked a fifty-rupee note on the counter. The first customer of the great Indian Cricket Season had arrived.

I folded my hands and looked at the sky. Thank you God, for the miracles you bestow on us.

★

'We have come to offer solutions, not just sell some balls,' I started.

I had delivered my first line perfect. The preparations until two last night better be worth it, I told myself. We were in the principal's office in the Kendriya Vidyalaya. The office was in a poor state, with rickety furniture and dusty trophies. Like most government offices and buildings old files piled up high on several cupboards. The lady principal and six teachers sat around a semicircular wooden table. It must be miserable to work here, I thought. It must be miserable to work for anyone else, I thought again.

'Go on,' the principal said, as my pause for effect became too long.

'So we have a district-level champion player who can design a package based on your needs and budgets,' I pointed at Ish and every teacher looked at him.

I passed out sheets that estimated the school's monthly needs based on eight hundred students. I had them laser printed at a computer shop for three rupees a page. A peon brought samosas and tea for everyone.

'How much will this cost?' the administrative head said.

'We did some calculations. Your average cost will be ten thousand a month,' I said.

'That's too much. This is a Kendriya Vidyalaya. Not a private school,' the administrative head said. He shut the notebook and pushed it towards me.

I took a deep breath. I had thought of an answer for this scenario. 'Sir, we can scale down.'

Ish interupped me, 'It is twelve rupees per child a month. Don't you think sport deserves as much as the cost of a fountain pen?'

The teachers looked up from their notebooks and exchanged glances.

'Frankly, no. We get judged on our results. The pass percentage and the first divisions. We have limited resources,' the head said.

'If everyone thinks that way, where will India's sportsmen come from?' Ish said.

'From rich families.' The head took out his glasses and wiped them calmly.

'But talent is not distributed only among the rich. We have to expand the pool.'

'Do you know half our classrooms leak in the rain,' the head said. 'Should we get shiny balls or fix the leaks?' He stood up to leave.

I mentally said the F-word a few times. C'mon Govind, save this. *You need business, any business.*

'Sir, we can do a plan for five thousand a month,' I said.

Ish raised a hand to keep me quiet. I could have killed him.

Ish stood up, to match the admin head's height. 'What are you here to do?'

'To give children an education,' the head said with a straight face.

'And all the education is in these books they read under the plastered roofs? What about the education that comes from sports?'

'What?' the admin head said.

'Sit down Jitin sir,' the principal said. 'Let us hear what they have to say.'

Jitin-sir, I mentally noted his name as he sat down again.

'Are you teaching your kids a subject called teamwork? Are you teaching them how to chase a goal with passion? Are you teaching them discipline? Are you teaching them focus?' Ish asked. I stamped his foot, signalling him to sit down. But he ignored me.

'What are you talking about?' This from one of the teachers.

'Sports teaches them all this. And tell me, who will be more successful in life? The kid who knows all the chemical formulae or the one who knows teamwork, passion, discipline and focus?'

'Sit down, son,' the principal said. Ish took his seat but did not keep quiet.

'I'm not settling for a scaled-down version. Eight hundred kids and they want to keep them locked in classes all day. We will chase useless first divisions but not spend two samosa plates worth of money on sports.'

He pointed to the samosas on the plate. All the teachers stopped eating midway. The pause continued until the principal spoke again. 'Fine, ten thousand is ok for a trial. Let's see how it goes. You are on for six months.'

We stood up to shake hands. Six educated, fifty-somethings stood up to shake hands with me. Yes, I had become a real businessman.

'If this works, why don't you come to a meeting at our Belapur school?' the oldest gentleman in the group said.

'Oh, yes. This is Mr Bhansali, headmaster of the Belapur school. He came for a visit, so I asked him to sit in this meeting,' the principal introduced.

I took his card. I mentally made a note to order business cards and wondered if I could do the fist pumping now or save it for later.

Eleven

'Goa, wow! Someone has a good life,' Vidya said with a pin in her mouth. She stood on a stool in her room, fixing a poster of Aamir Khan in *Dil Chahta Hai* on the wall. I, her tutor, held the pin tray. So much for my position of authority.

'Goa is your brother's idea. I really don't need this break from work,' I said.

'Of course, you do,' she said as she stepped down. 'It will help you get over the earthquake.'

'What will help me get over the earthquake is work, and the money I make to pay back those loans. This trip is costing us three thousand bucks.' I came back to her desk.

She took her seat, opened her book and slapped each page as she turned it over.

'Can you act more interested?'

'I am not a good actor,' she said.

'Very funny. So did you do the calculus chapter in your so-called self-study mode.'

'I did self-study as you did not have time for me,' she said.

'Anyway, I don't understand it. As usual, I suck. What is all this "dx dt", and why are they so many scary symbols?'

'Vidya, you are appearing for medical entrance. Don't talk like…,' I stopped mid-sentence. I opened the calculus chapter. Some spoilt brats have to be spoonfed even the basics.

'Don't talk like what?'

'Like a duffer. Now pay attention.'

'I am not a duffer. Just go to Goa, manage your business, make money, insult people who don't salivate for maths and don't make any time for friends. I can manage fine.'

The last word 'fine' had the loudest volume.

'Excuse me. Is there a problem?' I said after a pause.

'Yes, calculus problems. Can we please start?'

I explained calculus to her for an hour. 'Try the exercises in the end. And read the next chapter by the time I come back,' I said as I finished class.

She kept quiet.

'Vidya, why is it that sometimes making you talk is like extracting teeth.'

'I am like this only, you have a problem? Only you have the right to ignore people?' she threw back. Her eyes turned moist and her long fingers trembled. Before moisture turned to rain, I had to exit.

'I'll be back in four days,' I said as I headed to the door.

'Who cares?' she said from behind me.

★

'Eat on time and don't stay up late,' said Ali's dad as the train signal went off.

Ali was too excited to care for his dad's instructions. He reserved the top berth for himself and climbed up. Omi said his pre-journey prayers.

'Ali's ammi doesn't care. He is a piece of my heart,' Ali's dad said and his eyes became moist. 'Sometimes I wish I had not married again.'

I wrapped the cash and tickets in plastic and placed it inside my socks. Travelling with a twelve-year-old, and two other grown-up kids, this responsibility had to fall on me.

'It is ok, chacha. See now you can go to your election rally in Baroda,' I said.

'That's right. I cannot leave Ali with his ammi for four days.'

'Are you getting a ticket this year,' I said as I chained our suitcase to the lower berth.

The train began to move.

'No, no. I am not that senior in the party. But I will be helping the Belrampur candidate. Ali beta, don't jump between berths, Ali…' his voice trailed off as the train picked speed.

Ish pulled Ali's arm and drew him into his lap. 'Say bye properly,' Ish said.

'Khuda Hafiz, abba,' Ali called out as the train left for sunnier climes.

★

'Organisers. We have to meet the organisers. Let us go in,' I said. A hairy arm stopped me. The arm belonged to a security guard outside the VIP stand.

'Thirty thousand people here want to go in there. Who are you? Autograph hunters?'

'Say it,' Ish said to me in a hushed voice.

'Get your senior. I want to talk to him.'

'Why?' the hairy guard said.

I flashed out a card. It said 'Zuben Singh, Chairman, Wilson Sport.' Pandit-ji had once met the chairman of the biggest sports company in India. I had borrowed the card from his trunk.

'I own Wilson Sports. We want to talk about some endorsement deals. Now will you cooperate or…'

The security guard broke into a sweat and called his manager. I repeated the story to him. He called the senior-most security person who came in a suit. I made a fake phone call pretending to talk about ten-crore-rupees business orders. He remained sceptical. I ended another call in Gujarati and his face softened.

'Gujarati?' he said.

I stared at him, trying to decipher the better answer. In India you don't know whether someone will like you or hate you because you are from a certain place.

'Yes,' I said guardedly.

'Oh, how are you?' he said in Gujarati. Thank God for India's various regional clubs.

'I just landed from Ahmedabad,' I said.

'Why have you come without an appointment?' he said.

'I came to see the match. I saw the Australians play and thought maybe we could find a brand ambassador.'

'Why Australian? Why don't you take an Indian?'

A totally irrelevant question, but it hinted at his growing belief is us. 'Can't afford the Indian team. The good players are too expensive. The bad ones, well, tell me, will you buy a bat endorsed by Ajit Agarkar?'

The guard nodded. He spoke into a microphone hanging from his ear and turned to us.

'One of you stay with us,' the security head said.

'He will,' I said and pointed to Omi.

'One guard will accompany you. What about the kid? He has to go?'

'Oh yes, he is in the campaign. You see, we are doing a coach and student theme.'

The gates creaked open. The guards frisked us to the point of molestation. Finally, we made it to the enclosure. We walked through the posh, red fibreglass seats and sat down in an empty row. We had the best view in the stadium. We came after the Indian innings had ended. Australia would bat now. Apart from the batsmen on crease, their team would be in the stands soon.

'Omi will be ok?' Ish whispered.

I nodded.

'We will wait for the Australian team to come, ok?' I said to the security guard lest he became suspicious again. He nodded.

'Are you from Gujarat?' Ish asked him.

'No,' the guard said. He looked upset, as if a Gujarati girl broke his heart.

'Hey, look slowly five rows behind,' Ish said.

I turned. There was a young Sikh boy in a burgundy turban wearing the Indian team dress.

'Sharandeep Singh, the twelfth man. He may be in the team soon. Should I go shake his hand?'

'Don't be nuts. One suspicion you are star-struck and they will kick our asses out of here,' I said.

'Can I take that?' Ali said as waiters in white uniforms walked around with soft drinks.

'Pretend you own a two-hundred-crore company. Go for it Ali,' I said.

Soon we were all drinking Fanta in tall glasses. Thank God for sponsors.

Murmurs rippled in our stand. Everyone turned back to see men in yellow dresses emerge from the dressing room. Ish clutched my hand tight as he saw the Australian team members. They came and sat two rows ahead of us.

'That is Steve Waugh, the Australian captain,' Ish whispered in my ear. I could hear his heart beat through his mouth.

I nodded and a deep breath. Yes, everyone was there – Bevan, Lehman, Symonds and even McGrath. But we didn't come here to check out the Australian team like awestruck fans. We were here for a purpose.

'Ish bhaiya, there is Ponting, in the pads. He is one down,' Ali's scream ruined my effort to act placid.

A few people noticed, but looked away as Ali was a kid. True VIPs never screamed at stars even though they liked to hang around them.

A young white man, whom I did not recognise came and sat one row ahead of us. He wore the Australian team shirt, but had a pair of casual khaki shorts on. With curly hair and deep blue eyes, he could not be more than twenty.

The VIPs clapped as Adam Gilchrist hit a six. In the general stalls, there was a silence of misery. Ish wanted to curse the bowler, but sense prevailed and he kept silent.

The Australian team hi-fived at the six. The curly haired boy-man in front pumped his fists.

Ali finished his third Fanta.

'Go talk. I have done my job,' I prompted Ish.

'After a few overs, let the match settle,' Ish said.

Australia lost their first wicket of Hayden at a score of seventy and there was a dignified applause in the VIP enclosure. Ponting was cheered by teammates as he went out to take the crease. Srinath dismissed Ponting three balls later.

Ish could not contain himself any longer. 'Yes, go Srinath go,' Ish cheered as I stopped him from standing up on his chair. A few people smirked at the quality of lowlife making it to the VIP stands these days. Bevan, already padded up, left for his innings. The curly haired boy-man turned around to look at Ish.

'Go, India go. We can do this. Series win, c'mon we are 2-2,' Ish said to himself.

The boy-man stared at us. Ish became conscious.

'It's ok. Good on ya, mate!' he said.

'Sorry, we…,' I said.

'I'd do the same thing if it were my team,' he said.

Here was a chance to talk. Maybe he was a team member's brother or something.

I nudged Ish with my elbow.

'Hi,' Ish said. 'I'm Ishaan, we have come from Ahmedabad in Gujarat. And he is Zubin, he owns Wilson sports. And this here is Ali.'

'Good to see ya. Hi, I am Fred. Fred Li.'

'You play in the team?' I asked Fred.

'Not right now, back problem. But yes, started playing for Australia a year ago.'

'Batsman?'

'Bowler, pace,' Fred answered.

'Fred, we need to talk. About this boy. We really need to talk,' Ish said, his breath short with excitement.

'Sure mate, I'll come on over,' Fred said and lunged over to sit next to Ish.

The security guard relaxed as he saw us with someone white. We must be important enough after all.

Ish finished his story in an hour.

'You want me to test him? Mate, you should show him to your selectors or something.'

'Trust me, if Indian selectors were up to the job, we wouldn't lose so many matches to a country with one-fiftieth the people. No offence.'

'We are a tough team to beat. There are several reasons for that,' Fred said slowly.

'Well, that is why I want you to test him. I have groomed him for almost a year now, and will continue to do so. We travelled twenty-four hours to meet someone in your team because I trust you.'

'And what would that do? What if I told he was good?'

'If you say the boy has world-class potential, I will give up my life to get him out there, I swear. Please, just bowl a few balls to him.'

'Mate, if I started doing that to everyone that came along…'

'I beg you, Fred. Sportsman to sportsman. Or rather, small sportsman to big sportsman.'

Fred stared at Ish with unblinking blue eyes.

'I played for my district, too. Never had the guidance to go further,' Ish continued. 'I wasted my studies, fought with my parents, threw away my career for this game. This means everything to me. Not everyone coming to you will be like that.'

Fred smiled at that. 'Mate, you Indians are good at this emotional stuff. Trust me, I gave up a lot for this game, too.'

'So you agree?'

'Four balls, no more. After the match. Stay nearby,' Fred said and loped back to his seat. 'And you better hope Australia wins so I remain in a good mood to keep my promise.'

Ish's smile froze. 'I can't do that. I can't wish against India.'

'Kidding mate. You guys are better at emotions. But we take the-piss better,' Fred winked.

Half the Aussie lingo was beyond me, but we smiled anyway.

'Call our friend, we need him,' I said firmly to the guard.

Two minutes later, Omi joined us. He came in so thirsty he grabbed Ali's drink.

'What the hell were you guys doing? I waited two hours?'

'Making friends,' I said, smiling back at Fred as Australia hit a four.

Australia won the match, but Ish didn't have time for remorse. He had to pad up Ali.

We came to the ground half an hour after the final match ceremonies.

'He is a pace bowler.' Ish turned to Ali, 'Do you want a helmet?'

Ali shook his head.

'Wear it.' Ish strapped the helmet on to Ali's head.

'Ready, mate?' Fred called from the bowler's end.

Ali nodded. Ish took the wicketkeeper's place. Fred took a ten-step run-up with a ferocious expression. The ball zoomed past Ali. Ish stepped back to catch it.

'Gifted?' Fred said to me as he prepared another run-up.

'Hey, what's up Ali?' Ish said.

'I cannot see. The ball is white. And the foreigner makes scary faces.'

'Ignore the face. Look at the ball,' Ish said as he pulled out the helmet. Omi ran to adjust the black screen on the boundary.

Fred bowled a perfect second delivery. Ali struck this time. The bat deflected the ball forty-five degrees. The ball stayed low but did not bounce until it crossed the boundary. Six.

'Bloody hell! Where did that come from?' Fred said.

'Two more balls,' I said. I was aware of what was happening inside Fred's head. The feeling of being trampled, mutilated and vanquished by a mere boy had only begun.

Fred's third ball went for a four and the last one for a six. His face looked more humiliated than scary. And no matter how many times he said 'mate', his tone had turned from calm to anxious. He looked like someone who had been shaken of all his convictions about cricket.

'How did he do that?' Fred muttered, tugging at his curly hair.

We looked at Ali. He sat down on the floor and held his head.

'You ok?' Ish said. The pressure had gotten to Ali.

'What's up?' Fred said.

'Being extra focused takes a lot out of him. He needs to recoup after a few big hits. I taught him to play a full innings in the neighbourhood but today...'

'Stress, mate, all that travel and you shove a scary white guy in his face,' Fred said.

'He has to face this,' Ish said. He bent down to remove Ali's pads.

'Yep, needs stamina and training, but will go places,' Fred said.

'You think so?'

'That's Fred's verdict.'

'Hey guys can you hang on, I need to make a call.' Fred said and stepped away to dial a number on his cellphone. I couldn't hear Fred but he had a ten-minute animated conversation before he returned to us.

'Thanks, Fred,' Ish said. I could see the pride in Ish's face.

'Goodonya. Why don't you guys bring him down to Australia for a while? Hang out and practice in my academy,' Fred invited like going to Australia was as simple as taking an auto to Navrangpura.

'Really?' Ish said.

Yeah right, I thought. We had scraped to get second-class tickets for Goa. We were leaving the same night to save money. Yet, Ish wanted to go to Australia.

'We can't, Fred,' I intervened.

'Why?' Fred asked.

'Can't afford it. I don't own a cricket business.'

'What?'

'I run a small cricket shop. We lied to get into your enclosure for this.'

The air became tense.

'Holy Moly,' Fred smiled, 'You guys! Some gumption. Anyway, I am no rich guy either like your Indian team players. So that's cool by me. But you could have got into trouble there if caught.'

'I had to make sure Ali gets tested by the best,' Ish said.

'Then get him to Australia. I leave India tomorrow. How big is your business?'

'It is kind of small,' Ish said. 'And tickets are expensive.'

'Well, one of my ex-girlfriends works with Qantas. Let me see what I can do,' Fred said as we walked back. 'It is just Ish and Ali right?'

'That's fine,' I said quickly.

'No, we are partners Fred. Either we all come together or not. We need four tickets,' Ish said.

'Hang on,' Fred said as he stepped away to make another call.

'All right,' Fred said as he returned, 'I can do four tickets.'

'Wow,' Ish exclaimed, 'look Ali, this is because of you.'

Ali smiled.

'But July is better,' Fred said, 'it is winter in Australia and tickets are cheaper.'

'July works,' I said. 'We can't come in the summer vacation, that's peak sales season.'

I figured apart from the tickets, there would be expense on passports, visas and living expenses during the trip. I needed some time to save for that. I didn't have to do it, but it's not every day you get to go international.

Twelve

'There is some junk around here. But it will be a great store for your shop,' Mama said, opening the door of a dilapidated godown.

Sunlight hit the room for the first time in years. Two rats scurried across on unsteady legs. We navigated our way through empty gunnybags, stacks of bricks and abandoned masonry.

'It will take weeks to organise this. Omi, we will need six lights on the ceiling,' I said.

'It's fifteen feet by fifteen feet. A good size,' Mama said.

'Mama, what rent do you want for this?' I said.

I had decided to go into wholesale business. I was quite certain that the recent cricket series would increase demand bigtime. As long as I could secure goods on credit, I could make money.

'Nonsense. A father does not take rent from his son,' Mama said.

I hated such form of benevolence. I had estimated the godown's rent as half of the shop. It had no frontage to make it suitable for retail.

'And speaking of sons, I want you to meet my son today,' Mama said and shouted, 'Dhiraj! Dhiraj!' Dhiraj, Mama's fourteen-year-old son, came running from the temple compound. His Spiderman T-shirt and jeans contrasted with the plate of vermillion and saffron paste that he was carrying in his hand.

'Baba, here you are. Let me put the tilak,' Dhiraj said.

Dhiraj put a tilak on Mama's forehead. 'Meet your brothers,' Mama said. 'Govind, Ishaan and, of course, Omi.'

'Hi,' I said.

'The cricket shop owners. I love cricket,' the boy said in a voice that had just broken into adolescence.

'So young, yet he helps me with my campaign after school,' Mama said with pride in his voice. 'Two trips to Ayodhya already. Put tilak on your brothers, son.'

Dhiraj put tilak on our foreheads too. 'I have to finish puja. Ish bhaiya, you have to give me cricket tips someday.'

'Sure, run along,' Mama said.

We came out of the godown. Mama bolted the door.

'How is it going, Mama? You need me?' Omi said.

'Elections are only six months away. In a few months, the rallies will start. I have to show Parekh-ji what a brilliant job I can do.'

I took out ten one-hundred-rupee notes and placed them in Mama's hand.

'Rent for the godown, Mama,' I said.

'Leave it no,' he said.

'Don't say no, Mama. I am already obligated to you. Business is looking up. We will repay your loan soon, too,' I said.

★

'Hello, Pandit-ji? Can you hear me?' I said. I received a call from Pandit-ji a month after I had opened the godown. The temple bells made it hard to talk and I had to strain my ears to hear his voice on the horrible line.

'I have had enough, Govind. I want to marry my daughters off and go back to my Kashmir.'

'I know Pandit-ji,' I said. He had told me this story a dozen times.

'Yes, but last week a nice family came to our house. They have two sons, both based in London. They will take both my daughters. Want to do it as early as possible.'

'In one ceremony?'

'Yes, imagine the saving. But if it is one ceremony, they want it in style. I have sold the godown, but I need a buyer for the goods.'

'How much is the stock worth?'

'Two lakhs of sale value. Of which retailers like you took twenty per cent margin, and I kept another ten per cent. The true cost is around one lakh forty thousand.'

'I'll take it for one lakh,' I said on impulse. Ish and Omi looked at me in suprise. What crazy scheme was I up to now?

'One lakh forty is the cost, and now you want to buy it off me at a loss?'

'I am buying everything.'

'Give me the money by next month, you can take it for one ten,' Pandit-ji said.

'I said one lakh. No more.' I said in a firm voice.

'When can you take the stock? The godown buyer needs possession fast,' Pandit-ji said.

'Today,' I said.

When I told Ish and Omi about the deal later, worry lines crisscrossed their foreheads. I saw a gold-mine trade. India had performed great in the recent series. The summer vacations would start in a few weeks. If I sold it all, I could double my money.

'You know what you are doing, right?' Ish was doubtful.

I looked at him. My risks had let him down before. Yet, you can't do business without taking bets.

'Yes, I do. Do you trust me?'

'Of course,' he said. 'But his daughter is gone.'

'What?' I said, puzzled.

'You had a thing for her,' Ish reminded me.

'Oh,' I said and looked away. You have no idea who has a thing for whom buddy, I thought.

★

Business exploded in the next three months. Every Indian kid played cricket in May and June. Experts had called the India-Australia series historic. The actual matches had taken place during the exams. The pent-up cricket fix came out properly only in the vacations.

'Is this how Harbhajan grips the ball?' a seven-year-old tried to fit the cricket ball into his tiny fist.

'Laxman and my batting styles are identical,' said another boy in the park.

Customers at the temple shop tripled. Our wholesale business fared even better. Retailers never stopped calling.

'What? Pandit-ji is going back to Kashmir? Anyway, two boxes of balls in City Mall sports shop?' said one.

'I've taken over Pandit-ji's business. Call us, we deliver in two hours,' I told another large shop in Satellite.

'No, cash down only. Ahmedabad has no quality stock. You want now, pay now,' I said to a credit seeker.

I kept track of cash, Omi did deliveries, while Ish manned the shop. When schools reopened, he also looked after the monthly supply business. We now supplied to four schools. It took a national holiday on 15 August for us to have a quiet day at the shop.

'We should have kept kites. Look at the sky, that's easy money,' I said as I counted cash.

'Hurry up with the accounts,' Omi said. 'Mama wants us there by four.'

Mama had planned his rally on Independence Day, the same day as Ali's dad had planned a speech for his party's candidate. What's more, both the rallies took place at the same venue, at the opposite ends of Nana Park.

'We will get there by four. But guess what's our profit for the last four months,' I faced the two.

Both shrugged.

'Seventy thousand,' I said.

'Seventy what?' Ish said.

'That's right. Out of which forty thousand will be used to repay our loans. The remaining thirty is ours,' I said and passed on a bundle of notes to each of them.

'Who decides how to cut this money?' Ish said.

'I do, any problem?' I said and realised I had come across too firm.

'Nope. So, how many loans do we have left?'

'Only twenty thousand more, if you count the interest. We will repay all by the end of the year,' I said and locked the safe. I kept the key in my shirt pocket. I stood up to do a stock inventory in the godown.

'Hey, Govind,' Ish said as he pulled my arm down.

'What?'

'Australia,' he said.

'C'mon, we have discussed it. Yes, it was nice to meet Fred and Ali is good. Just the visas cost three thousand each.'

'Fred is giving the tickets,' Ish said.

'But we will still spend a lot. I'd imagine at least ten thousand a head, or forty thousand for the four of us,' I said. I wanted to go as well, but I couldn't afford to spend so much on a junket.

'Here is my ten,' Ish said and tossed the bundle back to me. 'My contribution to the Australia fund.'

I looked at Ish and Omi. These guys are nuts. Super nuts.

'Take this money home and toss the bundle at your dad. You need to.'

'Dad is only going to find another reason to curse me,' Ish said.

'Here's mine.' Omi tossed in his bundle, too.

'C'mon Omi,' I said.

'I don't work for money. I'm with you guys and don't have to be a priest. That's good enough for me.'

'Well then let's save it for the business and...,' I was interrupted immediately.

'No, this money is for Australia only.'

'Just when the business was looking up! Oh well,' I said and tossed my bundle too.

'There you go,' Ish said, 'we've got thirty grand done. Now if only you don't pay the loan this time.'

'No way Ish. The loan has to be repaid.'

'We will repay it – later,' Ish said.

'Ish, you don't listen. What if the other expenses end up higher?'

'We will spend as little as possible. We'll take enough theplas and khakras to eat for the stay. Fred will arrange the stay. Think about it man, the Australian cricket team,' Ish said.

I sat down and sighed. My financially clueless partners looked at me like kids waiting for candy.

'All right. Who is the bloody travel agent, let me bargain with him,' I said.

'Yes, here we go,' Ish said as he dialled the agent's number.

'One week, I can't leave the business anymore and everyday will be expensive there,' I said as I took the phone.

Omi disconnected the phone.

'Later, let's go to Nana Park now,' Omi said.

★

'Twice. They dug up the Ayodhya site twice.' Mama raised two fingers.

His voice echoed, more due to the poor quality of loudspeakers than the impact of his words. Ish and I sat at one end of the first row. Omi stood on stage. He felt important wearing a party badge, though he only had an errand-boy status. His responsibilities included placing mineral water bottles for everyone sitting on the stage.

Mama had done a good job of publicity. Two hundred people had shown up, not bad for a neighbourhood gathering. The candidate, Hasmukh-ji, a veteran of state politics and a longtime associate of Parekh-ji, sat centrestage. Mama was enjoying his five minutes of mike fame before Hasmukh-ji's speech.

'As far back as 1978, ASI, the government's own entity, found temple evidence. But the secular government hid it. Then in 1992, our dear kar sevaks were pushed into breaking the structure. And they found something.'

Ish started cracking knuckles, punctuating Mama's words.

'They found a Hari-Vishnu inscription that established without doubt that there was a temple in the past. But the secular party buries that news, too. The focus shifts to the kar sevaks as vandals. But what about that evidence? Can a Hindu in India demand justice or not? Where should we go? To America?'

Everyone applauded as Mama left the stage. Mama had candidate potential, I thought.

Hasmukh-ji came to the mike. He requested everyone to close their eyes to say the Gayatri Mantra, thrice. It always worked. The crowd became involved. They liked Hasmukh-ji before he had spoken a word.

Omi stepped off the stage and came to me. 'Govind, Mama wants you to spy on Ali's dad's rally. And Ish, can you come backstage, the snacks need to be distributed.'

'But why?' I was bewildered.

'You promised to help Mama, remember?' Omi said, his silk badge fluttering in the breeze.

I walked over to the other end of the park, to the other rally. The decorations here were less saffron and more white.

'Gujarat is a place of intelligent people,' Ali's dad was speaking, 'who know politics and religion are separate.'

I took a seat in the last row and eyeballed the crowd. Unlike Mama's hundred per cent Hindu, this was more of a mixed bunch. If the secular party was so pro-Muslim as Mama suggested, why were so many Hindus sitting here?

'The gods we pray to, stayed away from politics in their time. If we truly want to follow our gods, we must keep our religion separate from politics. Religion is private, politics public,' Ali's dad said.

'You a party member?' someone asked me. I shook my head. I guessed he was Hindu.

'How about you?' I said.

'Yes, for generations,' he said.

Ali's father invited the main candidate, Ghulam Zian, on stage.

As the septuagenarian began to talk, the microphones turned silent and the pedestal fans conked off. Murmurs ran along the crowd. Was it a power failure? No, as the event had its own generators.

'It's sabotage. The Hindu party did it,' said one person in the crowd. Tension filled the air. People talked about raiding the Hindu rally.

'Let's teach those guys a lesson,' a muscular man led the pack and lifted his chair. I wondered if I should run back and warn Mama.

'It's back. Ladies and gentlemen, please sit down. The power is back,' Ali's father came to the stage with folded hands. The fans whirred again.

I remembered the kissing chimpanzees and reconciliation mechanisms. But right now, there were no kisses. Only chairs that could be thrown everytime the power went off.

I stepped outside. I called a travel agent. 'We want to apply for four passports and visas to Australia. And don't give me a crazy price.'

I returned to Ghulam Zian's speech. Ali's dad spotted me and came over. 'Inaayat, Govind bhai. What brings you here? Welcome, welcome.'

'You speak well. You know Ish's plans to take Ali to Australia?' I said.

'He told me, Inshallah, you will go. Ali mentions Ishaan bhai's name at least ten times everyday. Sometimes I feel Ishaan bhai is more his father than me. Goa, Australia, I never say no to him. Why isn't he here?'

'Well he and Omi are...'

'At the other rally, isn't it? Don't worry, I understand. Your choice.'

'I am a businessman. I have no interest in politics,' I said. 'In fact, I'll go now.'

He fell into step with me. 'I'll come and say hello to Ishaan bhai.'

I wanted to tell him it was a terrible idea for him to come to Mama's rally. Politics may be his pastime, but for Mama it was life and death. I kept quiet as we walked back to Mama's rally. Hasmukh-bhai was still on, with lots of hand gestures. 'Put your hand on your heart. Don't you feel wronged as Hindus? And if we had the best culture and administration thousands of years ago, why not now?'

Mama saw us from the stage and pointed a finger. A few people in the crowd looked at me and Ali's father.

'Hey, who is that?' a party worker said.

The crowd booed at us. Ali's dad's beard looked extremely out of place.

'Get lost, you traitor,' said a person from the crowd.

'Let's teach him a lesson,' said another.

Hasmukh-ji stopped talking. Luckily, he kept quiet.

Ali's abba raised his hand to wave to Mama and Hasmukh-ji.

'Go away, Ali's abba,' I murmured without looking at him.

Omi came running to me and grabbed my hand. 'What the hell are you doing? I sent you to spy and you bring back another spy?'

Ali's dad heard Omi and looked at me. I shook my head. He gave me an all-knowing smile and turned to walk back.

'I don't give a fuck about this,' I shouted back. I doubt he heard me.

Thirteen

'First Goa, now Australia. What business do you do?' said Vidya, her eyes the size of the new one-rupee coins.

'Fred kept his promise when Ish wrote to him again. We received tickets in the mail,' I said. We had finished class and I wanted to tell her about my impending absence.

'So who are the two people going?' she said.

'Not two, four. Ali and the three of us are going,' I said.

'Lucky bums,' she laughed.

'So, I will be away for ten days. But your books won't be. Vidya, all my students do well. Don't let me down.'

'You also don't let me down,' she said.

'How?'

'Forget it. So where are you going in Australia?'

'Sydney. Fred is from there. Ali will practice in his academy for a week. When your brother sets his mind on something, he goes real far.'

'Unlike me. I can't focus. I'm sure I will flunk my medical entrance. I will be stuck in this hellhole home even in college. And then I will get married into another hell-hole in some backward part of Gujarat.'

'Gujarat is not backward,' I retorted.

'Maybe I am too forward.'

We locked eyes again. In an entrance exam for insolence, Vidya would top easy. I opened her guide books.

'Why are studies so boring? Why do you have to do something so uninteresting to become something in life?'

'Vidya, philosophical questions, no. Mathematical questions, yes,' I said and stood up to leave.

'Will you get me something from Australia?'

'Ask your brother, he will get you whatever you want.' I restacked the books. No way would I spend more cash than I needed to.

'Anyway, we are on a tight budget,' I clarified.

She nodded as if she understood.

'So, will you miss me?'

I continued to look down.

'You have a budget for how much you can miss people, too?' she asked.

'Do your sums, Vidya. Focus,' I said and left.

'You guys tired or wanna hit practice?' were Fred's first words of welcome at the airport.

'Where is my bed?' I wanted to ask.

We had taken an overnight train from Ahmedabad to Mumbai, waited six more hours to board a fourteen-hour flight to Sydney via Singapore. Thirty hours of travel in cramped environments and I wanted to kill myself with sleep.

'Oh, so we made it in time for practice?' Ish looked out at the streets of Sydney. At 7 a.m. in the morning, joggers clogged the pavements. Picture-postcard coffee shops advertised delicious muffins.

I patted the khakras in my bag. We couldn't afford any cakes in this town.

'I go to the academy ground in the morning,' Fred said as he stepped on the gas. 'I've put you up in a hostel. Take a nap first I'd say. Philip will pick you up for the evening practice.'

★

'Guys, this is Ali. He is a batsman,' Fred said to the other players who came for practice. Apart from Philip, there was a beefy guy called Peter and a spectacled spinner called Steve. I forgot the other names instantly.

Fred screamed, 'Five rounds everyone. Close to the boundary line, no short-cuts.'

The first two hours of our Australian practice was the practice of death. Five rounds of the academy grounds equalled twenty rounds of Nana Park and fifty rounds of the bank's courtyard. After the run, we did innumerable sit-ups, push-ups and crunches. Three personal trainers supervised five students each. The first time I groaned, one came running to me. The next time he said, 'Cut the drama, mate.'

We came to the pitch after endurance training. I told them I was no player, but I had to field anyway.

'Here, bowl,' Fred tossed the ball to Ali.

'He doesn't really bowl,' Ish said.

'I know, give it a burl,' Fred clapped his hands.

Philip took his fielding place at the boundary near me.

'What's burl?' I asked him.

'Aussie slang, mate,' Philip laughed. 'It means give it a try.'

Ish offered to be the wicket keeper, but Fred told him to stay at the slip instead. Ali's bowling was no match for these state level players. Roger slammed the ball towards the boundary several times. Once the ball came between Philip and me, and we had a tough time catching it.

'Rattle your dags, mate,' another fielder shouted at me. No one had to translate 'hurry up' to me.

I threw the ball back. What was I doing in the middle of this Australian ground?

As the day progressed, so did my Aussie vocabulary. 'Onya' was short for 'good on you', which meant well done. An easy ball was a 'piece of piss', while a good one 'packed a wallop'. The mosquitoes were 'mozzies', and soft drinks 'coldies'. When I took a loo break, Philip broke into some more slang. 'You got to siphon the python, is it?'

It started to get dark.

'Pack-up time,' announced Fred though Ali hadn't batted yet.

Fred raised his eyebrows at a glum Ish in the locker room.

'I am fine,' said Ish. Omi and Ali were taking a walk outside the club.

'Fair dinkum?'

Ish looked up from his wooden stool.

'He is asking if you are telling the truth,' I showed off my newfound linguistic skills.

'When is practice tomorrow, Fred, in English if you can,' Ish said.

'You a whinger?' Fred said.

'Whinge means...,' I said as Ish interrupted me.

'I know what whinge means, can someone please explain the point of calling a batsman from thousands of miles away and not making him bat?'

Fred smiled, 'Oh, you wanted your little discovery to bat. What for? So he can hit a few sixes. You want the kid to be a show-off from day one?'

'That's not what I...'

'Mate, I see a lot of talent. Every AIS scholarship kid has tickets on himself. If I don't break their pride, they will stay hoons for the rest of their life. Sportsmen aren't movie stars, mate. Even though your country treats them like that.'

'But Fred...'

'You Indians have good talent, but the training – trust me on that mate.'

'We are only here for a week,' Ish sounded helpless.

'I'll make the week productive. But today's lesson was important. If he isn't humble, he won't last long,' Fred said, then looked at his watch. 'Promised the missus some time. I'm off like a bride's nightie.'

★

'Cheers!' everyone cried. We clanged our dark brown bottles of XXXX beer, also known as 'fourex' stubbies.

'Hi!' our server Hazel, too hot to be a waitress, hugged Fred.

'Oooh...,' Fred's students egged him on after she left.

'No way, mate. The missus won't tolerate me making eyes at anyone else,' Fred said. 'But you guys are single. You must have pretty girls all over you in India.'

Everyone looked at us.

'We don't have girlfriends,' Omi said.

'Why not? Indian women are *hot*,' said Michael, rolling his eyes.

'Too busy with work,' I said.

'Busy? Never heard a bloke too busy to root, mate,' Roger said.

Everyone laughed. Root meant, well, whatever.

'Check those honeys out,' Michael said as four girls walked in.

'The one in brown, she's ain't bad,' Michael said. 'NCR 5.'

'NCR 10,' Roger said.

'And the blue one?' Philip said.

'She's NCR 0. Bring it on, man,' Roger said. Everyone laughed.

'What's NCR?' I asked as there was a whiff of maths in the air.

'NCR is Number of Cans Required. The amount of beer you need to drink to want to have sex with a girl,' Fred said.

'Michael dated an ugly bitch once. He admits it, NCR 40,' Roger said. Everyone roared with laughter.

'Here you go, hungry boys,' Hazel said in a flirtatious tone as she passed the plates.

The Australians mainly ate meat dishes. We had stuck to a pizza as it was the only recognisable choice.

'You got to do more protein,' Michael said, his biceps flexing as he ate.

Omi said, 'I drink two litres of milk everyday.'

Ish sat next to Fred. I could not hear their conversation. However, I saw Ish's frequent nods. I left the Aussie rooting stories and moved to Ish.

'If you're the bowler and you've got the ball in your hand, you're controlling the game. You've got to make sure the batsman knows who's the boss,' Fred was saying. 'Same for Ali. He doesn't just need to hit shots, he needs to show the other team who is the boss.'

'Right,' Ish said.

'My players will eventually figure out new ways to bowl to Ali. A determined mind can counter a gift. A champion has both.'

Ish nodded.

'Hi Govind!' Fred had spotted me. 'Don't want rooting tips? We are just doing boring coach talk.'

Ish's chest swelled with pride as Fred had called him equal in role.

I remembered something. 'You mentioned a scholarship yesterday. What's that? In fact, how does the whole sports thing work in Australia.'

'You want to know why Australia always wins?'

'It doesn't always win,' Ish said.

'Not always, thank goodness. We love to dominate opponents, but also love a fight. When there's a challenge, it brings out the best.'

'Yeah, even if not every time, Australia does win a lot. Every Olympics, there is pile of medals for Australia. In cricket, the domination continues. How come, Fred?' I said.

'Plenty of reasons, mate. But it wasn't always like this.' Fred sipped his sparkling water. 'In fact, in the 1976 Olympic games in Montreal, Australia didn't win a single medal.'

'But you guys did well last year,' Ish said.

'Yes, in Sydney 2000. Australia won 56 medals, only after USA, Russia and China. All these countries have ten times as many people.' He paused. 'Aussies saw the Montreal fiasco as a national shame. So the government set up the Australian Institute of Sports or the AIS and initiated the world's best scholarship programme.'

Fred finished his glass of water and continued:

'And today the AIS has hundreds of staff – coaches, doctors and physios. They get two hundred million dollars of funding and have excellent facilities. And at the heart of it all, they offer seven hundred scholarships a year.' Fred pushed the spaghetti plate towards me.

I listened as I struggled with the ribbon-like pasta. I calculated how seven hundred scholarships for twenty million people would equate to for India. That was the equivalent of thirty-five thousand sports scholarships a year for India to match the ratio.

'What's the scholarship? Money?' Ish wanted to know.

'Not just money, mate. It is full on. Expert coaching, accommodation, travel to tournaments, sports science, medicine – you name it. And the best part is to be part of that community, where everyone has a singular commitment to their sport. I can't describe that feeling,' Fred said, as his eyes lit up.

'I know the feeling,' Ish said. Even though Ish's eyes aren't blue, they shone as bright.

The waiters cleared our plates as we finished our food.

'Any famous players from this scholarship programme?'

'Heaps. Michael Bevan, Adam Gilchrist, Justin Langer, Damien Martyn, Glenn McGrath, Ricky Ponting, Andrew Symonds, Shane Warne...'

'What are you talking about? These are all cricketing legends,' Ish said.

'Legends – that's a good word,' Fred laughed. 'Hope I get there someday.'

'You have a scholarship, too?' I said.

Fred nodded.

'You are already a legend, Fred,' Ish said.

'Nah, I'm starting out. And let me tell you boys, the whole legend bit is far-fetched. You take a bit of talent and mould it properly, and good stuff happens. In that sense, Australia can create legends.'

'And we can't,' Ish asked.

'Well you could, though right now you rely on talent more than training. You have a big population, a tiny number of them are born excellent. Like Tendulkar, or may be like Ali.'

'Yeah, but,' Ish boxed his left palm with his right, 'imagine what would happen if we could have this kind of training in India.'

'Cricket would be finished. India would dominate and teams like us would be nowhere. At least for now we can call ourselves "legend".' Fred hooked his fingers around the last word.

Ali did bat the following days. Every bowler went through the shock of being slammed for sixes. However, Ali kept the showbiz low and played a steady game. He crossed fifty runs in a couple of innings. On Friday morning Ali hit the ball for a defensive shot. The ball didn't go far. Ali decided to stay at the crease.

'Run, it is a single,' Ish urged from the boundary line.

'Run Ali,' Ish said again. Ali looked surprised at the instruction but ran.

'Faster,' Ish screamed, 'don't sleep.'

Ali ran faster as the fielder returned the ball to the bowler.

'Jump,' Ish said. Ali dived. He made the crease but fell with his full body weight coming down on his left ankle. As everyone rushed towards him, he lay on the ground clenching his teeth and holding back tears.

'Oh, get up. No time for drama,' Ish said.

'Easy, mate,' Fred said to Ish and signalled for a physio. Within minutes, a paramedic arrived and placed an ice pack on Ali's swollen ankle.

'Lucky it is not a fracture or dislocation. Looks like a ligament got some wear, mate,' the physio said, applying painkillers and wrapping a crepe bandage. Ali leaned on the physio as he tried to hobble. 'Give the game a rest for two days. You'll be fine.'

'Don't worry, he'll play in a few hours,' Ish said with a sheepish expression. Guilt bubbled up his eyes.

'Everyone,' Fred clapped his hands, 'let's sit down.'

We sat down on the pitch around Fred in a circle.

'You are big boys and tough players. You want to give it your all. But I can't emphasise it enough – respect your body's limits.'

'I do,' Ish said, feeling compelled to speak, 'but there was a single there. And that is what we Indians miss. We don't want to dive. We don't want to take risks.'

'The game is not about being macho. You can't get caught up in the moment so much that you forget.'

'Forget what?' I said.

'Forget that you got one fragile body. Lose it, and you are gone. You must safeguard it. And Ish, you must protect your student.'

Ish hung his head low.

'I had just started my career when my nasty back almost finished it,' Fred said. 'I'd have been selling suits at a store for the rest of my life, as that is the only job I could get.'

He added, 'I made the same mistakes, wanting to kill myself for the game I played that day. But if you want a career, think long term. Yes, passion is important. But the head has to be clear during the match.'

Ish apologised to Fred later in the locker room. 'I'd never let Ali get hurt.'

'The kid is good. I have a little surprise for him. You leave Sunday evening, right?'

'Yes, in two days,' Ish said. 'Can't believe the week went by so fast.'

'Sunday breakfast is on me. I want you guys to meet someone important.'

★

Bondi beach is so beautiful that it needs a coffee table book of its own. First, the sky. The Australian sky is a different colour from India. It actually looks the same as the sky blue colour in paint shops and is so crisp that your eyes hurt. There is no pollution. The sea is visible for miles. At the shore, the Pacific Ocean meets the powdery sand to create perfect waves. They are strong enough to surf on, yet soft enough to make you relax.

But that summer, the nicest part about the beach was its people – those who were not men. That is, those who were women. Gorgeous and topless. And if you've never seen a topless woman in your life before, places like this did things to you.

'There must be a hundred women here,' Ish whistled. 'And each one a knockout!'

It was true. It was like all the beautiful women in the world emailed each other and decided to meet at Bondi.

'You want an umbrella?' I said as we parked ourselves at a scenic spot. Six topless women played Frisbee there.

'Wow, you can actually see their ni … wow,' Omi pointed out helpfully.

'There are a hundred women here. So we have two hundred breasts to look at,' I said and was teased for bringing maths everywhere.

Having grown up in a place where sleeveless blouses cause scandals, tops-off is what an MBA type would call a 'paradigm shift'.

'I could not play with them. I'd never look at the Frisbee,' Ish said.

'Check that blonde one, wow, she is massive,' I said. Oh well, when in Disneyland, play.

'This is what heaven must look like. My eyes are tired from not blinking,' Omi said.

It is funny but the bare-breasts became routine in a few minutes. I guess you get used to good things fast. I'd much prefer to see one topless woman every day for hundred days, rather than a hundred at once. I sat down on the sand. Ish and Omi soon went for a swim in the sea and to see if wet and topless women looked even hotter wet. Yes, we are a sick bunch.

I noticed a brunette in an umbrella next to me. She wore a shirt on top of her bikini and had her back to me. Her long black hair fell over her thin back. She applied something in her hair, probably oil or lotion or any such thing that girls feel is essential to their existence.

Something hurt inside me. I felt like someone pounded my chest. The brunette rubbed her hair exactly like Vidya. I saw Omi and Ish splashing in the water at a distance. They laughed as they pushed each other down.

Random thoughts circulated in my head, like oiled fingers in hair. Wouldn't it be nice if Vidya was here? Isn't this what she longed for most? Freedom above all else? Didn't she have the Bondi spirit, even though I'd have killed her if she walked around in a bikini. Wait a minute, I'd kill her or her brother Ish would kill her? Why should I care? But I did say I would kill her? And why am I thinking of her when there are so many beautiful topless women to distract me right now? And why do I think of her every night before I go to bed? And why does my mind not stop asking stupid questions?

If you began to miss a girl thousands of miles away even with naked breasts around you, something is seriously wrong. I opened my notebook that I carried everywhere. I wanted to make a budget for the next three months. I found a long strand of hair. It didn't belong to Ish or Omi or me. Only one person that I knew had long hair. The notebook I had opened to forget her made me miss her even more.

Omi came running to me. Water dripped from him and fell on my legs. I closed my book.

'The water is amazing. C'mon inside,' he said, catching his breath.

'No, I have work. I have to make a call,' I said.

'Call who?'

'Suppliers,' I said without making eye contact.

'From here? Isn't it expensive?'

'Short call, need some coins,' I said as I collected the change.

'You are working on Bondi? Whatever, I am diving in again,' Omi said and ran back to the sea.

I collected my belongings and walked back to the beach shopping area. I found a public phone.

I dialled her number.

Fourteen

The phone rang twice. I disconnected it. I thought about leaving the booth. I re-inserted the coins and dialled again.

'Hello? Ishaan bhaiya?' Vidya said as she picked up the phone.

The phone gobbled two dollars worth of coins.

I cut the phone again. *Fuck, what the hell was I doing?*

I called again with fresh coins. She picked up instantly.

'Bhaiya, can you hear me?'

I did the cheesiest thing possible. I just breathed. I must have come across as a pervert, but I could not find anything better to say.

'Govind?' she said, her voice careful.

Had she guessed my breath? What is with this kid?

'Hi,' I said. I could not contain myself any longer.

'Govind, wow. I saw the international number. So, tell me?'

Of all the phrases ever said on the phone, I hate 'tell me' the most. Do I have to tell something just because I have called?

'Well, I…'

'How is Australia? Having fun? Tell me?'

I could kill her if she said tell me again. But maybe I should just tell her something, I thought.

'Yes, it is nice. You will like this place,' I said.

'Which place? Tell more no? Where are you now?'

'Bondi beach. It is beautiful. Such a perfect place,' I said. Of course, I gave stupid descriptions. But you try to call a girl you are not supposed to call for the first time.

To add to the nervousness, the phone consumed coins at a ferocious pace. I kept adding more change as the damn phone ate a dollar every thirty seconds.

'Wow. I have never seen a real beach in my life. How is it? Does the water never end? Can you keep looking until forever?'

'Yeah, and the sky is endless too.' *Duh! Say something more than borrowing from her phrases.*

'Where are Ish and Omi?'

'They are in the water. I am in a booth,' I said.

She asked the one question I did not want her to ask.

'So, how come you called?'

'Oh nothing. How is the preparation going? Integration is quite important you know.'

'You called about integration?'

'Well, and other…'

'Do you miss me?'

'Vidya.'

'What?'

'Don't ask silly questions.'

'I miss you. A lot actually,' she said. Her voice became heavy.

'Ok, that's well, that's … wow,' I said, champion of nonsensical, monosyllabic responses.

'Yeah, and not as a tutor. As a friend. As a very good friend.'

A 'very good friend' is a dangerous category with Indian girls. From here you can either make fast progress. Or, if you play it wrong, you go down to the lowest category invented by Indian women ever – rakhi brother. Rakhi brother really means *'you can talk to me, but don't even freaking think about anything else you bore'*. A little voice in my mind shouted at me, *'tell her you miss her stupid, or you'll be getting rakhis for the rest of your life.'*

'I do. If you were here, Sydney would be more fun.'

'Wow, that's the nicest thing you ever said to me.'

I kept quiet. When you have said something nice, don't be in a hurry to speak again and ruin the good line.

'Can I get you anything from here?' I said.

'Tight budget, isn't it?' she said.

'Yeah, but a little something won't hurt…,' I said.

'I have an idea. Get me some sand from the beach you are on right now. That way I will have a piece of Sydney with me.'

Sand? Now that was a weird request. At least it was cheap. Free, rather.

'Really?' I said.

'Yeah, bring me a matchbox full of sand. And put some feelings in it if there is space,' she said.

The phone display blinked. It threatened me to feed it with more money or my first romantic conversation would be murdered. I had no coins left.

'Listen, I have to go now. No more change,' I said.

'Sure, come back soon. Someone's missing you.'

'Back in three days. I miss you too,' I said and cleared my throat. Wow, I could actually say what I felt after all.

'And I want to tell you something…,' she said.

'What?'

Beep. Beep. Beep. A stupid Australian company called Telstra ruined my first romantic moment.

I walked back. I thought about the girl who only wanted sand. I also thought how much money telecom companies must make given a tiny call cost me as much as a meal.

I passed a trendy outdoor restaurant called Blue Orange Café. Australians give the word laid-back new meaning. People sit with a glass of beer for hours. Beautiful waitresses scampered around getting people burgers and toasted sandwiches.

I took a match box from the bar and emptied the sticks in a dustbin. I walked back to the shore until the surfy water touched my toes. I looked around and bent over. I stuffed some sand in the matchbox and put it in my pocket.

'Hey, what are you doing?' Omi said as he emerged from the waves like the world's ugliest mermaid.

'Nothing, what are you doing this side? The waves are better at the other end,' I said.

'I came to meet you. Can I borrow a few coins for a Coke. I feel thirsty.'

'Coins are finished. Have some cash left for today, but let's use it to eat lunch.'

'Finished?' Omi said.

'Yeah,' I said, irritated. I don't like it when people less sensible than me question me.

'Who did you call?' Omi said.

'Supplier.'

'Which one?'

'Fuck off Omi, let's go get lunch. Will you get dry first.'

'Vidya?'

I looked at him dumbstruck. What a random guess. And what the hell is his business anyway.

'What?' I said, surprised.

'Don't lie to me.'

'C'mon Omi why would I call Vidya?'

'I'm not that stupid.'

'You are,' I said.

We walked towards the restaurant with me three steps ahead of him.

'I've seen the way you guys look at each other,' he said as he tried to catch up with me.

'Get lost,' I said and walked faster. We came to Campbell Parade, a strip of bars and cafés near the beach.

'And I've noticed. You never talk about her since you started teaching her,' he said.

I went inside 'Hog's Breath Café'. After five days in this country, the name didn't seem weird anymore.

We sat facing each other. I lifted the menu to cover my face and avoid conversation.

'You can hide if you want. But I know.'

I slid the menu down.

'It's nothing, ok maybe something. But nothing to worry about,' I said.

I hid behind the menu again.

'There is an unspoken rule among Indian men, and you broke it.'

'What rule?' I said and slammed the menu on the table.

'You don't hit upon your best friend's sister. You just don't. It is against the protocol.'

'Protocol? What is this, the army? And I didn't hit on her. She hit upon me,' I said.

'But you let her hit upon you. You let her.'

'Well, it wasn't exactly like being hit. It didn't hurt. It felt good,' I said.

I played with the toothpicks on the table to avoid eye contact.

'Fuck man, how far are you guys?'

'What? Hey Omi, go call Ish for lunch. We are here and he has no idea.'

'Yes, he really has no idea,' Omi said and left.

A noisy gang played on the pool table near us. I had five minutes until Ish came back. Thoughts came to me. *Will Omi say something stupid to him? No, Omi was not that stupid.*

Omi and Ish walked in laughing. Ok, all is good.

'Hog's Breath? Can you think of a worse name for a restaurant?' Ish said and laughed.

'I can,' Omi said.

'Don't say it. Anyway, where's the toilet? I have to go siphon the...,' Ish said.

'Over there,' I interrupted him and pointed to the corner. I had enough of Aussies for a lifetime.

'Are you intimate with her?' Omi continued.

'Did you say anything to him?' I said.

'You think I'm stupid?'

'Yeah.'

'I didn't. Now tell me, what stage are you in the relationship?' Omi said.

'Stage?' I said.

'Yes, there is a "we-just-look" stage, the most common stage in the old city. Then a "we-just-talk" stage. Then a "hold-hand" stage. Then a...'

'It's not like that. It's different between us.'

'Fuck, that's an advanced stage. When you think your relationship is different from any other in this world. Don't do anything stupid ok?'

'Stupid?'

Omi leaned forward to whisper.

'You know stupid. Ish will kill you, or her dad will. Or any man who is related to her will. Remember that guy in the car? Trust me, you don't want to be that boy, or that car.'

'Well, it's nothing really. Just good friends,' I said and looked towards the toilet.

'Just good friends should be a banned phrase. There is nothing more misleading. You are her teacher damn it. And how old is she? Seventeen?'

'Turns eighteen in a few months.'

'Oh great,' Omi said.

Ish came out of the toilet. He cracked a joke with the Aussie guys playing pool.

I turned to Omi.

'I don't want to talk about it. Don't worry, I won't do anything stupid. She sucks at maths. I don't know why I agreed to teach her in the first place.'

'Then stop teaching her no?' Omi said.

'Can we get lunch, I really want to get lunch,' I said and flipped the menu.

'I am just saying...'

'Ish,' I screamed across the bar, 'What do you want? Garlic bread is the cheapest item on the menu.'

'Whatever, I trust you,' he screamed back as he continued to play pool with the Aussie guys.

His last phrase bobbed up and down in my head like the surfboards on Bondi beach.

★

'These houses are huge,' I said as we drove past a rich neighbour-hood called Double Bay.

Fred had picked us up for breakfast on Sunday, our last day. Ish, Omi and Ali sat at the back in Fred's Saab convertible while I rode in the front. Cool air blew through our hair as we drove past Sydney's early morning streets.

'But most people have modest places,' Fred said. 'In Australia, we don't brag about how much money we make or what car you drive. Heck, people don't even ask what job you do. Do you know what people ask the most?'

'What?' Ish said.

'What do you play, that's what they ask,' Fred said.

'I love Australia. I wish India approached sports with the same spirit.' Ish leaned forward.

'Here sports is a national obsession,' Fred said. 'What's the obsession in your country then?'

'There's a lot of people. And there's a lot of obsessions. That's the problem,' Ish said.

'But religion and politics are pretty big. And them together, even bigger,' I added.

'I stay out of that stuff. Aussie politics are a joke anyway,' Fred said, killing the engine.

We parked in an area called Paramatta Park. Fred had brought us to Lachan's Restaurant in the Old Colonial House. We went inside the restaurant to find two men waiting for us.

'Good morning Mr Greener and Mr Cutler.' Fred introduced us to the two older men.

'And this is the talented boy?' Mr Greener patted Ali's back.

'Yep, as talented as the man above sends them,' Fred said as we settled at the table.

'These are the gentlemen who helped me get your tickets. Not my ex-girlfriend,' Fred said and winked at us.

'What?' Ish said as we understood the purpose of Fred inviting us. It wasn't to just play for a week.

'Remember my phone calls from Goa? To these gentlemen,' Fred said.

'Mr Greener is the chairman of the Australian Sports Academy and Mr Cutler is head of the AIS scholarship programme.' Fred buttered some toast. 'I told them about Ali. How he is good, really good, and how with proper training he has the potential to go really far.'

I saw Ish's face tighten in anticipation. Were they going to sponsor Ali?

'If he is as good as Fred and his boys who played with you say you are,' Mr Greener said, 'we should do whatever we can to help.'

'Thank you, thank you,' Ish said as Fred shushed him. Over-excitement was a constant problem with Ish. His sister as well. Maybe it was hereditary.

'You see,' Mr Cutler cleared his throat, 'the AIS selects from the nominations of the various state academies. I can get Ali selected. However, Ali doesn't live in any Australian state.'

'So?' Ish said.

'Under AIS rules, the scholarship holder must be an Australian resident, or at least a person in the process of becoming a resident.'

'Can't we make an exception?' I said. Omi was too busy eating to talk. Omi and Ali had hardly spoken during the entire trip. The Aussie accent stumped them.

'Well, the only way we can do it is this,' Mr Cutler said and took out a file. He opened it and laid out some forms on the table.

'Ol' Cutler had to pull serious strings at the immigration department for this,' Mr Greener laughed in a friendly manner.

'Well, this is the Australian citizenship forms. As you may know, a lot of people in the world want it. But here, given the great talent, we are offering Ali an Australian citizenship.'

Ali and Omi stopped eating as they saw the forms on the table.

'He'll become Australian?' Omi said.

'He'll become a champion,' Fred said.

'His parents will have residency rights, too. And Ish, you can ... your friends here, too, can apply. We will assist you in every way. Chances are good,' Mr Cutler said.

'You love Australia.' Fred winked at Ish.

'Think about the child's future. From what I hear, his means are rather, er, limited,' Mr Cutler said.

They meant poor. I nodded. Ali's life would transform. 'They have a point,' I told Ish, who still looked shell-shocked.

'Why don't you ask Ali first? It is his life and his decision,' Mr Greener said.

'Yes, no pressure,' Fred said, turning over both his palms.

We explained the offer in simple terms to Ali while a waiter cleared our plates.

'So, Ali ... what do you want?' Ish said.

'If I make it to the team, who will I play for?' Ali said.

'Australia,' Mr Cutler said.

'But I'm an Indian,' Ali said.

'But you can become an Australian as well. We are a multi-cultural society,' Mr Greener said.

'No,' Ali said.

'What?'

'I am an Indian. I want to play for India. Not for anyone else.'

'But son, we will give you the same respect as your own country. And some good coaching,' Mr Greener said.

'I have a good coach,' Ali said and looked at Ish. Ish beamed at his proudest moment ever.

'It will be tough to make it in your country. You coach knows that,' Mr Cutler said.

Ali spoke slowly after a pause.

'It's ok if I don't become a player, but it's not ok if I am not an Indian,' Ali said. Maybe he never meant it to be profound, but that was his deepest statement yet.

'But,' Mr Cutler said. He leaned forward and put his hand on Ali's shoulder.

Ali slid next to Ish and hid against him.

The officials tried for another half an hour. They asked if we could speak to Ali's parents, but realised this wasn't going to work after all. I maintained the polite conversation.

'We are sorry. We do realise that this is a big, big honour,' I said, 'sorry Fred. What you have done for us is huge.'

'No worries mate. Your kid is good and he knows it. If you can make a billion people proud, why bother with us down under?' Fred said and laughed. He didn't show if he was upset. Sportsman spirit, I guess.

We saw the officials off to their car.

'Never mind mate. Maybe next time, next life in this case. You could be Australian, who knows?' Mr Greener said as he slid into the driving seat of his silver Honda Accord.

'I don't want to,' Ali said, his face emerging from hiding behind Ish.

'What?'

'I don't want to be Australian in my next life. Even if I have a hundred next lives, I want to be Indian in all of them,' Ali said.

A plane flew above us. I looked up in the sky. I was glad I was going home tonight.

Fifteen

Vidya. Vidya. Vidya – her name rang like an alarm in my head. I ran through tomato sellers and marble playing kids to reach her house on time.

I had tons of work. There were waiting suppliers, stuck stocks and unattended orders. However, Vidya's thoughts dominated them all. A part of me, the logical part, told me this was not a good idea. Businessmen should not waste time on stupid things like women. But the other irrational part of me loved it. And this part controlled me at the moment. *Where is Vidya?* I looked up at her window as I pressed the bell downstairs.

'Govind,' Vidya's dad opened the door. I froze. Why does every male in the family of the girl you care about instil a fear in your soul?

'Uncle, Vidya … tuitions,' I said.

'She is upstairs, on the terrace,' he said as he let me in. He picked up a newspaper from the coffee table. Why do old people like newspapers so much? They love reading the news, but what do they do about it? I went to the internal staircase to go up to the terrace.

He spoke again as I climbed the steps. 'How is she? Will she make it to the medical entrance?'

'She is a bright student,' I said in a small voice.

'Not like her useless brother,' uncle said. He buried himself into the newspaper, dismissing me.

I climbed up to the terrace. Vidya stood there with an air-hostess smile. 'Welcome to my al fresco tuition place.'

She went and sat on a white plastic chair with a table and an extra chair in front. 'I had so many doubts,' she said, flipping through her notebook.

Smoke came out from under the table.

'Hey, what's this?' I said.

'Mosquito coil,' she said.

I bent under the table to see the green, smouldering spiral coil. I also saw her bare feet. She had her trademark pearl-white nail polish only on the toenail tips. 'The coil is not working,' I said as I came up, 'I see a mozzie party on top of your head.'

'Mozzie?'

'It is what they call mosquitoes in Australia,' I said.

'Oh, foreign returned now. How was Australia?'

'Great,' I looked at her. I tried to be normal. I couldn't, not after that call. I had opened my cards already. No matter how close I held them to my chest now, she had seen them.

I noticed her dress. She wore a new purple and white bandhini salwar kameez today. Her necklace had a purple teardrop pendant and matching earrings. She had freshly bathed. Her hair smelt of a little bit of Dettol soap and well, her. Every girl has a wonderful smell right after a bath. I think they should bottle it and sell it.

'You brought my gift,' she said to break the pause, or rather to fill up the silence as I checked her out.

'Yeah,' I said.

I stood up to take out the match box from my jeans pocket.

'Blue Orange Café, cool,' she said. She took the box and slid it open with her thin fingers.

'Wow, an Australian beach in my hands,' she said. She held it up with pride as if I had presented the queen's stolen diamonds.

'I feel silly. I should have brought something substantial,' I said.

'No, this is perfect. Look there is a tiny shell inside,' she signalled me to lean forward. Our heads met in a dull thud as we looked into the matchbox's contents.

Her toes touched mine as we inched closer.

'Ouch,' she said as she pulled her feet away.

'What?' I said.

'Nothing, the mosquito coil,' she said, 'I touched the hot tip.'

I sat back upright. Water droplets had passed from her hair to mine. Half the mosquitoes hovering over her head had shifted over to mine as well.

'Why am I so cheap?' I said.

'It's fine. The call would have cost something.'

'Yeah, five dollars and sixty cents,' I said and regretted talking like an accountant the next second.

'There you go. Anyway, life's best gifts are free,' she said and pulled her hair back to tie them with a rubber band.

I nodded. Ok, enough is enough, my inner Mr Logical told me. Time to study.

I opened the books. She asked the dreaded question. 'So how come you called?'

'I told you,' I mumbled.

'Did you really miss me?' she said and put her palm on my hand.

I pulled it back in reflex. She looked surprised.

'I am sorry, Vidya. I shouldn't. I have my business to focus on and this is really not my thing, but...,' I said and turned away. I couldn't talk when I looked at her. Or rather, I couldn't talk when she looked at me.

'It's ok, you don't have to be sorry,' she said.

'It's not ok. I don't have time for emotions,' I said in a firm voice, 'and this is not the place anyway. My best friend's sister? What the fuck ... oops, sorry.'

She giggled.

'Be serious, Vidya. This is not right. I am your teacher, your brother trusts me as a friend, I have responsibilities – loans, business and a mother. You are not even eighteen.'

'Two months,' she wiggled two fingers. 'Two months and I will turn eighteen. Time to bring me another nice gift. Anyway, please continue.'

'Well, whatever. The point is, significant reasons exist for me not to indulge in illogical emotions. And I want...'

She stood up and came to my side. She sat on the flimsy armrest of my plastic chair.

She put her finger on my mouth. She cupped my face in her palms.

'You don't shave that often eh? Ew,' she said. She threw a tiny spit ball in the air.

'What?' I said and looked at her.

'I think a mosquito kissed me,' she said and spit again, 'is it still there in my mouth?'

She opened her mouth and brought it close. Her lips were eight millimetres apart from mine.

Soon the gap reduced to zero. I don't know if I came towards her or she came towards me. The tiny distance made it difficult to ascertain who took the initiative. I felt something warm on my lips and realised that we have come too close, or maybe too far.

We kissed again. The mosquitoes on our respective heads rejoined.

I'd love to say I saw stars and heard sweet music during my first kiss. But the dominating background sounds were (a) Vidya's mom's pressure cooker whistle from downstairs in the kitchen, (b) the campaign sounds from the autos of various parties for the upcoming elections and (c) the constant buzz of the mozzies. But when you are in the middle of a kiss, sound and sight get muted. I checked once to see if the other terraces were empty. Then I closed my eyes.

'Vidya, what are we doing,' I said, not letting her go. I couldn't stop. Probability, algebra, trigonometry and calculus – the passion held back in all those classes came blazing out.

'It's fine, it's fine,' she kept reassuring me and kissing me.

We broke away from each other because even passionate people need oxygen. She looked at me with a big grin.

I packed my pens and books. No maths tonight.

'Why aren't you making eye contact?' She remarked, mischief in her voice.

I kept silent.

'You are older than me and a hundred times better than me in maths. But, in some ways, I am way more mature than you.'

'Oh, yeah?' I challenged weakly, collecting the textbooks.

She pulled my chin up.

'I am turning eighteen. I can do whatever I want,' she said. The loudspeaker of a campaign auto continued in the background. 'I can vote in that election,' she continued, 'I can have a bank account, I can marry, I can...'

'Study. You can also try to get into a good college,' I interrupted her.

She laughed. We stood up and walked over to the watertank on the terrace. We leaned against the tank and saw the sunset. We talked about everything other than maths. I told her about the academy, the dinner with Fred, the blue Australian sky and the foamy water on Bondi beach.

She listened in excitement. She said she wished she could have a home on the beach and how she would colour the walls inside pink and yellow. It is amazing how specific girls can get about hypothetical scenarios.

'Want coffee?' she said.

'You'll have to go down?' I said as I held her hand on instinct. A voice in me still protested, but now that voice had no volume.

'No, I have a secret stash under the water tank. Come,' she said and pulled at my hand.

The five feet cubical cement water tank was raised from the ground on reinforced concrete pillars. Between the tank and the ground, there was a gap of four feet. We could sit on the ground under the tank.

'This is my favourite place since I was a kid,' she said.

I bent on my knees and slid inside, following her. She pulled out a picnic basket. It had a thermos flask, red plastic cups and Marie biscuits.

'Welcome to Vidya's rooftop café sir,' she said and passed me a cup.

I looked at her. She is too beautiful to study maths. Maths is for losers like me.

I took a sip. My lips still felt the sensation of her lips. I rested on my elbow but the concrete surface hurt.

'I'll get cushions next time,' she said.

'It's fine,' I said.

We finished our coffee and came out. We switched on the terrace bulb. I flipped through the textbook to forget the kisses and coffee. The symbols of integration looked dull for the first time in my life. At one level, maths does suck.

'Thanks,' I said.

'For what?' she said.

'For the coffee and the ... you know.'

She leaned forward and kissed my cheek. 'Thanks for the gift, the gift of true close friendship.'

True-close-friendship, another hyphenated tag. It meant progress.

I came down the steps passed through the living room on the way out.

'What a good, responsible boy. Ish hasn't learnt anything from him,' Vidya's father was saying to his wife as I shut the door behind.

★

I could have done my accounts much faster if I didn't have the parallel SMS conversation. My phone beeped a fifth time.

'Who the hell are you SMSing?' Omi asked from the counter.

It was six in the evening, almost time to shut the shop. Ish had gone to one of the KVs and Omi had to leave soon for the evening aarti. Two dozen invoices, notebooks, pens and a calculator surrounded me.

'Nothing, I am bargaining with a supplier,' I said. I turned the phone to silent mode.

'Call him,' Omi said.

'I'll look desperate. I'd rather he calls first.'

'Do the accounts first, Govind. So many unpaid orders, it is a complete mess,' Omi said, popping a candy from the jar into his mouth. I let it pass. Anything to get his mind off the SMSs.

My phone flashed again.

itz my bday.
i celebr8 my way.
u'll get cake or not??

I had saved Vidya's number as 'Supplier Vidyanath' in my phone, in case anyone picked it up. Also, I deleted her messages as soon as I read them.

'I hope you are staying away from Ish's sister?' Omi said. My hands froze as I manipulated the messages. I told myself, *It is a coincidence. Omi doesn't know who I am messaging to. Be cool.*

I replied to the SMS.

Ok, u win. will get a small 1.
now let me work. you study 2. ☺

I kept the phone aside. Smiley faces had entered my life.

'I teach her, Omi. Just a few months for her entrance exams,' I said. I dug myself deep into the paperwork.

'Does she…,' Omi began.

'Can I do the accounts or should we gossip about my students?' I glared at Omi.

Mama came running to our shop. 'Switch on the TV fast.'

'Two planes crashed into the World Trade Center Twin Towers located in New York,' the BBC news channel reader said. The live visual was incredible even by sci-fi movie standards. The hundred-storey tall twin towers had deep incisions in the middle, like someone had cut through loaves of bread.

'Two planes in a row suggest a planned terrorist attack,' a military intelligence expert said on the TV. 'The world will never be the same again,' the Israeli prime minister said.

We half-closed the shutters. Everyone in the temple gathered around TV sets where the towers crumbled down again and again in replay. Smoke, soot and concrete dust filled the streets of New York. Reports said thousands may be dead.

'What the...,' Ish said as he returned to the shop.

'Muslim terrorists, I guarantee you,' Mama said as his phone rang. He saw the number and stood in attention.

'Parekh-ji?' Mama said, his voice subservient.

I couldn't hear Parekh-ji's words.

'I am watching it,' Mama said, 'They are turning into a menace. Yes, yes sir we are ready for the elections Parekh-ji, yes,' Mama said, wiping sweat off his chest, 'Belrampur is not a problem ... yes, other neighbourhoods need work but you know Hasmukh-ji. He doesn't spend as much time...'

Bittoo Mama stepped away from us. Parekh-ji gave him tips on the elections next week.

Later at night, pictures of the first suspects were released. Four Muslim boys had joined a flying school a few months back. They had hijacked the plane using office box cutter knives and caused one of the most spectacular man-made disasters of the world. A stick-thin old man called Bin Laden released an amateur video, claiming it was all his big idea.

'What's up?' Omi asked Mama as he ended his call.

'Hasmukh-ji takes everything for granted. He doesn't pound the streets of his constituency.'

'Parekh-ji is not happy?' Omi said.

'He is fine with me. He isn't too worried. The bye-election is only for two seats in Gujarat. The real elections are next year.'

'Mama, so next year,' Omi said and patted Mama's back, 'we will have an MLA in the family.'

The temple bells rang to signify time for the final aarti. Omi and Mama stood up to leave.

'I have to show Parekh-ji I deserve it. Winning this seat will help,' Mama said.

'You need any more help?' Omi asked. 'You already did so much,' Mama said and kissed Omi, 'but we must put extra effort next week. Parekh-ji said these attacks could work in our favour. Let's tell everyone at the puja.' They left the shop and went inside the temple.

'Your phone flashed. Is it on silent?' Ish said. He collected all the invoices scattered on the ground. We were closing the shop for the night.

'Oh, must be by mistake,' I said and picked it up, 'a supplier is sending me messages'.

I opened supplier Vidyanath's message.

when I study, I think kisses
u and only u, v misses

I put the phone in my pocket.

'What? Trying to sell you something?' Ish said.

'Yes, wooing me, hard,' I said as I locked the cashbox.

★

'I knew it, that old man wouldn't listen,' Mama said.

His mood alternated between anger and tears. It was hard for a tough, grown-up man like him to cry. However, it was even harder to work for months and lose an election. We stood outside the counting booths. Electoral officers were still tallying the last few votes, though the secular party had already started rolling drumbeats outside.

'Look at the Belrampur votes,' Mama pointed to the ballot boxes. 'Clean sweep for the Hindu party. That's my area. The two other neighbourhoods given to me, we won majority votes there, too.'

His group of a dozen twenty-something supporters held their heads down.

'And look what happened in the other neighbourhoods. That Muslim professor has nothing to do all day. He even met the old ladies. But Hasmukh-ji? Huh, chip on shoulder about being upper caste. Cannot walk the lanes and feels he can win elections by waving from the car. And look, he ran away two hours into the counting.'

Mama wiped his face with his hands and continued. 'Am I not from a priest's family? Did I not go to the sewer-infested lanes of the Muslim pols? Aren't there Hindu voters there? Why didn't *he* go?'

The secular party workers jeered at Mama's team. Tempers rose as a few of Mama's team members heckled the drum player.

'It's going to get ugly,' I told Omi in his ear, 'let's get out of here.'

'I can't go. Mama needs me,' Omi said.

A white Mercedes drove up infront of the vote-counting station. A jeep of bodyguards came alongside. The guards surrounded the area as the Mercedes' door opened. Parekh-ji stepped outside.

Mama ran to Parekh-ji. He lay down on the ground and touched Parekh-ji's feet.

'I am your guilty man. Punish me,' Mama said, his voice heavy.

Parekh-ji placed both his hands on Mama's head. 'Get up, Bittoo.'

'No, no. I want to die here. I let the greatest man down,' Mama continued to bawl.

Parekh-ji gave the youngsters a firm glance. Everyone backed off. Parekh-ji lifted Mama up by the shoulders, 'Come, let's go for dinner to Vishala. We need to talk.'

Mama walked towards Parekh-ji's car, his head still down.

'Come son,' Parekh-ji said to Omi. Ish and I looked at each other. Maybe it was time for Ish and me to vanish.

'Can Ish and Govind come along? They came to Gandhinagar,' Omi said. I guess he wanted us to have a treat at Vishala, normally unaffordable for us.

Parekh-ji looked at us and tried to place us. I don't know if he could.

'Hop into the jeep,' he said.

The Vishala Village Restaurant and Utensils Museum is located at the outskirts of Ahmedabad, in the village of Sarkhej. Along with a craft museum and village courtyards, there is an ethnic restaurant that serves authentic Gujarati cuisine.

We took a semi-private room with seating on the clay floor. Parekh-ji's security staff sat outside, near the puppet show for kids. Their guns made the guest's importance known to the waiters and ensured us good service. Within minutes, we had two dozen dishes in front of us.

'Eat, and don't get so sentimental about politics. Emotional speeches are fine, but in your mind always think straight,' Parekh-ji lectured Mama.

We gorged on the dhokla, khandvi, ghugra, gota, dalwada and several other Gujarati snacks. I felt full even before the main course arrived.

'Now, listen,' Parekh-ji said as he finished his glass of mint chaas, 'things are not as they seem. Hasmukh-ji's defeat has a back story. We expected it.'

'What?' Mama said while Omi, Ish and I made valiant inroads into the food.

'Hasmukh-ji's seniority in the party earned him a ticket. But he is part of the old school. The same school as the current chief minister. Our high command in Delhi is not happy with them.'

'They are not?' Mama echoed stupidly.

'No. We might be a Hindu party, but it doesn't mean we preach religion all day and do no work. Gujarat is a place of business, it is not a lazy place. The high command did not like the way the administration handled the earthquake. People lost a lot in that. I know you boys did too,' he turned to us.

We nodded. The mention of the earthquake still hurt.

'The by-elections for these seats came as a boon. The old school put their candidate. We knew they were weak. Of course, hardworking people like Bittoo tried their best. But, a dud candidate is a dud candidate. So we lost both the seats. With the main elections in twelve months, the entire party machinery is shaken up. And the high command finally gets a chance to make a change.'

'What change?' Mama said.

'They are replacing the chief minister.'

'What? For losing two seats?' Mama said, 'the total number of seats is…'

'A hundred and eighty plus,' Parekh-ji said as he broke his bajra roti, 'but like I said, it gave a reason to change. And Gujarat is vital to our party. We can't afford to lose it.'

'Who is the new chief minister?' Mama said.

'They'll announce the name in a few days. He is an old friend of mine. He is tough, determined and honest. With him I feel confident about going to the elections next year.'

'We'll do whatever it takes, Parekh-ji. My life is yours,' Mama said as the servers replenished our daal and kadhi for the third time.

'I like you, Bittoo,' Parekh-ji said, looking at us.

'Parekh-ji, could I get a ticket for the elections next year? You know my commitment,' Mama said.

Parekh-ji's face turned firm.

'I am sorry if I overstepped,' Mama said.

Parekh-ji broke into a grin. 'No, we need ambitious people like you in the party. But Bittoo, there are only so many tickets. And we have tens of thousands of workers. You are good, committed and I want to help you. But...'

'But what, Parekh-ji? Guide me.'

'To break into the top rank, you need to not only do work, but do work that gets you noticed. Understand?'

Mama nodded slowly.

'I am not criticising you. I am giving you advice to get to the next level as you have the potential. Don't just follow, take initiative. That makes a leader, right?'

'I will take young people to Ayodhya on organised trips every month. We'll guide them on our heritage and increase our support base.'

'Good, keep doing that. Come with me to meet the high command when you have done more. And then I will give you an extra push. Deal?'

Parekh-ji put his hand forward to shake hands. Mama took his hand straight to Parekh-ji's feet, the preferred body-part for interaction with one's superiors in politics.

'No dessert here or what?' Parekh-ji said as there was a delay after the main courses were cleared.

'Who will get the aamras for the sahib?' Mama screamed at the waiters.

Sixteen

'Where's your smallest chocolate cake?' I was at Navrangpura's Ten, the best cake shop in Ahmedabad.

Vidya turned eighteen on 19 November 2001. She could now officially make her own decisions. Unofficially, she had done that since birth.

'No bag please,' I said as I kept the cake box in my rucksack of books. I kept the rucksack upright in my lap until I made it to Vidya's place.

Entering Vidya's house while hiding a cake was hard enough. Ish being in the house made it worse. India was playing England at Kolkata Eden Gardens in a day-night match. Ish had plonked himself in front of the sofa with sandwiches, milk, chips and biscuits – everything that he needed to survive for the next eight hours. Ish's dad sat on the dining table, continuing his PhD on the newspapers of India. As was often the case when Ish was around, uncle had a disgusted expression on his face.

I snuck the rucksack between my arm and side body to keep it horizontal.

'India's batting – Ganguly and Tendulkar. Seventy no loss after ten overs,' Ish said and screamed, 'Mom, sauce!'

Uncle picked up the ketchup bottle from the dining table and banged it as hard as possible on the coffee table in front of his son.

'Thanks dad,' Ish said. 'Can you move. Can't see the TV.'

Ish's dad gave his son a dirty look and moved.

'Sit no,' Ish said to me.

'Tuitions,' I said, pointing to Vidya's room.

'Oh, you've come for that. She's studying on her birthday, dedication dude.'

'Some people are serious about their lives…,' Ish's dad ranted while still reading his paper.

Ish pressed the volume button on the TV remote as loud as possible in protest.

'His mother has made him into a monster,' Ish's dad said and left for his bedroom. Tendulkar struck a four and the monster clapped.

'Don't worry, dad's fine,' Ish said as he saw my nervous expression. 'Hey, wish her and all. She'll like it. I forgot this morning.'

Ish grabbed a sandwich and topped it with lots of chips and ketchup. He took a big bite. My friend had found bliss. I had to find mine.

I climbed the stairs, my heart beating fast.

'Happy birthday, Miss Eighteen,' I greeted as I shut the terrace door.

She wore a shiny red kurti and white pants. The choice of clothes was a bit over the top but it was ok on a birthday I guess.

'Did you know eighteen is the only number that is twice the sum of its digits?' she said.

I took out the cake and placed it on the white plastic table.

'A cake from Ten! Someone is going high-class,' she teased.

'You like chocolate. They have the best.' I opened the box. She stood up from her chair and came next to me to see the cake.

'You've changed since we have had this thing.'

'What thing?' I peeped into her big eyes.

'This thing,' she said and came forward to kiss me. We kissed during almost every class since the last month, so it wasn't a big deal. Sometimes we kissed everytime she solved a problem. At other times, we took a kissing break every fifteen minutes. Once, we didn't kiss at all as she did a mock test. However, we made up for it in the next class where we spent the first ten minutes kissing and the rest discussing her mistakes. When we felt desire, we kissed. When we felt guilty, we studied. Somehow, we balanced mathematics and romance within the hour quite well.

We went to the edge of the terrace. The last bit of sunlight disappeared as the sky turned dark orange. The evening breeze held a chill. At a distance, we saw the dome of Omi's temple.

She entwined her hands with mine and looked at me. 'You tell me,' she said as she removed a strand of hair from her face, 'should I become a doctor?'

I shook my head.

'Then how do I get out?'

'Apply to whichever college and just go,' I said.

'How?' she said as she tugged my hand. 'How will I even get the application fee to apply? How will I support myself in Mumbai?'

'Your parents will eventually come around. They will pay for your studies. Until then…'

A loud roar went through the pol and startled us. India had hit a six.

'Until then what?' she said after the noise subsided.

'Until then I will support you,' I said. We looked into each other's eyes. She smiled. We took a walk around the perimeter of the terrace.

'So my tutor doesn't believe I need to figure out maths problems?'

'Figuring out the maths of life is more important,' I said.

'What's that?'

'Who you are, what do you want versus what people expect of you. And how to keep what you want without pissing off people too much. Life is an optimisation problem, with tons of variables and constraints.'

'Is it possible to run away and not piss off my parents?'

'You can minimise the pissed-off state, but can't make it zero. We can only optimise life, never solve it,' I said as we came to a corner.

'Can I tell you something weird?'

'What?'

'When you talk hardcore maths, like these terms that totally go over my head,' she said, her hand in take-off motion above her head.

'Yes.'

'It turns me on.'

'Vidya, your boldness...,' I said, shocked.

'Makes you blush, right?' she said and laughed.

'So we are cutting this cake or what?' I said to change the topic.

'Of course, follow me to Café Vidya,' she said.

We slid under the water tank and sat on the floor. She had brought six pink cushions and a rug. 'I brought them from my room, so we can have a little party here,' she said and passed a couple to me. Under the cushions, she had a stereo.

'Music?' she said, her face pretty as a song.

I nodded.

'I'll put on Boyzone, my favourite,' she said.

I took out the packet of eighteen candles that came with the cake.

'Let's light all of them,' she said.

I wanted to go switch on the terrace light as it had become dark.

'Let it be,' she said and pulled my hand as she lit the eighteenth candle.

'What if someone comes?'

'Both my parents have bad knees. They never climb up to the terrace. And Ish, well there is a match on.'

We heard two consecutive roars in the pol. The Indian innings had reached the slog overs.

She released my hand as I sat down again. She looked beautiful as the candlelight flickered on her face. A song called 'No matter what' started to play. Like with all romantic songs, the lyrics seemed tailor-made for us.

No matter what they tell us
No matter what they do
No matter what they teach us
What we believe is true

The candle flames appeared to move to the rhythm of the music. She cut the cake with the plastic knife that came in the box. I wished her again and put a piece of cake in her mouth. She held it in her mouth and leaned towards me. She pushed me back on the cushions and brought her mouth close to mine for my share of the cake.

She kissed me like she never had before. It wasn't like she did anything different, but there seemed to be more feeling behind it. Her hands came to my shoulders and under my shirt.

The music continued.

I can't deny what I believe
I can't be what I'm not
I know this love's forever
That's all that matters now

I don't know if it was the candlelight or the birthday mood or the cushions or what. But it was then that I made the second mistake of my life.

I opened the top button of her kurti and slid my fingers inside. A voice inside stopped me, I took my hand out. But she continued to kiss me as she unbuttoned the rest of her top. She pulled my fingers towards her again.

'Vidya…' By this time my hand was in places impossible to withdraw from for any guy. So, I went with the flow, feelings, desire, nature or whatever else people called the stuff that evaporated human rationality.

She took off her kurti. 'Remove your hand, they won't run away.'

'Huh?' I said.

'How else do I remove this?' she said, pointing to her bra. I moved my hands to her stomach as she took the bra off and lay on top of me.

'Take it off,' she said, tugging at my shirt. At this point, I could have jumped off the terrace if she asked me to. I followed her instruction instantly.

The music didn't stop, and neither did we. We went further and further as the tiny cake candles burned out one by one. Sweat beads glistened on our bodies. Vidya didn't say anything throughout, apart from one time in the middle.

'Are you going to go down on me?' she said, after she had done the same to me.

I went down, and came back up. We looked into each other's eyes as we became one. The screams from the pols continued as England lost wickets.

Only four candles remained burning by the time we finished. We combined the six cushions to make one mattress and lay on it. Only after we were done did we realise how cold and chilly it really was. We covered ourselves in my jacket and dug our cold feet inside the lower cushions.

'Wow, I am an adult and am no longer a virgin, so cool. Thank God,' she said and giggled. She cuddled next to me. A sense of reality struck as the passion subsided. *What have you done Mr Govind Patel?*

'See, I still have goosebumps,' she said and lifted her arm. Little pink bumps dotted her flawless, fair skin.

Fuck, fuck, fuck, Govind, what are you doing right now? Touching her goosebumps? The voice in me grew stronger.

'I am so glad this happened. Aren't you?' she said.

I kept quiet.

'Say something.'

'I should get going.'

'Don't you like it here?'

'Here? You realise we are on top of your dad and mom and brother?'

'Stop freaking out,' she said.

'I am sorry. I am nervous,' I said.

'Don't be,' she said and hugged me. She felt my body shake. 'You ok?'

I didn't know why, but I had tears in my eyes. Maybe I felt scared. Maybe because no one had held me like that ever and asked if I was ok. Maybe because I never knew it would be possible for me to feel like this. Maybe because I had betrayed my best friend. I normally never cried, but with so many reasons at the same time, it was impossible not to.

'Hey, I'm the girl. Let me do this part,' she said. I looked into her moist eyes.

I sat up and dressed. We came outside as the moon lit up the terrace. I checked my watch. I had overshot the class time by thirty minutes.

'I love you,' she said from behind as I opened the terrace door.

'Happy birthday,' I said and left.

'Hey, you missed the best part. We will win this. Stay on,' Ish said as I reached downstairs.

'No, I'm quite tired. I'll watch it at home,' I said as I reached the main door.

'Eat dinner, son,' Ish's mother said as she set the table. 'I've made special dishes for Vidya's birthday.

'No aunty, my mummy has cooked at home as well,' I said. I had already celebrated her daughter's birthday.

'Such a good boy,' she said fondly as I left the house.

Seventeen

'Hold it tight, it is shaking,' Omi said. He stood on his toes on a stool to reach the ceiling. We wanted to drop the tricolour ribbons from the ceiling fan. I held the legs of the stool. Ish stood next to us with glue and cellotape.

'I'll fall,' Omi warned, dangling his right foot off the stool.

'It's not my fault. The stool has creaky legs,' I said.

I never wanted to celebrate Republic Day, which came in a week. However, we did want to celebrate our resurrection after the earthquake a year ago. Though thoughts about that day still made me tremble, I was relieved to have fully paid off our loans. Our business had tripled from a year ago and it all happened from this shop.

'January 26 preparations? Keep it up,' Mama's entry distracted us all. Omi toppled from the stool and landed on the floor. The ribbons fell on his head.

'You let go!' he accused me as everyone laughed.

Mama placed a brown bag of samosas and some yellow pamphlets on the table. We grabbed a samosa each.

'One year since the horrible day,' Mama sighed. 'I am so proud of how your hard work has brought you back on your feet. Something else also changed. Govind, do you remember? Don't ever give it up, ok?'

I nodded. Yes, my faith in God had helped me last year. And I wanted to continue with it.

'When you believe in God, amazing things happen. And that is why I brought this,' Mama said and passed a yellow pamphlet to each of us.

I read the headline.

Chaitavani Yatra
All lovers of Rama are invited to come to Ayodhya

I read further. The Hindu party wanted to send wave after wave of people to Ayodhya temple. It would remind the secular government of the temple issue. The pamphlet had contact details of Mama, other party workers, the various dates of departure and how to sign up for the trips. 'We have a deadline,' the pamphlet said, without exactly mentioning one.

'Good, no?' Mama asked me.

'Yeah, Parekh-ji did say, take initiative. You will get noticed,' I said.

'You boys must come,' Mama said 'In fact, the February trip is only for young people. Even I am not going. My son is going this time. You will have good company.'

I kept quiet.

'It is easy to go. Direct train from Ahmedabad station, Sabarmati Express,' Mama said and looked at me eagerly. I had to look interested even if I didn't want to go.

'How long?' I said.

'Thirty-two hours one way.'

'Three days of just travel. How to go now, Mama?' I said, pulling a long face. 'So much work in the new year.'

'There is more to life than business,' Mama said. He stood up to leave.

I opened the cashbox and took out two bundles of notes. 'Here's the rent for the next three months.'

'Who has asked for money?' Mama said as he tucked the notes into his kurta pocket. 'Come with your little brother this time. He is so fond of you.'

'Mama, please don't feel bad. We will come when business is slow. Sometime in March during the exams,' I said.

'Don't back out then. March is fixed, eh?' Mama said.

We nodded. I picked up a broom and swept the samosa crumbs.

'Ok, I better leave. I have to book the tickets for this February trip,' Mama said and stood up.

'I can go book them for you, Mama,' Omi said.

'Will you? Thank you so much, son. I have to go to Gandhinagar today and there is no time,' Mama said. He took out an envelope from the other pocket.

'This has all the names and the money. Dhiraj and eight others. Sleeper class, leaving on 20th February and returning a week later,' Mama said.

Omi put the envelope in his shirt pocket.

★

'Six, seven, eight, no actually that time doesn't count as we didn't really,' Vidya mumbled to herself as she lay next to me.

Omi had gone to the train station to see off his cousin. Ish manned the shop. I, under the pretext of revising permutations and combinations, lay naked with his sister.

'What exactly are you counting?' I asked idly.

'The number of times we have made love,' she replied. 'Wow, our score is eight already.'

'You keep track?' I said.

'I keep track of a lot of things.'

'Like what?'

'Like today is 21 Feb, only five days to my period. Hence, it is a safe day.'

'It's safe anyway. I used a condom,' I said as I shifted my cushion for comfort.

'Oh? So now you trust physics over mathematics?' she said and giggled. She flipped over to rest on her elbows and poked her toes into my shins.

'Are you still embarrassed to buy condoms?'

'I get them from an unknown chemist in Satellite. And I have enough now for a while.'

'Oh really,' she climbed over me. 'So no problem in using a couple more then?'

With that, our score reached nine.

'Goodnight aunty,' I said to Vidya's mom. I always hated that part, the point when aunty offered me something to eat or asked me why I worked so hard.

I walked back home with my thoughts. Nine times in two months. We made love on an average of once a week. Nine times meant I had lost all benefit of doubt. I couldn't say that I had made love to her by accident, in an impulsive moment. You don't do things by accident nine times. Though sometimes, another kind of accident can happen. And I found out exactly five days later.

★

'There is something you should know,' she said.

We had come to the Ahmedabad Textile Industries Research Association's (ATIRA) campus lawns. She had SMSed me that we needed to go for an 'urgent walk', whatever that meant. We had said at home that we had to go and buy a really good maths guide. No one questioned us after that. The ATIRA lawns in Vastrapur swell with strollers in the evening. Several couples held hands. I wanted to but did not. We fixed our gaze on the ground and did a slow walk. Fat aunties wearing sarees and sneakers and with a firm resolve to lose weight overtook us.

'What's up?' I said and bought a packet of groundnuts.

'Something is late,' she said.

I tried to think of what she was referring to. I couldn't.

'What?' I said.

'My period,' she said.

Men cannot respond when the P-word is being talked about. For the most part, it freaks them out.

'Really? How?' I said, struggling for words.

'What do you mean how? It should have happened yesterday, the 25th, but hasn't.'

'Are you sure?'

'Excuse me? I wouldn't know if it has happened?' she said and stopped to look at me.

'No, I meant are you sure it was due on 25th Feb?'

'I am not that bad at maths.'

'Ok but…,' I said. I had created the problem. I had nothing of value to offer in the discussion. I offered her groundnuts. She declined.

'But what?' she said.

'But we used protection. And how does it work with girls? Are they always on time?' I asked. Nothing in the world was always exactly on time.

'Mine are. Normally I don't care. But now that I am with you, even a slight delay scares me. And the anxiety creates more delay.'

'Do you want to see a doctor?' I was desperate to suggest a solution.

'And say what? Please check if I am pregnant?'

Another P-word to freak men out. No, she did not say that. 'You can't be pregnant?' I said.

Sweat erupted on my forehead like I had jogged thrice around the ATIRA lawns. I rubbed my hands and took deep breaths.

'Why not?' she retorted, her face tense. 'And can you be supportive and not hyperventilate.'

'Let's sit down,' I said and pointed to a bench. I threw the packet of groundnuts in the dustbin. She sat next to me. I debated whether I should put my arm around her. My being close to her had caused this anyway. She kept quiet. Two tears came rolling out of her eyes. God, I had to figure out something. My mind processed the alternatives at lightning speed. (a) *Make her laugh – bad idea,*(b) *Step away and let her be – no,* (c) *Suggest potential solutions like the A word – hell no,* (d) *Hold her – maybe, ok hold her, hold her and tell her you will be there for her. Do it, moron.*

I slid closer to her on the bench and embraced her. She hid her face on my shoulder and cried. Her hands clutched my shirt.

'Don't worry, I will be there for you,' I said.

'Why, why is it so unfair? Why do only I have to deal with this?' she cried, 'why can't you get pregnant at the same time?'

Because I am biologically male, I wanted to say. But I think she knew that.

'Listen Vidya, we used the rhythm method, we used protection. I know it is not hundred per cent but the probability is so low...'

Vidya just shook her head and cried. Maths is always horrible at reassuring people. Nobody believed in probability in emotional moments.

A family walked by. The man carried a fat boy on his shoulders. I found it symbolic of the potential burden in my life. The thought train started again. *I am twenty-two years old. I have big dreams for my business. I have my mother to support. Come to think of it, I have to take care of my friends' careers too. And Vidya? She is only eighteen. She has to study more, be a PR person or whatever she wants to be. She couldn't move from one prison to the next. Ok, worst case I have to mention the A-word.*

She slid away from me. The crying had made her eyes wet and face pink. She looked even more beautiful. *Why can't men stop noticing beauty, ever?* We stood up to walk back after a few minutes.

'Let's wait for a day or two more. We'll see what we have to do then,' I said as we reached the auto stand.

'It's probably a false alarm. I'm overreacting. I should have waited for a day or two longer before telling you,' she said. She clasped my fingers in the auto. Her face vacillated from calm to worried.

We kept quiet in the auto for five minutes. Then I had to say it. 'Vidya, in case, just in case it is not a false alarm. What are we going to do? Or should we talk about it later?'

'You tell me, what do you want to do?'

When women ask you for your choice, they already have a choice in mind. And if you want to maintain sanity, you'd better choose the same.

I looked into her eyes to find out the answer she expected from me. I couldn't find it.

'I don't know. This is too big a news for me. I can't say what we will do. Pregnancy, abortion, I don't know how all this works.'

'You want me to get an abortion?'

'No, no. I said I don't know. What's the other option, marriage?'

'Excuse me, I am eighteen. I just passed out of school,' she said.

'Then what?'

'I don't know. I don't want to think. Please don't talk about it,' she said.

We kept quiet for the rest of the auto journey.

'Here, take this maths guide to show at home,' I said and passed her a book when she reached home.

Vidya and I exchanged ten 'are you asleep' and 'not yet' messages that night.

'What's up?' Ish said as I laid my head on the cashbox early morning.

'Nothing. Couldn't sleep well,' I said.

'Why? Thinking of Pandit-ji's daughter,' Ish laughed. I ignored him. Every few hours I had the urge to send Vidya a 'did anything happen' message. But she would tell me if something happened. I opened a calendar and tracked all the past dates of our intimacy. Apart from the first time several months ago, I had used protection every time. Could they be late for any other reason? I didn't know and I could not ask anyone. Ish and Omi probably didn't even know the P-word. And there was no other woman I knew apart from Vidya. And I couldn't ask mom anyway. I picked up my phone again. 'How is it going?', I sent a neutral message. 'Nothing yet', she replied back.

The next night I did get some sleep. I sprang out of bed early morning to SMS her again. I had an SMS from her already, 'a bit of pain, nothing else'.

I threw the phone away. I wanted to reach the shop early to take out supplies from the godown. Somehow, I hated being late anymore.

Eighteen

'Are trains ever on time?' Mama's loud voice interrupted us while we were at work. Ish dragged out a heavy box of wickets from the godown.

'Mama, you here so early?' Omi said.

Mama kept two pink paper boxes on the wicket box. He had a tikka from the morning prayers on his forehead.

'I had bought hot kachoris for my son and other sevaks. Their train was supposed to reach at 5 a.m. But it is five hours late. Now what to do? Thought I will have them with you,' Mama said and took out a kachori.

'So leftover breakfast for us?' Omi said and laughed.

'They are absolutely fresh. I'll get more when they come. Eat them while they are still hot, come Ish, Govind,' Mama said.

'Didn't know you boys come here so early,' Mama said. The shop's clock said eight o' clock.

'Had some work in the godown,' I said and took a bite of a kachori. It tasted delicious.

We ordered tea and sat on the stools outside the shop.

Mama talked to Omi about their relatives. Ish and I discussed the delivery plan for the day. The shop didn't open until nine. We could eat in peace.

'Third round of tea? Ok? Yeah good,' Mama said and called for the tea-boy again. I had two kachoris and felt full.

Mama stood up to leave at 9.30 a.m. I wrapped the boxes back for him.

'Keep them,' Mama said, 'I'll get more any way.'

'No Mama, we have had enough…'

Mama's phone ring interrupted me. Mama picked up the phone. His face became serious. His mouth opened and his eyes darted around.

'I don't know the coach number, why are you asking me?' Mama said.

'What's up Mama?' Omi said.

Mama put his hand on the phone and turned to Omi.

'It is a junior party official in Ayodhya. He put our sevak team in the train the day before. Now he wants the coach number. And he isn't telling me why,' Mama said.

'Wait,' Omi said and went inside the shop. He came out with a notebook.

'Here, I had noted the PNR number and other details while making the booking,' Omi said.

Mama took the notebook and spoke on the phone again.

'Ok listen, they were in S6 … yeah, it says S6, hundred per cent S6, hello listen … why are you praying while talking to me? Hey, hello…'

The person on the other end hung up the phone. Mama tried to call the number back but no one picked up.

'What's going on?' I said.

'I don't know. I have to … I'll go to the station,' Mama said.

'I'll come with you?' Omi said.

'No, it's fine. I had to go anyway. I'll find out,' Mama said and left.

Two hours later the whole country had found out.

'Stop flipping channels,' I screamed at Omi, 'they are all showing the same thing.'

We stopped at NDTV. The newsreader repeated the news for the tenth time.

'At least fifty people died and more than a dozen injured when miscreants set fire to a bogie of the Sabarmati Express near the Godhra station in Gujarat on Wednesday morning.' The channel dialled in a railway official from Godhra on the phone.

'Can you tell us what exactly is going on sir?' the newsreader said.

'We are still getting reports. But at around 8.30 in the morning Sabarmati Express arrived at Godhra station,' the official said as his voice waned.

'Hello, can you hear us?' the newsreader said several times.

'Yes, I can now,' the official said and continued his story.

From what the channels knew at that point, a mob stoned a bogie of the Sabarmati Express. The bogie contained kar sevaks returning from Ayodhya. The passengers shut the metal windows to protect themselves from the stones. The mob threw petrol on the bogie and set it on fire.

'What mob is this? Does it look premeditated?' the newsreader asked.

The railway official avoided controversy.

'The police has arrived and are investigating the matter. Only they can comment on this.'

Ish, Omi and I watched TV non-stop. We cancelled all deliveries for the day.

'Mama's not picking up, I've tried ten times,' Omi said and threw his phone aside.

TV channels had reached Godhra station. We saw the burnt bogie. The rest of the train had already left for Ahmedabad. A tea vendor revealed more than the railway official.

'The mob had Muslims. They had an argument with the Hindu kar sevaks and burnt everyone – women, children,' the tea vendor said.

'We have fifty-eight people dead and over twenty injured, as per reports from the Godhra hospital,' the newsreader said, 'and we have just received confirmation that the burnt bogie was S6.'

'Did she say S6?' Omi said, turning to me.

I kept quiet. I didn't want to confirm the bad news.

'Did she? My brother is in that bogie.' Omi said and ran out.

We came out of the shop. Every shopkeeper had a tense expression.

'They burn little kids, see what kind of a community is this,' a florist said to his neighbouring mithai shop owner.

'Early morning in a railway station. Look at their guts,' another shopkeeper said.

'They struck America in broad daylight too. Now the fuckers have reached Gujarat. And Delhi will suck their dicks,' the florist said. One rarely heard curse words in the temple, but today was different. Of all the days in my life, today was different.

Omi came out of the temple with his father, mother and Mama's wife. All shopkeepers, Ish and I gathered around them.

'Get my Dhiraj. I say get my Dhiraj,' Mama's wife's wails echoed against the temple walls.

'I'll go to the station and find out,' Omi said. He tried Mama's phone again, but it did not connect.

'Don't go, the city is not safe,' the florist said. Omi's mother clutched Omi's hand.

'There could be a curfew soon. Let's shut shops and go home,' a florist said.

The shopkeepers dispersed. Dhiraj's mother's tears didn't stop.

'Don't worry, Mama will call back. The news is sketchy. We don't know what happened,' I said.

'Come home son,' Omi's father said to Omi.

'I'll help them shut the shop,' Omi said.

We went back to the shop. We had no customers that morning, and didn't expect any more.

'Do you have gloves Ish bhaiya? Mine are worn out,' Ali's voice startled us. We had packed the shop by one o'clock.

'What the hell are you doing here?' Ish said.

Ali was taken aback. He wore a yellow T-shirt and an old pair of jeans. Luckily, he wasn't wearing his skull cap.

'I am getting ready for practice. We have one at 4.30 today no?'

'You haven't seen the news?' I said.

'We don't have TV,' he said.

'And your abba?'

'He took ammi to her parents in Surat. He will come at six.'

'And you didn't go?' Ish said.

'How could I? We had practice. Don't want to do hundred push-ups for missing practice,' Ali said and laughed, 'hey why are you shutting down the shop? My gloves…'

'Nothing, you come with us. Don't be alone at home,' Ish said as he downed the shutters.

'Us?' Omi said in a firm voice.

'You go Omi, your parents and aunt need you,' Ish said.

'And you?' Omi said.

'Am taking Ali home. I'll drop him off when his parents come back.'

Omi looked at me to say something. I shrugged my shoulders.

'You want to come to my place?' Ish said to me. We walked out of the temple compound.

I wanted to see Vidya. But it wasn't the best time, and Vidya would not be in the best mood anyway. I wondered if I should SMS her again.

'No, my mother would be worried too,' I said. She'd probably be in the kitchen, preparing dough for the evening dhokla.

I reached home. Over lunch, I told my mother what had happened at Godhra. My mother made me swear that I'd never fall in love with a Muslim girl. I felt tired after the two sleepless nights and the events on the TV, and took an afternoon nap. Omi's phone call woke me up.

'Hey what's up Omi? Got in touch with Mama?' I said and rubbed my eyes. The phone's clock showed it was 5.30 p.m.

'I lost my brother Govind. He died on the spot,' Omi said and his voice broke. He started crying. I lifted myself off the bed and stood up.

'Mama called. He is devastated,' Omi said.

'Is he at home?' I said.

'No, he went to the party office. All the workers are with him to support him. He told me not to tell his wife or anyone else. Like they haven't guessed.'

'It's horrible. Omi, it's horrible,' I said. I shuddered to think we almost took that trip.

'I can't keep silent at home and not show it. I have to get out,' Omi said.

'Then come home,' I said.

'Where is Ish?' Omi said.

'I don't know, can you stay on the line?' I said. I put Omi's line on hold and called Ish. He picked up after ten rings.

'Ish, where are you? Why do you take so long to pick up?'

'I am at the bank. I came with Ali to practice.'

'Is this the time to practice?'

'What? I became sick of staying at home all day. And dad gave me dirty looks because Ali was with me. So I said, screw it, let's hit some balls.'

'Ish, horrible news. Dhiraj is...,' I said and stopped mid-sentence.

'Oh no,' he said, 'really?'

'Yeah, Omi told me. Mama told him to keep quiet at home. He wants to get out.'

'Come over here then,' Ish said.

'Ok,' I said. I hung up on Ish and switched to the other line.

'Come to the bank. Leave now before it gets dark,' I said to Omi.

'Mom, don't cook for me. We'll make something at the bank,' I said as I left the house.

★

'Trouble has started in the city. I heard a mob burnt two buses down in Jamalpur,' Omi said.

We came to the tuition area of the backyard to have our dinner. Omi had cooked potato curry and rice.

'Rumour or true?' I said.

'True, a local TV channel showed it as I left,' Omi said, 'It's strange at home. Mami is still praying for Dhiraj's safety.'

Omi's body shook. He broke into tears. I held his hand as he hugged me.

Ali looked at us. I smiled back at him. I went to the room where we kept books and brought back three *Phantom* comics. I gave them to Ali as he happily read them with his meal.

We sat away from Ali so he could not hear us.

'The mob that burnt the Jamalpur bus, Hindu or Muslim?' I said.

'I don't know, I'm really scared,' Omi said.

We finished dinner and cleaned the kitchen by eight. We were planning to leave when Ish's phone rang. It was his dad. Ish hesitated to pick it up and did so only after half a minute.

'I had dinner. I'll be back in half an hour…,' Ish said, 'what?'

We turned to look at Ish. I could only hear his side of the conversation.

'Ok … Ok … listen, I am at the bank. We are safe here. Yes, I promise we won't walk out on the streets … yes we have bedding here. Don't panic.'

I gave Ish a puzzled look.

'A building in our pol caught fire,' Ish said.

'Wow, which one?' I said.

'The Muslim one at the corner,' Ish said.

'It caught fire? By itself?' I said.

'That is what dad is hoping. But it could be a Hindu mob. Dad said stay wherever you are.'

'Our moms will worry. Govind's would too,' Omi said.

'Call them,' Ish said, 'I can't take Ali to his home too. His parents don't even have a phone,' Ish said.

I called my mother and told her I would be safe at the bank. We had slept over at the bank several times in the past. Many booze parties had ended with us passing out on the mattresses in the branch manager's room on the first floor.

We sat on couches in the cashier waiting area and played cards after dinner. Ali slept soon. Ish brought a quilt from the manager's office and tucked him in on a separate sofa.

Omi dropped three cards. 'Three aces,' Omi said with an extra-straight face. He sucks at bluff.

I tapped the cards. I wondered whether to turn them. Loud chants disrupted my thought.

'What's that?' I said. I saw the time – 10 p.m.

'Those are Hindu chants,' Omi said.

'Angry-Hindu chants,' Ish said.

Calls to Shiva and Rama combined with drumbeats. We climbed the stairs two floors to reach the bank's roof. The city glowed orange in the thick winter night. One, two, three – I saw three balls of flame across the pols. The nearest flame came from a building fifty yards away. A crowd of people stood outside. They threw stones on the burning building. I couldn't see well, but could hear the screams of the people inside the pol. The screams mixed with celebratory chants. You may have heard about riots several times or even seen them on TV. But to witness them in front of your eyes stuns your senses. My neighbourhood resembled a calamity movie film set. A burning man ran across the road. The Hindu mob chased him. He stumbled on a stone and fell, around twenty yards away from us. The mob crowded over him. Two minutes later, the crowd moved away while the man lay still. I had witnessed someone's death for the first time in my life. My hands, face, neck, legs – everything turned cold. My heart beat in the same irregular way as it did on the day of the earthquake. Nature caused that disaster, man made this one. I don't know which is more dangerous.

'Come inside,' Ish tugged hard at my sleeve.

We went downstairs. My body shivered.

'It's fine. Let's go to sleep. The police will come soon. By morning it will be ok,' Ish said as he put his arm around me.

'Can we sleep together?' I said. Yes, I admit it, I felt super scared.

Ish nodded. He picked up Ali from the couch. We went to the branch manager's room on the first floor and shut the door. I checked my phone before going to bed. Vidya had given me a missed call. I was in no state of mind to call or SMS back. Ish lay next to me anyway. I kept the phone in my pocket.

I took three quilts and slept in the middle next to Ali. Omi and Ish surrounded us. We switched off the lights at 10.30 p.m.

At 11.30 p.m. I woke up again. We heard a shattering noise. Someone shook the main gate of the bank.

'Who is it,' I said. Ish stood up and wore his shirt.

'Let's find out,' Ish said and shook Omi's leg, 'come Omi.'

We went downstairs. I switched on the main lobby lights. Ish looked through the keyhole.

'It's the mob,' Ish said, one eye still on the keyhole, 'Mama is leading the pack.'

We looked at each other. Ish turned the door knob and opened the door.

Nineteen

'**M**y sons,' Mama screamed.

We unlocked the bank's main gate and opened it slightly. Mama opened his arms. He held a fire-torch in one hand and a trishul in the other. I expected him to cry when he saw Omi, but he didn't. He came close to us for a hug. He took the three of us in his arms. 'My son, the bastards killed my son,' Mama said as he wouldn't let go of us.

I looked into his cold eyes. He didn't look like a father who had just lost his son. Alcohol and marijuana smells reeked from his mouth. Mama appeared more stoned than grieved.

'My brother, Mama,' Omi said and held back his tears.

'Don't cry. Nobody will cry today,' Mama screamed and released us. He turned to address the mob, 'we Hindus have only cried. While these mother fuckers come and keep killing us over the centuries. In a Hindu country, in a Hindu state, the fuckers can come and burn our kids in broad daylight. And we don't do anything. We just cry. Come rape us, loot us and burn us. They think they can terrorise the whole fucking world but we will have no guts to do anything.'

'Kill them,' the mob replied. The shaky body movements of the mob showed their intoxication. By blood or alcohol, I could not tell.

'But the bastards made a big mistake. They tried to rape Gujarat today. Mother fuckers thought these vegetarian people, what will they do? Come let's show them what we can do?'

Mama paused to take a sip from his hip flask. We stepped back towards the bank.

'I hope they won't expect us to join. I won't,' I whispered in Ish's ear.

'Nor am I, and let's take Omi inside too,' Ish said. We told Omi to hide behind us. In a delicate movement, Ish shut the bank gate again and locked it.

'What are you whispering?' Mama said and almost lost his balance. His fire torch fell on the floor. The mob cleared around it. He lifted the torch back.

'Where is my other son? Open this gate,' Mama said as he couldn't see Omi.

'What do you want Mama? Can we talk tomorrow?' I said.

'No tomorrow, I want something today.'

'Mama, you know Omi needs to get home…,' I said. Mama brushed me away.

'I don't want Omi. I don't want any of you. I have many people to help me kill the bastards.'

Ish came next to me. He held my hand tight.

'So leave us Mama,' Ish said.

'I want the boy. I want that Muslim boy,' Mama said.

'What?' Ish said.

'Eye for an eye. I'll slaughter him right here. Then I will cry for my son. Get the fucking boy,' Mama said and thumped Ish's chest. Ish struggled to stand straight.

The blow torches lit up the dried grass on the entrance of the bank. A thick lock kept the gate shut and the mob outside.

'Mama, you are drunk. There is nobody here,' Omi said.

'You lose a son first. Then I will tell you about being drunk,' Mama said, 'and I know he is here because he is not at his home.'

'Mama, your dispute is with his father,' I said.

'I've taken care of his father,' Mama said, 'and his whore step-mother. I killed them with this.' Mama lifted his trishul to show us. The tips had blood on them.

I looked at Ish and Omi. We made an instant decision. We ran inside the bank. I shut the main entrance door and bolted it.

★

I sucked in long, deep breaths.

'Relax, relax ... we have to think,' Ish said.

'I will join them and take them away,' Omi said.

'No, it won't work,' Ish said.

'They killed his parents?' I said and continued to breathe fast.

The mob banged against the gate. They didn't like our vanishing manoeuvre. I wondered how long the lock would hold.

I sat down on the couch. I had to think despite the deafening gate noise.

'What are our options,' I said.

'We can try to negotiate with them,' I said.

Nobody responded.

'They have madness in their eyes, they won't talk,' Omi said.

'We could try and escape. Or fight them,' Ish said.

'You want to fight forty people who are under a spell to murder?' I said.

'Then what?' Ish said.

I looked at Ish. For the first time in my life, I had seen him scared. I kept looking at him hoping he would consider all options. Even the worst one.

'Don't even think about giving up Ali,' Ish said to me as his pointed finger poked my chest.

'What else can we offer them?' I said.

'Money?' Ish said as his body shivered, 'you say people always talk if there is money involved.'

'We don't have that much money,' I said.

'But we will make it and give it to them,' Ish said.

'For Mama it is not about the money,' Omi said.

'That is true,' Ish said, 'but if we buy the rest of them, Mama won't be able to do it alone. We need to scatter the crowd.'

I paced around the room. We didn't have money. Yes, the rioters would be poor people in the neighbourhood with nothing to lose. But still, how and who would do the talking?

'You are the best at money talk,' Ish said.

'It could backfire. How do I separate Mama from them?' I said.

'I'll do that,' Omi said.

We opened the main door again. The crowd stopped banging their trishuls at the front gate lock.

'C'mon son, open the gate. You boys can leave, we will do the rest,' Mama said.

'Mama, I want to talk to you. Just you,' Omi said in a sympathetic voice.

'Sure, open the gate son,' Mama said.

I went forward and opened the gate. I raised my hand to calm the crowd. I had to appear confident.

'Move back. Mama wants to talk to his other son,' I said.

Omi took Mama to the side and hugged him. Mama consoled him. I looked through the crowd to see any influential person. A man with a turban had six men behind him. He wore a gold chain.

'Can I talk to you?' I said.

The man came to me. He held a fire torch in his hand. My cheek felt the heat.

'Sir, I want to offer you a proposal.'

'What?'

'How many of these men are yours?'

'Ten,' he said, after some hesitation.

'If I promise you ten thousand, can you slowly step back and walk away?' I said.

'Why?' he said.

'Please, don't ask. Consider it an offering. And keep it quiet as I don't have enough for all.'

'Why do you want to save the boy?' he asked.

'Fifteen thousand last. My shop is at the temple. You can ruin it if I don't pay.'

The man in the gold chain went back to his group. He spoke to them as they stepped backwards. He turned to me and nodded. Twenty-five per cent of my problem was over.

Mama left Omi and came to me.

'What's going on here?' Mama said. He did not notice forty people turning to thirty in his drunk state.

'Mama think again. You have a future in the party. Parekh-ji will not approve of this,' I said.

Mama laughed. He took out his mobile phone and dialled a number.

'Parekh-ji won't approve?' Mama said and waited for the phone to be picked up.

'Yes, Parekh-ji, I am well. Don't worry, I will grieve later. Right now it is war time. Oh and someone thinks you are not happy with me ... here talk ... yes talk...'

Mama passed his phone. The crowd waited behind us.

'Hello? Who is this,' Parekh-ji's voice came at the other end.

'Govind, Parekh-ji. One of Omi's friends. We came to Vishala with you...,' I said.

'Oh yes. Son, trying day for us Hindus. So are you supporting us?'

'This is wrong, sir,' I said, not sure why I called him sir, 'this is wrong.'

'What? The train burning, isn't it?'

'Not that Parekh-ji, they want to kill a boy.'

'So what can I do?' he said.

'Stop them.'

'Our job is to listen to people and do what they tell us. Not the other way round.'

'People don't want this,' I said.

'They do. Trust me. Today, the cooker needs a whistle to release the pressure.'

'But kids? Women?' I said.

'Doesn't matter. Whatever it takes to quench the hurt feelings. People in pain want to feel better. Unfortunately, today I can't think of a better way.'

'This is a horrible way,' I said.

'This will last a day or two, but if we stifle it, it could explode into a huge civil war.'

'Your party will be blamed for it,' I said, trying to appeal to their self-interest.

'By who? A few pseudos? Not the people of Gujarat. We are making people feel better. They will elect us again and again. You wait and see.'

'Sir, this boy. He could be in the national team someday.'

Mama snatched the phone from me.

'Don't worry Parekh-ji, I'll take care of all this. You will be proud of me tomorrow,' Mama said and hung up.

I looked around for another mini-leader in the pack. I walked up to him and took him aside.

'Fifteen thousand, you take your people and walk away,' I said.

This time my lure did not entice.

'Mama, he is trying to buy me,' the mini-leader screamed at the top of his voice.

'No, no you heard me wrong, what are you mad or something?' I said and moved back towards the bank.

'What's going on Omi? Get the boy here,' Mama screamed.

Omi nodded to Mama. He went to the main door. The crowd remained at the gate and only the porch separated us. However, the gate did not have a lock anymore.

Omi knocked on the main entrance. Ish opened it after confirming the person. Both of them disappeared inside.

I stood alone with the rioters. They suspected me of offering bribes. I wanted to run inside too. However, someone had to keep the crowd out.

'Are they getting him?' Mama asked me.

'I think so,' I said.

I offered to check inside as Mama asked twice. I went to the door and knocked. Ish opened it for a nanosecond and I slipped inside.

I let out the loudest sigh ever. Ish bolted the door and blocked it with the sofa from the waiting lounge.

'They are waiting. If one of us doesn't show up in two minutes, they will attack,' I said.

'Ali woke up,' Omi said.

'Where is he?' I said.

'I locked him in the manager's room. How many people?' Ish said.

'Thirty,' I said.

'Let's fight,' Ish said.

Twenty

'Ish, I want to talk to you,' I said.

'We don't have time,' Ish said.

'Omi!' Mama's scream came through the main door.

'Coming Mama. Give us five minutes,' Omi screamed back.

'Get him fast,' Mama said.

I made Ish sit on the sofa that blocked the main door.

'Ish, can I offer a bit of logic in the current chaos,' I said.

'What? We have no time,' Ish said.

'I know. But I also know what will happen if we fight thirty people. We will all die. They will get Ali and kill him too,' I said.

'So what are you trying to say,' Ish said and stood up.

'Giving up three lives to possibly save one. Can you show me the maths in this?'

'Fuck your maths. This isn't about business.'

'Then what is it about? Why should we all die? Only because you love the kid?'

'No,' he said and turned his back to me.

'Then what?'

'Because he is a national treasure,' Ish said.

'Oh, and we are national filth? So maybe one day the kid will hit a few sixes and Indians will waste the day watching TV and get thrills out of it. So fucking what? What about my mother? What about Omi's parents? What about...,' I said and turned quiet. I almost said Vidya.

'I'm not giving him up. You want to run away. Open the door and run. Omi, you are welcome to go too,' Ish said.

'I am not going. But how do we fight them Ish?' Omi said.

Ish told us to follow him. He led us to the kitchen. He told us to lift a kerosene canister each. He also picked up three buckets that we used to chill beer. We fell in step behind him as we took the steps to the roof.

'It's heavy,' I said.

'Twenty litres each. That's heavy for sure,' Ish said as we reached the roof.

Fires dotted the neighbourhood skyline. The weather didn't feel as cold as a February night should be.

'We are coming!' Mama said as his group pushed the rusted metal gate of the bank open. They came to the porch and banged on the main entrance door.

'Stop shouting Mama,' Ish said.

Mama looked up to the roof.

'Where are you hiding sister-fuckers,' Mama said. The crowd hurled fire torches at us. We stood two stories high. Nothing reached us. One fire torch fell on a rioter and he yelped in pain. A mob maybe passionate, but it can also be quite stupid. They stopped throwing torches after that.

Ish kept Mama engaged.

'Mama, I was born without fear. See,' Ish said and climbed on the roof ledge.

The crowd became distracted. If they weren't, they'd attack the main door. Despite three bolts and a sofa in front, they would break it in ten minutes flat. After that, they'd have to break the first floor entrance door and then the flimsy one at the roof. In fifteen minutes, we would be roasted in blowtorches. Ish's plan better be good.

'Say Jai Sri Ram,' Ish shouted. It worked perfectly, the crowd had to participate. Most of the crowd did not know whether we supported them or not. At least not yet.

Meanwhile, Omi and I poured the kerosene out of the canisters into the buckets. The canisters had a narrow neck and the kerosene wouldn't flow out fast. We needed a big strike.

Ish struck Siva's poses on the ledge. A few drunk members of the mob even bowed to him. Perhaps Siva had come down tonight to bless the rioters.

'One, two, three and go,' I whispered as Omi and I upturned the buckets. We threw the oil forward to keep it away from the bank building.

The blowtorches in the rioters' hands acted as the ignition. A river of fire fell on the bank's porch. Panic spread in the mob. They took a few moments to realise we had attacked them. Ish stepped off the ledge. We hid ourselves under the parapet. I raised my head high enough to watch the happenings below. A few mobsters ran out of the bank gate as their clothes caught fire. I suppose it is much more fun to burn people, than get burnt yourself.

'How many ran away?' Ish said.

'Quite a few. There's panic downstairs.' The remaining people started jabbing trishuls on the main door. I popped my body up to count the people. I estimated more than ten, but less than twenty.

'We have to go down,' Ish said.

'Are you mad?' I said.

'No. Let's reduce the people further,' Ish said.

'Ish, we are hurting people. Some of them may die. We threw a lot of kerosene,' I said.

'I don't care,' Ish said, 'we have to hurt some more.'

We came down to the first floor. Ish unlocked the branch manager's office door with the bunch of keys in his pocket. Ali awaited him inside and ran to hug him.

'I am scared,' Ali said and broke into tears.

'Don't worry, it's going to be fine,' Ish said.

'I want to go home to abba.'

I ran my fingers through Ali's hair. Home was no longer an option.

'Ali, you will be fine if you listen to me. Will you listen to me?' Ish said.

Ali nodded.

'Some horrible people want to get you. I need to lock you up in the vault. They will never get you there,' Ish said. He pointed to the claustrophobic six by six room.

'There? It's so dark?' Ali said.

'Here, take my phone. Keep the light on. I will be back soon,' Ish said and gave him his cellphone.

Ish put Ali in the safe. He gave him a few pillows. Ali switched on the phone light. Ish shut the door and locked it. He kept the keys inside his sock.

'You ok?' Ish screamed.

'It's dark,' Ali said.

'Hold on ok?' Ish said.

'Ok, we have to cook one more dish in the kitchen. Come fast,' Ish said.

We left Ali in the vault and ran to the kitchen. The jabs at the main door continued. I estimated we had five more minutes before the door gave away.

Ish unplugged the LPG cylinder. 'Carry this to the main door,' Ish said.

Omi and I carried the LPG cylinder. We kept it under the sofa blocking the main door.

'Omi where do we keep the fireworks?' Ish said.

'Top shelf,' Omi said.

Ish came back with boxes of leftover Diwali crackers. We usually burst them when India won a match. Ish emptied a box of bombs on the cylinder.

He took two bombs and opened the fuse to make it last longer. The crowd banged at the door. One main door bolt became loose.

'I open, you light and all run up. Clear?' Ish said to Omi.

Omi nodded. Ish climbed on the sofa and tried to get hold of the bolt. It vibrated under the impact of the mob's jabs.

Omi lit a matchstick and took it to the fuse. As the fuse tip turned orange, Ish opened the bolt. The sofa would keep the door in place for a few more seconds, the time we had to save our lives.

'Run,' Ish said as he jumped off the sofa.

We ran up the stairs. I was four steps away from the top when the door came loose.

'Mother fuckers we won't leave you. Killing your own people,' the mini-leader I had tried to bribe opened the door. Him and three more men entered the room.

'Hey stop,' they shouted at me as I continued to climb. I looked behind, eight men had entered the bank.

I was one step from the top when my ears hurt. The explosion rocked the cupboards on the ground floor as the main door blew away. I think the mini-leader took the worst hit from the cylinder. The other eight men couldn't have been much better off.

I didn't know what we were doing. Preventing someone from taking revenge by attacking them ourselves. I had never seen body parts fly in the air. I didn't know if any of the rioters remained. I used the two way switch at the top to switch on the ground floor tubelight. Smoke and bits of paper from the old files filled the room. Ish and Omi came behind me.

'All gone?' Ish said.

The smoke cleared in thirty seconds. A few men lay around the room. I could not tell if they were injured or dead. The erstwhile main door was now an empty gap. Mama entered the room with five other people. Maybe he was lucky, or maybe he had the foresight to send others to open the door first. The five people ran to the injured in the room. Mama looked up. His eyes met us.

Twenty one

'Traitors, you bastards,' Mama screamed. I noticed his left hand. It bled and the kerosene had burnt part of his kurta's left sleeve.

'Catch them,' Mama shouted. He and five other men ran up the stairs. Ish, Omi and I ran into the branch manager's office and shut the door.

'Hold these,' Ish said. His hands trembled as he shuffled through the cricket equipment we kept in the manager's office. Ish picked up a bat. Mama and his group had reached the branch manager's office door.

'Open or we will break it,' Mama said, even though they didn't bang the door. They continued to threaten us but didn't act. Perhaps they were afraid of what we would blow up this time.

My heartbeat sounded almost as loud as their screams.

'I don't have my phone. Give me yours, I'll call the police,' Ish said to me.

'We will not leave,' Mama's voice reverberated through the door.

I passed my phone to Ish. He dialled the police number.

'Fuck, no one is picking up,' Ish said and tried again. Nobody answered.

Ish hung up the phone and shook it in frustration.

Beep Beep, my phone said as a message arrived.

'It's an SMS,' Ish said as he opened it.

Hey, stay safe tonight.
By the way, just got my period!! Yippee!!
Relieved no? C U soon my hot teacher. Love – me.

The message came from supplier Vidyanath. Ish gave me a puzzled look. I shrugged my shoulders and reached to take my phone. Ish moved the phone away from me. He looked at me in shock. He turned to the message and went into details. He saw the number. He dialled it.

I came close to a cardiac arrest.

'Hey, cool no? I never thought I'd be celebrating a period,' Vidya rattled off on the other side as she saw my number. I could hear her cheerful voice even though Ish held the phone.

'Vidya?' Ish said as his brows became tense.

'Ish bhaiya?' she said.

Ish looked at me. He cut the line and kept the phone in his pocket.

For a moment we forgot that we had murderers at our door. Ish stepped forward towards me as I backtracked until I reached the wall.

'Ish I can explain...,' I said even though I couldn't.

Ish dropped the bat on the ground. He lifted his hand and then – slap! slap! He deposited two of them on my face. Then he made his hand into a fist and punched me hard in the stomach.

I fell on the ground. I felt intense pain, but I felt I had lost the right to say anything, including screaming in agony. I clenched my teeth and closed my eyes. I deserved this. I had to pay for the second mistake of my life.

'What the hell are you doing?' Omi said even though he understood the situation well.

'Nothing, selfish bastard. He is a snake. He'll sell us if he could. Fucking businessman,' Ish said and kicked me in the shins.

'Hey Ish, you want to get killed?' Omi said.

'Fuck you Mama, come in if you have the guts,' Ish shouted and walked up to the door.

Omi lent me a hand. I stood up and leaned on him. I wondered if my intestines had burst.

'I told you. Protocol,' Omi said.

'I didn't do anything wrong,' I said. I don't know why I said that. I had unprotected sex with a barely legal student and my best friend's sister. It must be up there in the top ten morally wrong things one could possibly do.

Mama's patience ran out after five minutes. He ordered his minions to break the door. They pressed their trishuls against the door, but kept their distance.

'Right now, aim is to survive, not to settle scores,' Omi said.

Omi handed Ish the bat again. I held my wicket tight. We monitored the door. A few more jabs and it would open.

'I'll let them in anyway,' Omi said and released the bolt.

'You want to kill me? Mama, go on, kill me. Why wait,' Omi said and opened the door.

'Move aside Omi. Just tell me, where is the boy,' Mama said.

'You won't get any boy here,' Ish growled.

Mama's five men held up their trishuls. We lifted our cricket weapons. One man attacked Ish. Ish blocked him with his bat. Ish struck the bat on the man's arm, leg, thigh and groin. The man fell on the floor.

My hands shivered as I tackled another fat man. My wicket got stuck in his trishul's blades. Our conjoined weapons hurled in the air as we tried to extract them apart. He kicked me in my right knee and I lost my balance. He came forward and pinned me to the wall.

The third man hit Ish on the neck with the blunt end of the trishul. Ish fell forward. The man took Ish captive and pushed him against the wall.

Omi had crushed the toes of the fourth man with the bat. The man winced as he fell on the floor. Omi kicked his stomach but the fifth man punched hard on Omi's back. The man grabbed Omi from behind.

'Buffalo, you can't get free now,' the man said.

'Tch, tch. Stupid bastards. Like playing with fire eh?' Mama said as he sat on the branch manager's table. The three of us were pinned to the wall. The three remaining able men had blocked our bodies with their trishuls.

Mama sat on the branch manager's table and looked at us.

'I want blood. Give me the boy, or it will be yours,' Mama said. He took out his hip flask and had a big sip of whisky.

'There is no boy here,' Ish said, 'as you can see.'

'You are not to be trusted, as I have seen,' Mama said. He threw the empty flask at Ish. It hit him in the chest.

Two injured men lay on the floor. Mama kicked them.

'Go search,' Mama said.

The men hobbled and left the room.

'Nobody here,' they screamed as they traversed the various rooms of the bank. Their voice had pain. Something told me they'd had enough.

Mama went close to Ish. He pulled Ish's hair hard.

'Tell me you bastard,' Mama said.

'He is not here,' Ish said.

'I will...,' Mama said as a phone ring interrupted him.

The phone didn't belong to me or Omi. The ring didn't come from Mama and his men either.

Mama followed the sound. The sound came from the manager's table. Mama went to the wall behind the manager's table. It had the vault. The sound came from within the vault.

'Open this,' Mama said as he pointed to the wheel shaped lock of the vault.

We kept quiet. Ish's phone rang again. I guessed Vidya had called to explain things to her brother.

'I said open this,' Mama said.

'This is the bank's vault. We don't have the keys,' I said. I wanted to do my part to help Ish. I wanted to do anything to make me less of a creep.

'Oh yes. The smart boy has spoken. No keys,' Mama said.

My head turned to Ish. Ish looked away from me.

Mama grabbed my chin and turned my face to him.

'So we are idiots isn't it? You don't have the keys, but how did the fucking phone end up inside? Search them.'

Mama's minions began the most violent search possible. The man searching me ripped open my shirt pocket. He slapped me once and asked me to turn around. His nails poked me as he frisked me from top to bottom. I told him I didn't have the keys more than ten times, but he wouldn't listen. He searched my pant pockets and grabbed my groin twice to check. Whenever I tried to squirm, he jabbed me with his fist.

The other men did the same to Omi and Ish. The man searching him ripped off Ish's shirt. He took a trishul and poked him in his rib cage.

'This bastard doesn't have it,' my man said and gave up his grip. He pinned me to the wall again.

'This one neither,' the man with Omi said.

'This one needs to be tamed,' the man with Ish said as he tried to take off Ish's pants. Ish kicked hard in the man's shins. I noticed the blood on Ish's chest.

'Should I help,' Mama said from the branch manager's desk.

'Don't worry I'll tackle him,' the man said even as Ish bit his arm.

Mama came to Ish. He jabbed the blunt end of the trishul again at his chest wound.

Ish screamed in pain and fell. The man searching Ish slapped him a few times. Ish clenched his teeth and continued to kick. Mama reached into Ish's pockets. He felt something. Ish had worn practice shorts underneath his pants. Mama took his hands out of the pants and slid it again into Ish's shorts. He pulled out a bangle sized keyring. It had two six inch long keys.

Ish lay on the floor taking heavy breaths from his mouth. His eyes looked defiant even as his body refused to cooperate.

Mama twirled the key ring in his hand.

'Never looted a bank before,' Mama said, 'and what a prize today. Father and son, I'll root out the clan.'

Mama took a minute to figure out the vault keys.

'Don't Mama, he is a child. For my sake,' Omi said.

Mama paused and turned to look at us.

'My Dhiraj was also a child,' Mama said and went to the vault.

Ish sat on the floor. The man guarding him suffocated Ish with the trishul rod around his neck.

'Don't touch him. He is national treasure,' Ish growled. The man suffocated him further.

'I'll pay you, whatever you want,' I said.

'Businessman, go sell your mother,' Mama said to me as he turned the wheel of the vault.

'There is the bastard,' Mama said.

Mama yanked out Ali from the vault. His thin body in the white kurta pajama shivered intensely. His smudged face told me he had been crying inside. Mama grabbed Ali by the neck and raised him high in the air.

'Ish bhaiya,' Ali said as his legs dangled.

'The more innocent you look now, the bigger devil you will be in ten years,' Mama said and brought Ali down. He released his grip on Ali's neck.

'Stop it Mama,' Omi said as Mama lifted his trishul.

'You won't understand,' Mama said and folded his hands to pray.

'Run Ali, run,' Ish screamed.

Ali tried to run out of the room. Mama opened his eyes. He ran after Ali and jabbed the trishul into Ali's ankle.

Ali screamed in pain and fell down.

Mama kneeled down on the floor next to Ali.

'Don't you try and escape son of a bitch. I can kill you in one clean shot. If you try to be clever I will cut each finger of yours one at a time. Understand?' Mama roared. His eyes were red, the white barely visible.

Mama closed his eyes again and mumbled silent chants. He took his folded hands to his forehead and heart and tapped it thrice. He opened his eyes and lifted the trishul. Ali stood up and tried to limp away.

Mama lifted the trishul high to strike.

'Mama no,' Omi screamed in his loudest voice. Omi pushed the man blocking him. He ran between Mama and Ali. Mama screamed a chant and struck.

'Stop Mama,' Omi said.

Even if Mama wanted to stop, he couldn't. The strike already had momentum. The trishul entered Omi's stomach with a dull thud.

'Oh ... oh,' Omi said as he absorbed what happened first and felt the pain later. Within seconds, a pool of blood covered the floor. Mama and his men looked at each other, trying to make sense of what had occurred.

'Mama, don't do it,' Omi said, still unaware that the trishul blades had penetrated five inches inside him.

'Omi, my son,' Mama said.

Omi writhed in pain as Mama yanked the trishul out.

I had never seen so much blood. I wanted to puke. My mind went numb. The man who pinned Omi earlier now held Ali tight and came close to Mama. Mama had Omi in his lap.

'Look you animal, what did you do,' Ish screamed. Ish had seen the scene from behind. He never saw the trishul inside him. Only I had seen, and for years later that image would continue to haunt me.

'Call an ambulance you dogs,' Ish screamed. Ish's captor held him super-tight.

Ali put his free hand on Omi's chest. It moved up and down in an asymmetrical manner.

Omi held Ali's hand and looked at me. His eyes looked weak. Tears ran across my cheeks. I had no energy to fight the man holding me. I had no energy left to do anything.

'Leave us you bastards,' I cried like a baby.

'You'll be fine my son, I didn't mean to,' Mama said as he brushed Omi's hair.

'He is a good boy Mama, he didn't kill your son. All Muslims are not bad,' Omi said, his voice breaking as he gulped for breath.

'Love you friend,' Omi said as he looked at me, a line that could be termed cheesy if it wasn't his last. His eyes closed.

★

'Omi, my son, my son,' Mama tried to shake him back to life.

'What? What happened?' Ish said. He had only witnessed the drama from behind.

Mama put his head on Omi's chest. Ish started kicking and shoving the man holding him. The man jabbed Ish with his elbow. Ish gripped his trishul rod and pushed back hard until he could slip out. He gave the man a kick in his groin. The man fell down as Ish kicked him again thrice in the same place. Ish pounded his head with his foot until the man became unconscious. Ish ran to Omi.

Mama left Omi's body on the ground and stood up. Ish went over and touched Omi's face. He had never touched a dead body before, let alone his friend's. I saw Ish cry for the first time. He sniffed back hard but the tears wouldn't stop.

'See what you made me do you bastard,' Mama said, 'made me kill another son. But I am not weak. I haven't cried yet, look.'

Ish ignored Mama. He went through the same numbness I did a few moments ago. He touched Omi's body again and again.

'Hindus are not weak, am I weak?' Mama said as he turned to his men. The men looked nervous, as things had not gone as planned. The man who held Ali's arm looked at Mama, looking for guidance for the next step.

'Hold him back, next to this mother pimping businessman,' Mama said.

The man brought Ali next to me and held him back with a trishul.

Ish's captor had recovered from the groin attack. He woke up and ran to Ish from behind. He struck the blunt end of the trishul on Ish's head.

'Ah!' Ish said in pain as he fell down, semi-conscious. The man dragged Ish back to the wall.

Ish faced Ali and me.

'No more chances,' Mama said as he came in front of Ali. Mama asked Ali's captor to release him. I looked at Ish, around fifteen feet away. His captor looked extra-alert. Ish looked at me. His eyes tried to tell me something.

What? I asked myself, *What is he trying to say?*

I squinted my eyes to look at Ish. He moved his eyeballs from centre to left in quick succession. He wanted me to run out and block Mama. Just the way Omi had, unsuccessfully.

I examined my captor. He blocked me but his eyes watched Mama and Ali. It is hard to take your eyes of a live murder. I could slip out. However, what was the point of getting killed?

'Get ready you pig,' Mama said as he lifted his trishul and took five steps back.

Maybe I could extract myself and try to pull Ali towards me. That way Mama's strike could hit the wall. Ish could push his captor away, come from behind and protect us all. Is that what Ish had tried to say? I had limited data beyond the eye movement. I had limited time. I couldn't analyse, I had to do first and think later. The exact opposite of when I slept with Vidya. There, I should have thought first and done later.

Mama ran towards Ali. I knew I had to get out of the captor's grip, grab Ali and pull him to my side. I got ready to move. However, I looked at Mama. The sight of his huge frame and a sharp weapon sent a fear inside me. And I wasted precious time thinking when I should have acted. Ish and I exchanged another glance and he saw my fear mixed with self-interest. What if the trishul ends in my stomach? The what-ifs made me hesitant, but I snapped myself out of it and made a dive to my left. I grabbed Ali and pulled him towards me. Mama struck, but missed Ali's torso. One blade of the trishul jabbed Ali's wrist. Ali would have been completely unhurt only if I had dived a second earlier. And here it was, something I didn't realise then, the one second delay being the third big mistake of my life.

Of course, I didn't know I had made a mistake then.

Ish did exactly as I thought, and banged his head against the captor's to set himself free. It would have hurt Ish, but I think Ish was beyond pain right now. Ish took his captor's trishul and struck it into the man's heart. The man screamed once and turned silent.

Ish ran to us.

'He's ok, he is ok,' I said turning to Ish. I held Ali tight within me in an embryo position.

★

There were two captors left and Mama. We did not want to kill anyone.

'We just want to go away,' Ish said as he held his trishul, facing Mama. Mama had a trishul too. Their eyes met. Mama's men watched the impending duel. I ran with Ali to the other end of the room. The men came running after us.

'Stop you bastards,' the men said as we reached the end of the room. One of the men went and bolted the door.

Ali lifted a bat from the floor. I picked one too, though not sure if I could really fight right now.

Ali winced as his right wrist hurt when he lifted the bat.

'Heh? Want to fight?' the two captors said.

Mama and Ish were still in their face off. Each had a stern gaze. Mama rotated his trishul in his hand.

One of the men turned to go back to Mama.

'I'll take care of him, you finish the boy Mama,' he said.

'Sure,' Mama said as he moved away. As he left, Mama struck his trishul at Ish's toes. Ish didn't expect it. He lost his balance and fell down next to the manager's desk.

'You are fucking weak, you know that,' Ish said.

'I can finish you now. Thank your stars you were born in a Hindu house,' Mama said as he spat on Ish's face. Mama came to Ali.

'Oh, you want to play eh? You want to play bat ball with me,' Mama said and laughed as Ali held up his bat.

'Move away,' Mama said to his men, 'the boy wants to play. Yeah, you son of a whore, play with me,' Mama said as he danced around Ali, just out of the striking distance of Ali's bat.

Ali pranced around as he stumbled on two cricket balls kept on the floor. Mama picked one up.

'You want me to bowl? Eh? Play bat ball?' Mama said and laughed, 'one last ball before you die?'

Mama tossed the ball in his hands.

'Yeah, bowl to me,' Ali said.

'Oh really?' Mama said and laughed.

Another ball lay next to Ali's foot. Ali brushed the ball with his feet towards Ish. The ball rolled to Ish. Ish sat on the floor leaning against the manager's table. His toes whooshed out blood and he couldn't get up.

'Don't come near me,' Ali said to Mama.

'Oh, I am so scared of the bat ball,' Mama said and pretended to shiver in jest. He tossed the ball in one hand and held the trishul in the other.

Ish picked up the ball slowly. Ali's eyes met with Ish. Ali gave the briefest nod possible.

Ish lifted the ball in his hand. The captor noticed but didn't react. Ish threw the ball towards Ali with all his strength.

Slam! Ali struck the ball with the bat. He had one shot, and he didn't miss it. The ball hit Mama's temple hard. Mama released the ball in his hand to hold his head. The ball fell on the floor and Ali kicked it to Ish. Ish threw it again, Ali connected and slam! The ball hit the centre of Mama's forehead.

Ali's shots were powerful enough to get balls out of stadiums. At five feet range, they hit Mama like exploding bricks. Mama fell down. His trishul fell on the floor. Ish used it as a stick to get up. The captors ran towards Mama. Ish came from behind and stabbed one in his neck. The other captor saw the blood gush out, the killer look in Ish's eyes. He opened the bolt and was out of sight in ten seconds.

Ali kneeled down on the floor. He held his right wrist with his left hand.

'Oh my God,' Ali said, more in pain than surprise at what he had done.

Mama lay on the ground. His temple had burst. Internal bleeding had made his forehead dark and swollen. He barely moved. Nobody wanted to go close to check his breath. His eyes shut after five minutes and I checked his pulse.

'It's stopped. I think he's dead,' I said. I had become an expert in dead bodies.

Ish's arms wrapped around Ali.

'It's hurting a lot Ish bhaiya. Take me home,' Ali said. His body still trembled in fear.

'C'mon move that wrist. Ali, you need that wrist, keep it alive,' Ish said. He hobbled towards the door to leave. He used a trishul as his walking stick.

'We saved him, Ish we saved him,' I said as I shook Ish's shoulders from behind.

Ish stopped. He turned to me. He didn't give me a dirty look, but something worse than that. He gave me the look of indifference. Sure, I had let him down for lots of reasons. But why was he behaving like *Who was I?* Like he had nothing whatsoever to do with me. Ish turned and started to walk.

'Hey Ish, wait for me. I'll help you open the door' I said. I reached the door.

Ish hand gestured me to get out of the way.

'Ish, c'mon Ish, he is alive. We, we did it,' I said.

Ish didn't say anything. He left me like I was one of the dead bodies and walked out.

Epilogue

*T*he heart rate monitor beeped fast. Govind's pulse had crossed 130 beats a minute.

The nurse came running inside.

'What did you do?' she said.

'I am fine. Just chatting,' Govind said. He sat up a little on the bed.

'Don't make him exert himself.' The nurse wagged her finger at me. I nodded and she left the room.

'And from that day, exactly three years, two months and one week ago, Ish has not spoken to me again. Everytime I try speaking to him he snubs me.' Govind ended his story.

I gave him a glass of water as his voice faltered.

'So what happened in the three years – to the shop, to Vidya, to Ali?' I asked.

He turned his gaze down and played with the heart rate monitor wire attached on his chest. He swallowed a couple of times to keep his composure.

I did not prod further. If he wanted to tell me, he would. I checked the time, it was five in the morning. I stepped outside the room. The early morning sunlight filled the hospital corridors. I asked someone where to get tea from. He pointed me to the canteen.

I came back with two cups. Govind refused as he wasn't allowed one after a stomach wash. He didn't make eye contact.

'I need to find the Singapore Airlines phone number. I have to confirm my return trip,' I said, to change his mood.

'Omi's parents,' Govind said, his gaze and voice both low. 'I can't tell you how ... destroyed they were. For weeks, the temple had visitors from the neighbourhood and the only prayers were for Omi, Dhiraj and Mama. At the funerals, Omi's father cried as five thousand people descended from all over Ahmedabad. Omi's mother became ill after not eating for a week. She had to be in the hospital for a month.'

I debated whether to place my hand on Govind's hand lying pale on the covers.

'I didn't go to the shop for two months. I tried to contact Ish, but ... If I went to meet him, he'd shut the door on my face.'

'Did you speak to Vidya?'

Govind shook his head. 'Speaking to Vidya was out of question. They put her under house arrest. Her dad slammed her mobile phone to pieces. The TV channels moved on after the Godhra news and the riots. But my life collapsed. I lived through all that. I didn't pop pills then. Don't think I am not strong ... just because I am here today.' He paused. 'Three months after the incident, Omi's mother came home. She told me to reopen the shop. Omi had told her it was his favourite place in the world. Mama was gone, so the shop belonged to Omi's mother now. And she wanted to give it to us to keep the memory of her son alive.'

'So did you agree?'

'Initially, I couldn't meet her eye. The guilt ... of letting Omi die, of my part in Mama's death, of celebrating Mama's death. But she knew nothing of my nightmares and I had to make a living

anyway. The business was losing money. We had defaulted many supply contracts. So I came back to the shop. Ish told Omi's mother he would come, too, but didn't want anything to do with me. Omi's mother wanted us both, so there was only one solution.'

'What?'

'We split the shop into two. We put a plywood wall right in the middle. Ish took the right side and continued the sports shop. I took the left and turned my portion into a student stationery and textbook store. His customers often came to my store and vice versa. We offered studies and sports at the same place but we never, not once, spoke. Not even when India reached the finals in the 2003 World Cup. Ish watches matches alone now, and never jumps at a six.'

'Did you ever contact Vidya again? And what happened to Ali?' I realised I was asking more questions than offering support. But I had to know.

'They sent Vidya to Bombay, to do a PR course. That was the one positive thing for her. They wanted her away from me, medical college or not. So Vidya did get to fly out of her cage. She had instructions to never speak to me again. However, she loves breaking rules and did try to contact me a couple of times from there. But this time I never replied. I couldn't do it … I saw her brother everyday. All I wanted to do was make as much money as possible and save it for Ali.'

'To bring him up?' I said and took a sip from my cup. Why does hospital tea taste like Dettol?

'Ali stays in Ish's house now, so he will be brought up well anyway. But we need the money for his wrist operation. A lot of money,' Govind said.

The nurse came to the room for the morning checkup. Govind requested he wanted to use the toilet. The nurse agreed and took off the drips and monitor cords attached to him.

I waited anxiously for ten minutes, my mind riven with doubts about his stability, when he returned.

'What kind of operation?' I asked.

'Ali's wrist is damaged. That means his ability to turn the bat at the right time is gone. I saved his life, but my one second of delay cost him his gift. I told you, that delay was the third mistake of my life.'

'You did your best. It was a moment's delay,' I reassured.

'But a conscious moment. I was selfish. Like I was with my ambition when I wanted to make the mall, or when I was with Vidya. They are right, you know. I am not a businessman, I am a selfish bastard,' he said and paused before speaking again.

'He needs reconstructive surgery. The trishul gouged out some of the muscle from the wrist. So doctors have to cut up a piece of muscle from the thigh and attach it to the wrist. Then, they have to hope that it works. It isn't a synthetic skin graft, but a muscle transfer. It only happens abroad. And it costs a bomb.'

'How much?'

'Don't even talk about the full price. Ish wrote to every big hospital in the UK and USA for subsidies. The best deal he has is from a hospital in UK, which has promised us an operation for five lakhs. Of course, Ish never told me all this. That is all I could hear from the thin plywood wall.'

'You have the money?'

'Ish saved two lakhs in the past three years. I saved another three. Last week I went to him with the money. I said let's pool our resources and get Ali operated. I said we must act now as it takes nine months to get an appointment at that hospital anyway. And then he…,' Govind's voice choked again.

'You ok?' I said.

Govind nodded. 'You know what he did? He refused to touch my money and wore cricket gloves while handing the envelope back to me. In fact, he offered me his cashbox and said he could give me money if I needed it to satisfy my greed. He said he didn't want to get Ali operated with a dishonest man's money.'

Govind voice began to break. 'I am not dishonest. I'm selfish and have made mistakes, but I'm not dishonest. And I don't only care about money. I care about Ali, too.'

I sat on his bed put my hand on his arm. He pulled it away.

'After three years of saving every rupee I could, Ish calls my labour dishonest. I can't take it anymore. Dr Verma had given me pills as I had trouble sleeping at night. That day I felt why not sleep once and for all. Maybe I had calculated life all wrong. It was time to quit the equation.' He smiled feebly.

The doctor came to Govind's ward at 7 a.m. The chemicals from the pills had been flushed out of Govind's system.

'I'd like the patient to sleep for six hours,' the doctor told me as he drew the curtains.

I left the room and went out. Govind's mother sat on a bench in the corridor. She looked up, worried.

'He is fine, just needs some rest.' I sat next to her on the bench.

'Such a brave boy I had. What happened to him?' she sighed.

'He thought he was being brave,' I said. 'Does Ish know?'

She looked at me sideways. 'They don't talk.'

'Can you tell him what happened. Don't force him to come to the hospital,' I said.

Govind's mother nodded. We left the hospital together. She had sat in an auto when I spoke again. 'By the way, do you know which college Vidya goes to in Bombay?'

'So many visitors? This is a hospital, not a club,' the nurse grumbled as she changed Govind's bedsheets in the evening.

Govind's hospital room was bustling with people. Apart from the nurse, there were Ish, Vidya, Govind's mother and I. We waited for Mr Sleepyhead to wake up from his second nap of the day. A lot of people had lost sleep because of his sleeping pills.

Govind's eyelashes flickered and everyone moved closer to the bed.

'Ish? Vidya!' Govind blinked.

'There are better ways to attract attention,' Vidya said.

'When did you come?' Govind asked, quite forgetting the others.

'I left my marketing class halfway,' Vidya said. 'But that doesn't mean I forgive you for not replying to me. Or for popping these pills. I never popped anything even when I was most scared, you know when.'

'Your parents told you not to speak to me again. Ish wanted the same.'

'So?' Vidya removed her college bag from her shoulder and placed it on the bed. 'What did your heart want?'

Ish stood silent, looking at Govind. Govind's mother looked shocked, probably dreading a firecracker of a daughter-in-law like Vidya someday.

'I am sorry, Ish. I didn't mean to hurt anyone. I l ... loved her,' Govind said.

Ish began to walk out of the room. Govind's mother went after him and pulled his arm. She placed Ish's hand on Govind's.

'You don't have to listen to parents, but I do think you should be friends again,' Govind's mother said.

Ish remained silent. Govind clasped Ish's hand. Govind's mother continued:

'Life will have many setbacks. People close to you will hurt you.

But you don't break it off. You don't hurt them more. You try to heal it. It is a lesson not only you, but our country needs to learn.'

'Remember the kissing chimpanzees?' Govind called after him.

Ish stopped and looked back at Govind.

'Take the money for Ali. For me, it's no longer just for the money. But what the money is for. Get Ali all right, it is important to me, too.'

Ish sniffed hard as he tried to resist tears.

'Can you forgive me, three times over?' Govind said.

Both Govind's and Ish's eyes turned moist.

'Aunty, isn't it strange that all the men in the ward are crying while the women are like, so, together?' Vidya said.

Govind's mother looked horrified. Confident women make terrible daughters-in-law.

I met Govind the next morning, right before I left for the airport. Govind was due for discharge that evening.

'Thanks,' he said emotionally.

'For what?'

'For dropping by. I don't know how I will ever repay you…'

'Actually, there is a way.'

Govind waited.

'Your story, it needs to be shared.'

'Like a book?'

'Yes, exactly a book. My third book. Will you help me?'

'I don't know. I only like stories with happy endings,' he said.

'You have a pretty happy ending.'

'I don't know yet about Ali. We are going for the operation, but the success probability is not hundred per cent. Fifty-fifty is what they told us.'

'You should have faith. Probability is best left to books,' I said.

He nodded.

'So I'll go back and we'll be in touch over email,' I said.

'Sure, we can work on it. But do not release the story until we know about Ali. Ok? It may mean your effort goes to waste,' he said.

'I agree,' I said and we shook hands.

I met Vidya at the hospital entrance as I left. She was wearing a green lehanga, probably her most cheerful dress, to lift Govind's spirits. She carried a bouquet.

'Nice roses,' I said.

'Law Garden has the best ones. I miss Ahmedabad, can't wait for my course to be over in six months,' she said.

'I thought you were a Bombay girl, trapped in the small city or whatever.'

'He told you everything? Like everything?' she, looked shocked.

'Pretty much.'

'Oh well, Bombay is nice, but my own is my own. Pao bhaji tastes much better in Ahmedabad.'

I wanted to chat with her more, but had to leave. They had let me into their world, but I couldn't overstay.

Epilogue II

I sat at my home computer in Singapore. My wife came to my desk at midnight.

'Can you leave this story for now? You have done what you could. He'll tell you if anything happens,' she said.

'Yes, but they are in London right now. The operation is over, Ali's doing physio exercises everyday. He could be ready for a batting test anytime.'

'You have been saying the same thing over and over since last month. Now can you please turn off the light?'

I lay down and thought about them. It was day time in London. Would the doctors agree to let him go to the cricket field for a test today? What would happen if he faces a ball after such a long gap? Will the new wrist be too delicate to play sports? Thoughts continued to swirl as I drifted off to sleep.

The next morning I woke up early. I had an SMS from Govind.

    doc approves ali 2 play.
    fingers X. pls pray.
    v hit pitch 2mrow

I went to office the next day. London is eight hours behind Singapore, and I checked my phone during my evening coffee at 4 p.m. I had no message. I left office at 8 p.m. I was in the taxi when my phone beeped.

    ish bowls 2 ali.
    ali moves fwd & turns.
    straight 6…!

FIVE POINT SOMEONE
What not to do at IIT

*On the bestseller charts for
four years!*

Five reasons why Hari, Ryan and Alok's life is in a complete mess:

1. They've messed up their grades big time.
2. Alok and Ryan can't stop bickering with each other.
3. Hari is smitten with Neha, who happens to be Prof Cherian's daughter, head of the Mechanical Engineering department.
4. As IITians, they are expected to conquer the world, something they know isn't likely to happen.
5. They're with each other.

Welcome to *Five Point Someone*. 'This is not a book to teach you how to get into IIT or even survive it. In fact, it describes how bad things can get if you don't think straight.'

Funny, dark and non-stop, *Five Point Someone* is the story of three friends whose measly five-point something GPAs come in the way of everything — their friendship, their love life, their future. Will they make it?

ONE NIGHT @ THE CALL CENTER

The new bestseller from the
award-winning author

In the winter of 2004, a writer met a young girl on overnight train journey. To pass the time, she offered to tell him a story. However, she had one condition: that he make it into his second book. He hesitated, but asked what the story was about.

The girl said the story was about six people working in a call center, set in one night.

She said it was the night they had got a phone call.

That phone call was from God.

Welcome to one *night @ the call center*, another contemporary novel from the award-winning author of the national bestseller *Five Point Someone*.

Are you ready to take the Call?